Ralph Compton: The Cheyenne Trail

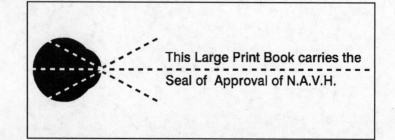

This Large Print Book carries the
Seal of Approval of N.A.V.H.

RALPH COMPTON: THE CHEYENNE TRAIL

JORY SHERMAN

THORNDIKE PRESS
A part of Gale, Cengage Learning

GALE
CENGAGE Learning·

Farmington Hills, Mich • San Francisco • New York • Waterville, Maine
Meriden, Conn • Mason, Ohio • Chicago

GALE
CENGAGE Learning·

LIBRARY OF CONGRESS CATALOGING-IN-PUBLICATION DATA

Sherman, Jory.
   Ralph Compton : the Cheyenne Trail : a Ralph Compton novel / Jory
Sherman. — Large print edition.
      pages ; cm. — (Thorndike Press large print western)
   ISBN 978-1-4104-6729-4 (hardcover) — ISBN 1-4104-6729-5 (hardcover)
   1. Large type books. I. Title.
PS3569.H43R347 2014
813'.54—dc23   2014012387

Published in 2014 by arrangement with NAL Signet, a member of
Penguin Group (USA) LLC, a Penguin Random House Company

Printed in the United States of America
1 2 3 4 5 6 7 18 17 16 15 14

THE IMMORTAL COWBOY

This is respectfully dedicated to the "American Cowboy." His was the saga sparked by the turmoil that followed the Civil War, and the passing of more than a century has by no means diminished the flame.

True, the old days and the old ways are but treasured memories, and the old trails have grown dim with the ravages of time, but the spirit of the cowboy lives on.

In my travels — to Texas, Oklahoma, Kansas, Nebraska, Colorado, Wyoming, New Mexico, and Arizona — I always find something that reminds me of the Old West. While I am walking these plains and mountains for the first time, there is this feeling that a part of me is eternal, that I have known these old trails before. I believe it is the undying spirit of the frontier calling me, through the mind's eye, to step back into time. What is the appeal of the Old West of the American frontier?

It has been epitomized by some as the dark and bloody period in American history. Its heroes — Crockett, Bowie, Hickok, Earp — have been reviled and criticized. Yet the Old West lives on, larger than life.

It has become a symbol of freedom, when there was always another mountain to climb and another river to cross; when a dispute between two men was settled not with expensive lawyers, but with fists, knives, or guns. Barbaric? Maybe. But some things never change. When the cowboy rode into the pages of American history, he left behind a legacy that lives within the hearts of us all.

— *Ralph Compton*

CHAPTER 1

Reese Balleen stared at the western horizon with apprehension. His wind-weathered face, tanned the color of red ochre, bore a worried look. And worry had etched furrows in his forehead and wrinkles around his pale blue eyes.

He turned to look at his foreman, Argus Dewitt, a lean, whip-thin man whose face was equally tanned, burnished the color of the sun-struck pair of buttes that rose in the prairie like ancient monoliths of some lost civilization. He sat astride a dappled gray gelding, a .45 Colt on his hip.

"A rider," Reese said. "From where? No ranch out thataway."

"It ain't just one rider," Argus said. "Old Cheyenne trick. There're at least four ponies in single file."

Reese cursed under his breath. "Is it that damn Silver Bear? He's getting on my nerves."

7

Reese was a tall man, a shade over six feet, with black hair, blue eyes that looked black, a hatchet face, an aquiline nose, and thin livery lips. He too wore a six-gun, a converted Remington .44 that was now a caplock survivor of the War Between the States. He had been a captain in the Confederate army and had served under Lee himself until he was found guilty of adultery with an enlisted man's wife and was sent to command a company of misfits under the command of Quantrill.

He had staked out more than one thousand acres in Wyoming after the war and driven off the Cheyenne after raiding their camp and shooting a number of their old men, women, and children. He was not a friend of the red man, but had gotten away with his slaughter because there were no survivors.

"Hard to tell at this distance, Reese. But way yonder, behind 'em, I see smoke from that mesa where all them buffalo bones is scattered."

"Smoke?" Reese said.

"Yeah, smoke signals. Like the Cheyenne are talkin' to some others way far off."

"I don't like it none," Reese said.

"They had a bad winter, boss. And old Silver Bear is a renegade. No damn reservation for him."

"I know," Reese said. He chewed on his lower lip, a habit from childhood when his family had lived in Kansas, near Guthrie.

"I count five ponies," Argus said. "All single file. Don't see no paint, though."

"So it's not a war party," Reese said.

"More like a palaverin' party. No lances, no saddles. Just five men wearin' feathers."

"You got good eyes," Reese said.

"Yeah, for redskins."

Reese laughed.

Argus had been a scout for the army under Fetterman and killed a lot of Sioux and Northern Cheyenne before coming to work for Reese. He had lived for a time with the Crow, and rumor had it that he had a squaw and maybe a half-breed kid somewhere up in Montana.

The band of Indians got closer, so close that now Reese could see the eagle feathers in their hair and make out that there wasn't just one man but at least three others. He wondered why they were trying to conceal their number by riding single file. It was an old Indian trick, according to Argus, who knew about such things.

"We ought to shoot 'em all for trespassing," Reese muttered, and stroked the stock of his rifle in its boot.

"I don't think that would be wise, Reese," Argus said. "That smoke means there are more of them than these few."

"You're right, of course. It was just a thought."

"Uh-oh," Argus said as the Cheyenne ponies separated and fanned out until there was a line of five distinct riders. They appeared to Reese as if they were in a battle formation. He kept his hand on his rifle stock, just in case.

But one of the Cheyenne raised his arm and displayed the open hand of greeting as the small phalanx came to within twenty yards and halted their ponies. The Indians were wearing only loincloths and carried bows, instead of rifles. Each had a quiver of arrows slung over his back.

"Silver Bear," Reese said. "You're trespassin' on my land. State your business."

The brave next to Silver Bear spoke to the man Reese had addressed. His name was Yellow Horse and both Reese and Argus knew him to be the Cheyenne's interpreter because he spoke English.

Silver Bear spoke words in his language to Yellow Horse.

"Silver Bear comes in peace," Yellow Horse said. "He wishes to have cattle from your herd."

10

Reese looked at all the Cheyenne as they sat their ponies, wide-eyed and mute. They were all skinny. Their ribs were showing through their bronzed skins.

"Does Silver Bear have money to buy my cattle?" Reese asked.

Yellow Horse shook his head. He did not ask Silver Bear the question in his native tongue.

"Our people are starving," Yellow Horse said. "We ask for cattle to feed our people. You have many cattle and we have no buffalo to hunt."

"That's not my problem," Reese said. He scowled as Yellow Horse mulled over the meaning of Reese's words.

"He means," Argus said, "that the buffalo are not his worry."

Yellow Horse translated Argus's words in his own language.

Silver Bear folded his arms across his chest and looked down at the two men. Then he spoke as Yellow Horse and the other braves listened.

Yellow Horse translated Silver Bear's words into English.

"Silver Bear tells you that he and his people are starving. You have cattle. He has nothing. He has no buffalo to hunt and the antelope are few. He wants only some cattle to feed his people. Five cattle. Winter is coming and he wants to live to see another spring."

"So Silver Bear wants cattle, does he? And he just wants me to give him five head. Well, I ain't gonna do it. I don't give a damn if he and his people starve to death. Let him learn the way of the white man and raise his own cattle, till his own ground, like we do."

Yellow Horse translated what Reese had told him. Silver Bear scowled and let his arms fall from his chest. Then he spoke to Yellow Horse in Cheyenne.

"Silver Bear says that if you will not give him cattle, he will take them. He will return with more braves and take the cattle."

"Tell him to go to hell," Reese said, and his face contorted in anger.

Yellow Horse spoke to Silver Bear. Then all of the Cheyenne turned their horses as if to leave.

But first, Yellow Horse spoke again to Reese.

"Silver Bear will keep his promise," he said. "He will return and take the cattle he needs. He warns you that to keep his people alive, he will kill any white man who rises against him. His true name is Silver Sky Bear, and he believes the sky people will

12

return and kill all the Long Knives."

With that, Yellow Horse spun his pony around and joined the others.

Reese watched them ride away and swiped a hand across his forehead to wipe away the rime of sweat above his eyebrows.

"That ain't the end of it," Argus said.

"What do you mean?" Reese asked.

"I mean we got trouble. Big trouble. That Silver Bear means business."

"I don't give a damn about them redskins," Reese said. "If they try and steal any of my cattle, they won't die of starvation."

He looked up at the sky as the riders diminished into small black dots on the horizon. There were long, thin clouds that drifted against the blue-gray tatters that floated like streamers from a distant battleground.

And Reese thought of war in that solitary instant. He wondered if there really were sky people. If so, they were beyond his comprehension.

CHAPTER 2

Reese and Argus rode to the vast north pasture of Lazy R near Bismarck, North Dakota. The grass was already sparse under a sky smeared with long dusky clouds like leftover banners after a parade. There was an early chill in the air, rising from the north like some wintry breath of warning.

Cattle were scattered in all directions, their white faces bobbing up and down as they grazed on the last of the summer grass.

The two men heard a piping whistle as they crossed through a bordering stretch of prairie and saw a prairie dog abandon its sentry post and disappear into a freshly dug hole.

"Them prairie dogs are comin' onto my land," Reese said. "You got to get rid of 'em, or we'll lose pasture right and left."

"We'll smoke 'em out, Reese," Argus said.

Reese surveyed the pasture where his cattle grazed. He saw bunches of whitefaces

14

all the way to the horizon. "What do you figure, Argus, better'n a thousand head of whitefaces?"

"Oh yeah," Argus said. "And a good crop of calves this spring."

"Chip wants to buy at least one thousand head from me, and now is the time."

"Why now?"

"I'm worried about Silver Bear stealin' cattle. Once he starts, he won't stop."

"Well, you need to generate some cash — that's for sure. What's Chip payin' per head?"

"Twelve dollars."

Argus whistled. "That's a goodly sum, Reese. Might get more at the stockyards in Salinas, but from one ranch to another, it ain't bad."

"No, and it's a standing offer. You make the gather and then we'll drive 'em down to Cheyenne."

"It won't be easy this late in the year, what with winter comin' on. It's a hell of a drive clear to Cheyenne."

"It's got to be done. And quick."

"I'll get right on it, Reese."

Reese grunted in satisfaction.

Leo Chippendale owned the Flying U near the foothills west of Cheyenne. The two had served in the war together and both had grown up on farms with cattle raising as the principal form of income for their parents. After the war, Chip had staked out land in Wyoming, while Reese had gone up to North Dakota. But the two had kept in touch and after pinkeye had wiped out most of Chip's herd, he was desperate to restock the Flying U and had asked Reese to sell him at least a thousand head of his Herefords. That had been a month ago, and at first, Reese hadn't wanted to thin his own herd that much.

But Silver Bear's threat had changed his mind. And, as Argus had told him more than once, he needed the money. He was cash poor and needed more horses and a chance to buy some yearlings at a good price.

"How soon can you finish the gather, Argus?" Reese asked as the two rode on over yellowing grasses and more signs of the prairie dog incursion. They rode to the creek that bordered the north pasture and let their horses drink from the flowing waters of Antelope Creek.

Argus looked up when he heard a horse nicker in the distance.

He saw a rider weaving his way through a large bunch of Hereford cows and calves. Heading their way.

"Here comes Roy Bledsoe," Argus said to Reese. "I sent him off this morning to track down those strays that went missing yesterday."

"Looks like he's carryin' something," Reese said.

"Yeah. Somethin' dead, looks like."

Bledsoe rode up to them and threw down the animal that was draped just behind the pommel. The animal was dead. It was a bobcat.

"Found this critter in that gulley with the missin' cattle," Roy said. "He was tryin' to bring down one of the new calves. Calf's got scratches all over its face. I shot the bobcat."

"What about the runaways?" Argus asked.

"George and Johnny drove 'em back up to the ranch house. Penned 'em up for a few days to teach 'em a lesson, maybe."

Argus laughed.

"You can't train cows like dogs," Argus said.

"I think you can," Roy said. "I remember one old Guernsey we had what was always gettin' into the chicken feed, knockin' down the door of the henhouse. We took a rooster to her what pecked her nose and cackled like it was the end of the world. Little old

Bessie never went near that henhouse again."

Both Argus and Reese laughed at Roy's odd little story.

"Go ahead, Argus," Reese said. "Tell him."

Argus knew what to tell Roy.

"We got to make another gather, Roy. Whole herd. And get a tally on 'em."

Roy looked up at the sky and across the creek at the trees. "What for? It ain't spring no more. Calvin's over with the cattle and they're all branded."

"Reese is sellin' off the herd. We got to drive 'em clear down to Cheyenne."

"Cheyenne?" Roy exclaimed. "Why, they ain't no railhead in Cheyenne, just tracks goin' past it to somewhere else."

"The Flying U," Argus said. "Chip wants 'em."

"Oh yeah, your friend, boss. He's buyin' up your herd?"

"Yep, Roy. He sure is. And we've got to move fast. I want a thousand head runnin' south in two days."

"Two days?"

Roy looked around at the scattered cattle. It would take a day just to round up those that he saw in the north pasture. No telling how long it would take to gather up the herds out of the south and east pastures, some seven or eight hundred head, at least.

"Can't be done, boss," Roy said. He stretched a bony finger to tilt his hat back on his head. He scratched a grimy fingernail against his scalp as if to stir the thoughts inside his skull.

He was a stubby mass of muscle and sinew, with a game leg that he broke in a stampede when he was a boy, skin turned leathery and brown from hours in the saddle, close-set blue eyes, and tallow hair, crooked nose from more than one bar fight, and lips stained brown by the tobacco he chewed day in and day out. His hands were gnarled and cracked, rough as sandpaper and scarred from those same fistfights in dim-lit saloons all across Nebraska and Kansas with some Colorado thrown in for good measure.

"Got to do it," Reese said. "Otherwise we'll be swarmed over by hungry redskins and start losin' cattle right and left."

"Huh?" Roy said.

Argus told him about Silver Bear and his threats.

Roy squared his hat and tightened up on his reins.

"That's different," he said. "I'd better get started right away."

"Can you do it, Roy?" Reese asked.

"I can do it. We got enough hands if I can beat the laziness out of 'em, put a burr under their blankets."

"Get to it," Argus said.

Reese and Argus watched Roy ride off toward the south pasture, weaving his way through clumps of bunched cattle that eyed him while they chewed their cuds.

"If anyone can get the hands to put their noses to the grindstone, it's Roy," Argus said.

"You'd better pitch in, Argus. We're goin' to move these cows out in two days."

"I'll go get Jimmy John and Lonnie," Argus said. "They should be cleanin' out that tank in the home pasture. I'll settle the gather in the south pasture and be ready to move 'em in two long, hard days."

Reese smiled.

"I'm countin' on it," he said. "I'll tell Checkers to stock up the chuck wagon for the trip to Cheyenne."

"I'll get the stomach remedy when I get to the bunkhouse," Argus cracked.

Reese knew what he meant. Orville Birdwell, the man they called "Checkers" because he was fond of the board game, had come with two dozen head of cattle looking for a job. And he had a chuck wagon that he said he'd driven and cooked from on a drive from south Texas to Salina, Kansas. He had done some cooking during roundup, and only a couple of the men had gotten sick. Seemed Checkers had used a soapy bowl when he made up a stew. One of the hands found a dirty sock in his bowl and promptly threw up his supper.

Reese rode off to the ranch house to tell Louella that she'd be alone for a few weeks. He wondered if she could manage without his help. She had broken her hip in a fall and was in constant pain. Limped around the house and had to lie down a lot. He had promised her that he would hire a maid to take care of her sometime, but he had not found one willing to leave Bismarck and live on the lonesome prairie. And the ones he had talked to were either too young or two old.

He hated to leave her alone while he helped drive the herd to Cheyenne, but she would want to keep an eye on the place.

He would not tell her about Silver Bear and his band. No need to worry her about a bunch of renegade redskins.

He should have killed Silver Bear while he'd had the chance. It was something he hoped he would not live to regret.

He looked to the west and saw puffs of smoke rising from a mesa. He wondered

21

what the smoke said. And on the same level, he saw something else. The glitter of a mirror flashing in the sunlight.

There was sure a lot of talk, and he didn't understand one word of it.

Chapter 3

Speckled Hawk read the smoke signals and the mirror as he and the others rode toward the mesa. He knew that Silver Bear was angry and not paying attention to what the smoke was saying and what the signaling mirror was telling him. That would be White Duck with the mirror.

Yellow Horse deciphered the coded messages too. His impassive face did not reveal his emotions as the messages sank in. He pulled his own mirror from a small leather pouch attached to his loincloth. He held it up so that the sun's rays struck it an angle. He moved his wrist to spell out a message.

"Go back to camp. I will tell Silver Bear what you have said."

One of the braves at the top of the mesa smothered the fire with a blanket and kicked sand onto it. The other man put his mirror in a pouch. The two walked off the mesa to their horses, which were ground-tied at the base of the limestone bluff.

Silver Bear looked up at the mesa and saw that there was no more smoke and that the men atop it were gone.

"We will gather at the camp and speak to one another of what to do," Silver Bear said to his fellow braves.

"Yes," Yellow Horse said. "It will be good to talk of these things."

"We will smoke the pipe and make offerings to the four directions."

"Yes. We have tobacco," Yellow Horse said.

"We do not have food," White Duck said. "We will have to eat our moccasins."

"We will get the food we need," Silver Bear said. "We will take some cattle from the White Eyes."

"Yes," Yellow Horse said.

They passed the mesa that rose from the prairie like some ancient monument. Tendrils of smoke still hung in the air and rose until it disappeared.

"There is bad news, Silver Bear," Yellow Horse said as they came within an arrow's shot from their camp above a deep arroyo beyond the mesa.

"Is there? Where did you hear bad news?"

"The shining glass. The smoke."

"What is this news, Yellow Horse?"

"Your woman, Bright Bead."

"Yes?"

"She is dead. She died of the empty stomach sickness. There is much wailing in camp."

Silver Bear said nothing. His stoic face did not show any emotion.

He closed his eyes for a moment and thought of Bright Bead. She had become very thin and her eyes had filled with water. She moaned in pain every night when they lay on the blanket together.

A deep sadness engulfed Silver Bear as he rode toward the Cheyenne camp. No more would he have his woman's tender touch when they lay down in their blankets at night. No more would he hear her soft voice as she spoke words of admiration for him. No more would he feel her warmth on cold winter nights when they clung to each other, their breaths intermingling as they whispered love words to each other.

He heard the women keening as they approached the branch-covered lean-tos of their camp. The women sang the death lament and poured handfuls of dirt over their heads and into their hair.

The trilling tongues of the women continued to shriek their grief as Silver Bear and the others dismounted.

He saw the body of his wife lying on a

buffalo robe under his lean-to.

One of the women, the oldest one of the females, approached him. It was Little Basket and her face was smeared with dirt, her hair clogged with sand and twigs.

"Silver Bear," she said. "I have sorrow for my sister, who lies in your shelter. She is with the Great Spirit now and no longer has hunger."

"That is so," Silver Bear said. "She is in the sky now, on the star path. She is going back home."

The women washed and painted the face of Bright Bead and then she was taken to a platform constructed of rocks piled upon one another. This would serve as her scaffold where she would allow her body to return to the earth as her sightless eyes stared up at the sky where her spirit made the trek along the star path to where the Great Spirit dwelled.

That night there was much chanting as the men and women vocalized their grief and expressed their sadness at losing a little sister. Through it all, Silver Bear remained impassive, thinking of the woman he had loved who was now gone, leaving a big emptiness in his heart.

Then the pipe was passed around as the women retired to their lean-tos. The campfire blazed high and spewed its sparks into the dark night sky so that they looked like golden fireflies winking their lights on and off as they died in flight.

"We must not have more of our women die of the hunger sickness," Silver Bear said. "There is plenty of food waiting for us on the white man's land. We will get that food and we will drive the Long Knife from his land."

"How will we do this, Silver Bear?" asked Whining Dog, who passed the pipe to the man sitting next to him.

"There is one thing the white man fears more than all other fearsome things," Silver Bear said.

"We have no rifles," Yellow Horse said. "We have only bows and a few arrows."

"We have knives and tomahawks," Iron Knife said as he blew a plume of smoke over the dancing fire.

"It is the cattle we want," Silver Bear said. "Not the scalps of the Long Knives. We must have cattle and we must chase them and catch them."

"So, we do not kill the Long Knives," Black Feather said. "We just steal their cattle. They are many. We are few."

Silver Bear listened to the talk and he thought about what they must do to get the cattle. He listened and he waited until the words died away and he had both their silence and their attention.

"There is a way," he said. "It came to me in a vision. I know how to drive the white man away from his land and take his cattle into our camp."

"Tell us, Silver Bear," Black Feather said. "Tell us of your vision and how we will drive the white man off his land and return the land to our people."

"Yes," Yellow Horse said, "when the Long Knives are gone, the buffalo will come back and blacken the prairie once again."

"We must do this fast and be careful," Silver Bear said. "In my vision, I saw the fires of the underworld, burning the grasses and running wild across the prairie until all the white men were running and all the cattle running right into our waiting arms."

"Fire?" Black Feather said.

"Yes. We will burn the White Eyes from their land. We will capture their cattle as they run away from the fire. The White Eyes will die. They will burn to death in their houses and on their horses."

"I have seen the prairie on fire," Yellow Horse said. "It was a terrible sight. I saw rabbits and prairie dogs caught by the hands of the fire and I saw antelope running and buffalo gallop for miles to try and escape the flames."

"Yes, that might work," Whining Dog said. "Fire. That is the way to drive the White Eyes from our land."

"We must carry the fire to the grassland and wait for the wind," Silver Bear said.

"How do we make the fire to burn the grass?" Yellow Horse asked.

"We will gather the bulrushes at the creek and dry them in the sun. They will give us fire."

Silver Bear's reply was acknowledged by grunts from the other men.

"The women can cut the reeds and lay them out to dry," Black Feather said.

"Yes. That is the way," Silver Bear said. "We will need many of the bulrushes."

"Two suns to dry," Yellow Horse said. "While we starve."

"Two suns, yes," Silver Bear said.

And in the morning, the women went to the creek with their knives and tomahawks. The cattails swarmed with redwing black-birds. The birds screeched in protest at being driven from their meeting place along the creek.

The women laid out the cattails. The stalks with their fuzzy crowns began to dry.

The warriors checked their arrows and bow-strings.

"We must know what the white eyes are doing with their cattle," Yellow Horse whispered to Silver Bear.

"Remember, Yellow Horse, we have eyes and ears in the white man's camp."

"But can you trust him?"

"I trust him, Yellow Horse. He will tell us all that we wish to know."

The warriors were hungry and weak.

They were tired and hungry.

But they were ready.

CHAPTER 4

The night birds were calling when the first riders rode out to the north pasture and began the gather. There was a chill in the air as the hands began to drive the cattle from their beds and head them south over the silvered prairie.

"Hard to see 'em all in the dark," George Billings hollered to Johnny Whitfield, who was driving two head into a black clump of cattle who were balking about leaving their night beds.

"You have to guess where they are," Lonnie Willets said. "Just look for something big that's blacker than the ground."

George laughed, and yelled at the cows as his horse danced back and forth behind them.

"Where in hell is Avery?" Johnny asked when the two cows were added to the bunch. "That half-breed bastard's always disappearin' when there's work to be done."

"He was just here a few minutes ago," said Lonnie.

"Likely he's chasin' after a lone head up at the crick," Johnny said.

But Vernon Avery was not tending to the gather. Instead he rode toward the Cheyenne encampment with news of the roundup and the cattle drive.

Reese had hired him on when he turned up one day saying he was down and out. It was only later that Reese found out that Vernon Avery had a Minneconjou mother and was, supposedly, an outcast from the Lakota, or Sioux, tribe.

Little did Reese know that Vernon was still in contact with several renegade warriors, rogue bands of Cheyenne and Lakotas, and that his loyalty was not to his father, a mountain man, but to his mother, Little Bird, who was still alive and living up in Minnesota.

Louella Balleen walked as if she was disjointed. One hip was higher than the other and she looked as if she were aboard a tilting ship at sea. It was painful for her, and painful for Reese to watch.

She carried two cups of coffee on a tray to their chairs in the front room after he had watched her painfully serve them both supper. And he knew that she would wash and dry the dishes without allowing him to help.

"Of course I'll miss you, Reese," she said as she set their cups on a small table in front of the cowhide-covered sofa. "I like to take care of you."

"I know you do, Lou," he said as he reached for his cup. "I just think you ought to let me get you help in the house."

"I won't have another woman in my house," she said. "I enjoy taking care of the house and you."

"But you take on too much, Lou. And you're in pain all the time."

"So do you take on too much, Reese. You're going on a cattle drive when you ought to be lying in a hammock and sipping a mint julep."

He laughed. "I'm not ready for that quite yet," he said.

They were comfortable together, Louella and Reese. They had been married a good long while and genuinely respected each other and enjoyed each other's company when they shared a final cup of coffee at the end of a day's hard work.

"Doesn't have to be a woman," he said.

Louella's face took on a blank look.

"What?" she said.

"I could have one of the hands come in

every day and sweep up, wash clothes, dust, and all that."

"Pshaw, Reese. You know I wouldn't stand for that. A man just doesn't know what to do in a house full of dust, dirty dishes, and clothes."

"You could train one."

"Like I would train a dog or a monkey? Don't be silly. The time I spent supervising a cowhand to clean my house would drive me bats. We won't talk any more about this. I make do and I'm happy."

Reese smiled.

He admired her for her determination and loyalty to him. It just pained him to see her suffer from that hip injury and limp around the house. She was a cripple, but she never would allow him to use that word or to acknowledge her disability.

She looked past him at the dark window and sighed. "I keep thinking of all those men out there, trying to round up cattle in the dark."

"They can do it," he said.

"Will you take all the hands with you, Reese?"

He shook his head. "I'm not going to leave you all alone, Lou. I thought I'd leave two men back here to look after the place."

"You mean look after me."

He chuckled. "We're not taking all the cows to Cheyenne. There will be a few head left here. For seed."

"Who will you leave here?" she asked.

"Maybe that kid, Tommy Chadwick, and Vernon Avery."

"Vernon Avery? Why him?"

"You don't like him?" Reese asked.

"I don't know him. But there's something about him that's not quite right. He doesn't seem to fit in. Like the other men."

"He's a half-breed."

"I know. But he seems, well, distant whenever I speak to him. As if he's off in some other place."

"I know what you mean. He takes some getting used to."

"Is that why you're leaving him here?" she asked.

"Partly. I want harmony and cooperation on the trail. Vern, well, he lives in his own world, like you say, quiet, reserved, almost . . ."

"Almost what?"

"Well, distant. I just don't think he'll fit in with the rest of the bunch."

"But you trust him enough to leave him here. With me."

"Oh, I think Vern's harmless enough. He's not part Cheyenne. His mother was a Sioux,

I think."

"What about his father?" she asked.

"His father, the way he tells it, was a fur trapper. A free trapper. He had a run-in with a bunch of company trappers, with American Fur, I believe, and one of them killed his father. Name was Benjamin, I think. Ben Avery. Yes, that's it. Vernon doesn't seem to know much about him, but that's understandable."

"Why is it understandable?" Louella sipped her coffee now that the steam was off and it had cooled.

"Trapper's life, I suppose. Indian squaw for a wife. Ben came and went, like the seasons. Vern doesn't talk about his father, but I knew a trapper or two. Strange bunch. Loners, mostly, obsessed with prime fur, traps, and wild game."

"They were out here first, weren't they?" Louella's face was beautiful, he thought. And she had ringlets in her soft hair. She kept it clean and washed. And combed. Sitting there, as she was, you'd never know that she was crippled. She looked perfectly normal when she wasn't trying to walk. He loved her this way. When he saw her walk, the pain she was in, he winced inside.

"Injuns was here first," he said, a twinkle in his eye.

"Oh, silly. You know what I mean."

"Yes, Lou, I know what you mean. The trappers really opened up this country. They were the first white men to come west of the Mississippi and see what riches were in the Rocky Mountains."

"In a way, then, that's how we came to own this ranch."

He saw that she was interested in the history of the land where they lived. So was he. Especially now that Silver Bear was demanding cattle because all the buffalo were gone. He would not tell her about the Cheyenne demand. It would be just another worry she didn't need while he was away on the cattle drive.

"Well, I'd better get some shut-eye. Early start in the morning."

"You're not leaving tomorrow, are you?" she said.

He shook his head. "No, but I've got to help with the gather. We got cattle scattered all over the place. Got to get 'em bunched and ready to head south."

"I'll miss you," she said.

"I'll miss you too, Lou."

The two embraced and he kissed her, long and lovingly.

Then with his arm around her, she turned down the lamp and they watched it sputter out. In the darkness, they walked to their bedroom.

Outside, they heard the lowing of cattle and the far-off cry of a coyote. It was a lonesome sound, a sound like the prairie itself, and it sang in their ears as they undressed in the hazy glow of moonlight streaming through their bedroom window.

That night, Reese and Louella made love, and it was as if all the cares of the world had faded into nothingness.

There were no disgruntled Cheyenne. There was no need to drive the cattle to Cheyenne. There was only the peace and calm of the prairie night.

CHAPTER 5

Jimmy John had chased the heifer for half a mile before he brought the calf up short with a well-thrown lariat around her neck. When he rode up on her, he saw that she wasn't branded.

Somehow, he figured, she had escaped the spring gather. More than once. He led her back to the south pasture and she fought him all the way.

"What you got there, Jimmy John?" Reese called when he saw the dancing heifer at the end of the cowhand's rope.

"Another unbranded calf," Jimmy John Nolan replied as the heifer dug all four feet into the ground to stop from being pulled.

"They're just startin' up a branding fire over yonder," Reese said. "Too dark to see where just now, but just keep goin' the way you're goin'."

"I know where they are," Jimmy John said. "They're going to put trail brands on every head, but there are Lazy B irons there too."

"Got it," Jimmy John said, and jerked the rope, which brought the heifer to its feet once again.

It was still dark, but already there were gray smears of clouds on the eastern horizon and a pale cream light in the eastern sky.

Reese made a circle and saw the first flames of the branding fire. He headed that way, wending his way through bunches of cattle that were grazing in small groups.

George and Roy were starting the branding fire in a ring of stones. Roy was fanning the small flame as Roy blew on it from the other side of the fire ring.

Other men, including Vern Avery, were roping cattle, and hog-tying them close to where the branding would take place. Reese noticed that most of the cattle already had Lazy B brands on their hips. Irons were stacked next to the fire ring, some of them with the trail brand, a bar *b,* at the ends. The brand was small and would go on the ears of the cattle they would drive to Cheyenne. The small *b* and the small bar were as Reese had ordered from the blacksmith, Ernie Wilson, who worked for him. Ernie kept the horses shod and the stables cleaned. He sometimes had to dehorn a bull

40

or steer and had some knowledge of veterinarian skills dealing with cattle and horses, and the occasional dog or cat.

"Vern, get your thumb out of your butt," Calvin Forbes said. "You got to tie them back legs tight."

"Up yours," Avery said as he wrapped rope around a steer's hind hocks. "If you can do any better, hop to it."

Reese frowned at the two men. The steer was kicking and Avery had more rope dangling than he did around the animal's ankles.

"We got a lot of cattle to brand, boys," Reese said. "By tonight."

"No way are we goin' to get this herd movin' by tomorrow," Jimmy John said.

"Boys, we'd better build another fire ring," Reese said. "We've got plenty of irons for two setups."

George nodded. "We can do that," he said.

Meanwhile, more riders were herding cattle onto the south pasture, their forms silhouetted against the western darkness as they chased cattle onto new pasture.

Calvin got off his horse and fell on the neck of the steer that Vern was attempting to hogtie. He grunted and glared at Avery.

"Now, just jerk them ropes tight as you wrap 'em, Vern," he said. "And tie it off."

41

"I'm doin' it," Avery said as he wrapped the rope around the steer's hind legs. He had to lean on the upper haunch to keep the animal from kicking.

That's when Calvin noticed something on Vern's shirt. "You got paint on your shirt, Vern. Where'd you get that?"

Vern looked down and saw a streak of red paint that went across the seam of his blue chambray shirt. He knew where it had come from and felt a flush of guilty embarrassment.

He had met with Silver Bear and told him of Reese's plans to drive all of his cattle to Cheyenne. In two days. When he had embraced the man, some of his paint rubbed off on his shirt. He just hoped nobody would figure out where the paint had come from.

Silver Bear had not liked the news.

He told Avery to do everything he could to slow down the start of the drive.

"We want some of the cattle," Silver Bear said. "And we want to drive the white man from our land."

"Maybe if you burn him out, he will not come back," Avery told Silver Bear.

"He must not take his cattle away," Silver Bear said.

And now Avery was wondering how he

could slow up the departure of Reese and all his cattle. Without getting caught or drawing attention to himself.

He wanted Reese and his kind off the lands of his forebears too. But he was just one man against many. And Silver Bear was at least two days away from carrying out his plan.

And in two days, all the cattle on the Lazy B would be headed south.

The fire grew hotter and men began to lay the branding irons into the flames while others dragged hog-tied cattle close to the fire pit.

Reese grunted in satisfaction as he watched his hands drive more cattle to the pasture. There were a lot of head to get trail brands on, but he thought that with at least two fires going, they would have the entire herd ready by late in the afternoon of the next day.

It was then, as the sun slid above the horizon and spread golden light over the prairie, that he noticed an ominous sign.

To the west, where the buttes and mesas rose like dark ships and castles, he saw the white puffs of smoke.

The Cheyenne were up to something. They were calling to more of their tribe.

Why?

He could only imagine that they meant to steal his cattle before he could move them.

He looked at his men. All were busy with the cattle. He could not spare a single one to stand guard or patrol the outer reaches of his ranch.

The seeping light of dawn widened his view so that he saw the gathered cattle as more than dark silhouettes. He was proud of his herd. The animals were healthy and fat on the rich prairie grass.

Avery hunkered down next to the first branding fire. He picked up one of the iron brands and poked its business end into the blazing fire. George picked up another iron and stuck it into the heart of the flames.

Roy and Johnny dragged two hog-tied cows over and left them near the fire.

"Ready to go," Roy said.

Other men were roping cattle, ready to lead them to the fire ring.

Avery turned the iron to heat it clear through. George did the same.

The morning air filled with a different smell, the aroma of new iron heating up, aromatic sage and dried sagebrush, cattle hides, and men's sweat soaking through cloth.

"How hot you gettin' them irons, Roy?" Johnny asked. "You goin' to burn both flanks at once?"

The men laughed.

All except Avery. He turned the iron to make sure that it was heated clear through the trail brand lettering.

He too saw the puffs of smoke rising in the morning sky. And he knew the meaning of the signals.

Silver Bear was sending out, to all who could decipher the meaning, a request for all warriors to come help him drive the White Eyes from their lands. The smoke talked about the return of the buffalo only if the white man was gone from Cheyenne hunting grounds.

There were a few Cheyenne, Lakota, and Crow who still roamed free. They might see the messages in smoke and join forces with Silver Bear. In the meantime, he would fight the white man in his own small way.

With that in mind, Avery lifted the hot iron and looked at its bright orange glow. He swung the iron toward Roy's face and landed the hot iron on his cheek.

Roy screamed and grabbed at the burning flesh.

The smell of burned human skin wafted to Avery's nostrils.

Roy stood up, a partial brand burned into the side of his face.

"Sorry," Avery said, loud enough for all those around him to hear.

Roy staggered a few feet, blinded by pain. He tapped at the burn and his fingers came away with blood and scorched tissue.

"What the hell?" George exclaimed. "Avery, you dumb numbskull, what have you done?"

"It was an accident," Avery said.

Reese rode over to Roy and watched him twitch and writhe with pain.

"Get some water," one of the men shouted.

"Water won't do any good," Reese said. "Avery, watch what you're doin'."

Avery bowed his head and put his iron back in the fire.

"I said I was sorry," he said. "I didn't see Roy when I picked up the iron."

"Well, that hot iron is lethal, so watch where you put it. On the cows, not on one of the hands."

All of the men glared at Avery, who stared into the fire as he turned the iron to heat it through.

George walked over and grabbed the iron from Avery's hand. He burned a brand into one of the cows' hide.

"Just find something else to do, Vern," he said. "You're too awkward with that iron."

Avery stood up. "What do you want me to do, boss?" he said to Reese.

"Maybe you'd better stay away from fire, Avery. We've got a lot of head to brand. Make yourself useful."

Avery assumed a look of innocence. He walked over to his horse and untied his lariat.

He had slowed the branding down. That was all he could do just then.

CHAPTER 6

Silver Bear inspected the drying cattails. They were still not dry enough. In the meantime, the women were gathering scraps of wood from sage and other prairie bushes and stacking them near their shelters. Others were sharpening flints and testing them on iron horseshoes they had saved from those old ones thrown away by the white man on his ranch.

Up on the mesa, Lean Wolf and Red Deer had used wet brush to build their signaling fire. Silver Bear had told them what messages to deliver in the white smoke. He looked up at the smoke signals now and grunted in satisfaction. He knew that there were like-minded Lakota, Crow, and both Southern and Northern Cheyenne who would heed his call. Maybe even some Kiowa who roamed the country in search of game in a land ravished by the intrusion of the Long Knives.

He longed for the days before the coming of the white man, when the prairie was black with buffalo and the deer and elk came down from the mountains each spring. There was plenty of food for everyone, and his people were free to roam without hunger in their bellies.

Now there were soldiers and settlers who hated the red man and were trying to wipe out all the people of every tribe. It was a sad time in the lives of the Cheyenne, and it had all started when they lost the Medicine Arrows and the Medicine Hat. That was the year when everything changed and the fortunes of his people worsened as they succumbed to defeat at the hands of their enemies, both red and white.

The Medicine Arrows and the Medicine Hat were sacred to his people. And when they were lost, the people were lost. Now they were scattered or penned up like sheep and the land had turned empty from the hide hunters who slaughtered the buffalo with long fire sticks and left their meat to rot in the sun while they stripped the animals of only the hair.

He sat by the bleak morning fire and smoked, his thoughts roaming through his past and drifting to the ranch owned by a man called Reese. A bad white man who would not give up just a few of his cattle to feed a starving people.

He could not understand such heartlessness. Nor did he understand how the white man could claim that the land was his. The red man did not believe that any man, white or red, could own something that had been given to the people by the Great Spirit and that none owned any piece of land. The land belonged to the people and they could not buy or sell it as the white man did.

Silver Bear looked up when he saw Yellow Horse walk up, leading his horse.

"Someone comes," Yellow Horse said.

"Who comes?"

"It is a Crow on a painted pony. He rides alone."

"Ah, maybe that is Crooked Arrow."

"I think it is Crooked Arrow," Yellow Horse said.

The rider came up and lifted his hand to show that it was empty.

"Come down off your pony," Silver Bear said. "It has been many moons since you came to my lodge."

"I have hunted and been with the Lakota. I saw your smoke."

Crooked Arrow had more than thirty summers. He was a slender man. His moccasins were worn and he wore U.S. cavalry trousers that were faded. He had the marks on his chest that showed that he had danced the Ghost Dance once. The scars were like welts on his bare bronzed chest. In his hair, he wore a single eagle feather that was frayed from wind and wear.

He dismounted and squatted by the fire, laid his bow across his knees.

"I come to fight the white man, Silver Bear," Crooked Arrow signed with slender hands that had ridges from rope burns beneath each finger.

Silver Bear signed back, "You have hunger?"

"Yes." Crooked Arrow rubbed his swollen belly. His ribs showed, like those of the others in the Cheyenne camp, and his face was drawn and taut.

"We have eaten our moccasins," Silver Bear said, "and the white man's bridles from the last soldier fight many moons ago."

"I have only the rope bridle, and my moccasins are skinnier than I am."

"We will have cattle to eat soon."

Crooked Arrow's tired eyes sparkled with sunlight that seemed to come from within. "You have cattle?" He made the signs and licked his lips.

"In one sun, or two, we will have cattle."

"Two Bows and Broken Knife follow me,"

Crooked Arrow said. "They come from the mountains."

"Ah, the Lakota," Silver Bear said. "Brave men. Good warriors."

Crooked Arrow watched the women come and go from the creek. They carried knives and brought back bundles of bulrushes that they laid out in even rows on flat ground. He saw these things but did not say anything. He wondered if the Cheyenne would eat the bulrushes. But he also saw the stacks of bushes, twigs, and small branches. Perhaps, he thought, the Cheyenne were eating those too.

Silver Bear saw the look on Crooked Arrow's face and signed his intentions with the bulrushes and the brush.

"That is a good plan," Crooked Arrow signed. "I will help you. I will take many scalps when you capture their cattle."

"The White Eyes are leaving," Silver Bear said. "They are taking the cattle away."

"Then what will you do?"

"We will take some cattle before they leave," Silver Bear said.

"And what if you do not take the cattle before they ride away?"

"We will follow them and steal their cattle when the stars fill the sky."

"Ah, that is a good plan too," Crooked

Arrow said.

When the Lakota came, Silver Bear welcomed them. They brought with them the dried meat of beaver and marten. There was enough food to chew on while the women cut the bulrushes and gathered firewood. There was enough for the women too.

The day passed in its slow way and Silver Bear felt the bulrushes.

"Tomorrow," he told Yellow Horse, "the reeds would be dry. We will go to the white man's ranch and set fire to the brush and the bulrushes."

"Now that we have more braves, we will need more cattle. We will need twice the number of fingers on my hands."

"We will take four times as many cattle as there are fingers on your hands, Yellow Horse. And we will go far away so that the White Eyes do not follow us."

That evening, Speckled Hawk and Black Feather rode into camp. They had been scouting the Lazy B Ranch, spying on the south pasture unobserved by the white men.

They reported to Silver Bear what they had seen.

"They burn the writing into the hides of the cows. They have many to catch and mark with the hot irons."

"Ah, then we have more than one sun to

catch the cattle and take them with us," Silver Bear said.

"Maybe one more sun," Speckled Hawk said. "There are many cattle that they must catch and take to their fires where the writing irons are burned."

"In two suns, the bulrushes will be very dry," Silver Bear said. "They will burn fast and set the grass on fire."

The Cheyenne chewed on dried berries and meat that night.

But their bellies were still empty and their eyes sunk deep in their faces.

The women moaned in their sleep and the horses nickered like the whispering ghosts of dead warriors from the time of the white man and the loss of the Medicine Hat and the Medicine Arrows.

CHAPTER 7

Reese did not like the way the gather was going. The branding was slow and the men chasing their scattered cows were complaining about the heat, the dust, and the meanness of the cattle.

"George, what's the tally so far?"

"You mean how many cattle we've gathered or how many we've branded?"

"Both," Reese said.

"We've rounded up four hundred thirty head and branded almost all of those."

"Can we head south by tomorrow?"

"We'll come close," George said.

Roy rode up and doffed his hat to wipe sweat from his forehead. "We'll have near a thousand head gathered and branded by morning," he said. "I got three fires goin' and hot brands in every one."

"Good," Reese said.

He felt the pressure as he watched his men drive more cattle onto the south forty, but he was gratified to see that the branding was going well. The bawling of cattle resounded over the forty acres, and there was the whisper of ropes and the sizzle of hides that were music to his ears.

No one saw Vern Avery sneak up on Jimmy John's horse when the rider left it to hog-tie a steer. Avery drew his knife and slit the horse's leg from belly to hock with one slash of his blade. Then he snuck back to where the other hands were wrestling cattle and blended in, unnoticed.

The horse made a ruckus and danced sideways, blood streaming from its leg.

Jimmy John saw that his horse was lame and spraying blood on the ground. He ran over to it and saw the wound down the length of its left leg.

"What the hell?" he exclaimed, and grabbed the bridle.

The horse tossed its head and neighed in pain.

"What's the matter?" Roy called over from the branding fire.

"Somebody cut my horse's leg. Look at it."

Jimmy John led his horse close to the other men. All could see the gash in its leg, a leg that dripped fresh blood.

"Who in hell could have done such a

thing?" Roy asked. "That was no accident."

"It damn sure wasn't," Jimmy John said.

He looked around, wondering which of the men had injured his horse. None of them looked guilty or suspicious.

"That's a deep cut," Lonnie Willets said as he stepped close to the injured horse. "He might lose that whole leg."

Roy got up and walked over to the horse. "You're going to have to put it out of its misery, Jimmy John," he said.

"I — I can't. Old Ned here is my best horse."

"He's lame and won't make the drive," Roy said.

Reese rode over to see what all the fuss was about. Jimmy John pointed to his horse's leg.

"See what somebody done?" he said.

Reese swore when he saw all the blood. And the horse was limping as it walked around in a half circle.

"That looks like a knife cut," Reese said. "And it's deep."

"Somebody sure as hell did it," Jimmy John said.

Reese too looked around at the men. Some were holding down cattle next to the branding fire. Others were pulling on ropes to lead the cows to be branded.

He saw Avery pulling on a rope, seemingly oblivious of what was going on near the fire. But there were other men there too, and they all carried knives along with their pistols.

"Somebody's tryin' to cause trouble," George said.

"Who?" Jimmy John asked.

"Somebody who don't want us to make this drive," Reese said. He dismounted and walked over to Jimmy John's horse. He looked at the deep cut in the horse's leg and shook his head. "You're going to have to put him down, Jimmy John," he said.

Blood suddenly began to spurt from the horse's leg as a rip in a major artery burst wider. The horse went to its knees, then lay on its side. Jimmy John looked down at the spurting blood, and tears welled up in his eyes.

"You're goin' to have to do it," Roy said. He touched the raw wound on his face and looked over at Avery. "You have anything to do with this, Vern?" he asked.

"Me? No," Avery said. "I been too busy to mess around."

"I wonder," Roy muttered. The burn on his face was still raw and the memory of it strong in his mind. And he had his suspicions.

The horse was losing blood fast and appeared to weaken considerably.

Jimmy John drew his pistol. He cocked it and held the muzzle up to his horse's head.

He pulled the trigger.

The explosion was loud and the horse's head jerked as the bullet penetrated its brain. It kicked all four legs and then lay still.

Tears flooded down Jimmy John's face. The other men around him hung their heads.

"Good-bye, Ned," Jimmy John murmured, and holstered his pistol.

"One less horse in the remuda," George said.

Reese's jaw hardened.

The long shadows of afternoon crept across the pasture. Cattle bawled and milled as riders kept them hemmed in on the dry grass that had lost its green and turned brown.

"First thing in the morning, George," Reese said. "Keep at it."

"What we don't brand with trail brands, we can catch up on the trail," George said.

"Ready or not, we go at first light," Reese said.

The longer they stayed on his ranch, he knew, the more precarious it became. Not only was there a threat from the Cheyenne, but he had every reason to believe that someone, perhaps Avery, was trying to prevent them from driving the cattle south to Cheyenne.

Past sunset and into the night, the hands, spurred on by seeing Reese was working alongside them, drove cattle to the branding fires. Gradually the herd began to expand until the final tally before dawn.

"We have purt near a thousand head," George told Reese. "Jimmy John tallies more than nine hundred and we still got a bunch or two headin' for the gather."

"That's more than I expected," Reese said.

"Cattle have a way of multiplyin', and we got good men out lookin' for 'em," George said.

"I'll get the chuck wagon rollin' by first light," Reese said. "Make sure everybody who's goin' to Cheyenne is ready to raise trail dust. Once we start out, we won't stop."

Orville Birdwell, the cook, had already caught the fever by the time Reese found him loading up the chuck wagon.

"You got enough grub, Checkers?" Reese asked as he watched Birdwell wrestle a keg of flour into the wagon.

"Reese, ain't no man goin' to go hungry on this drive," Checkers said. "Thanks to

Louella, I got enough stock for two drives."

"Well, there's always the return trip to think about, Checkers."

"I'm talkin' about a return to home and then some," Birdwell said.

He was barely puffing when Reese rode to the house to pack his duds for the drive and to say good-bye to Louella. She was awake and had coffee made with Arbuckle's.

"Will you want breakfast before you leave in the morning?" she asked as she set two cups on the table, both filled with steaming coffee.

"No, I want to leave on an empty stomach," he said.

"Why? You need your strength."

"Old habit. I always hunted on an empty gut and I have a feelin' we're going to get into weather right soon."

"Weather? What do you mean, Reese?"

"There's a north wind buildin'," he said. "When I come in, I could feel its bite."

"Snow?"

"Maybe," he said. "It's nigh into October and we've got a stretch to go before the herd settles down."

"I laid out your winter coat," she said. "I figured you might need it in a week or so."

"Might need it sooner than that."

The coffee warmed him, but he had felt a

chill just before coming into the house. He was sleepy and tired, but he was also keyed up about the drive south.

"Better pack your long johns too," she said.

"Don't want to take too much."

"I want you to be warm, Reese." She smiled and sipped her coffee.

"You're a dear, Lou," he said, and smiled back.

"What's a wife for if she can't take care of her husband?"

"You go beyond that with me."

She reached across the table and touched the back of his hand with hers.

"I want you back home in one piece," she said. "Not frozen up like a hibernating bear."

He laughed at the image that sprang up in his mind.

Half an hour later, he kissed Louella good-bye and checked his saddlebags and the bundle tied in back of his cantle. Louella had thought of everything, even his hair-brush and straight razor.

When he rode to the south pasture, he followed Checkers in the chuck wagon. It rumbled along, heavy and fat, with two horses pulling and two on lead ropes at the rear.

He waved good-bye to Checkers after he circled the herd. The herd was bawling and restless.

"All set," George told Reese.

"You got a final tally?"

"Better'n nine hundred head," George said. "Jimmy John done counted nine hundred sixty, and I come up with a hair more'n that."

"We'll likely lose a few head before we get to where we're goin'," Reese said.

"That's still a lot of cattle," George said.

"More than I expected."

The men started moving the herd well before first light. Reese watched the cattle begin to move and wet a finger. He held the finger up to test the wind.

They'd have the wind at their backs, he thought, as the chill struck his finger. It might not snow that soon, but he sensed a shift in the weather, even so.

Jimmy John rode point, and as Reese rode the left flank, his belly filled with butterflies. They were on the move with nearly a thousand head of cattle.

The drive was on.

CHAPTER 8

Black Feather heard the white men's voices and listened to the bawling protests of the cattle as several head began moving. Even in the dark, he knew that the white men had started their drive.

He saw the dark shapes of cattle rising from their beds and start to walk from view as men on horseback rode among them with lashing quirts and shouts of "Get along, bossy," and "Heeya."

Black Feather had seen enough. He walked to his tethered pinto and lifted himself onto its bare back. He tugged on the rope bridle and turned the horse toward Silver Bear's camp. He shivered in his light doeskin shirt as he rode over ground that the cattle had once occupied.

That's when he saw the dead horse. It was just lying there, near one of the fire rings the cowhands had used to brand their cattle. He looked around, but all the cattle in his vicinity were gone. And he saw no white man.

The dead horse was food, despite its strong smell.

He dismounted and drew his knife. Quickly he gutted the horse and cut out its heart and liver. He skinned the rear haunch by a cut across its belly and then cuts to its flanks. He then cut the horse's back from neck to rump and peeled the hide away from the backbone. He removed the hide on the left rump and laid it aside. Then he cut into the horse's left flank and removed a large chunk of meat. He wrapped the meat in the hide he had removed.

When he was finished, he covered the carcass with sagebrush. He tucked the organs inside his shirt and carried the hip meat between his upper legs after remounting his pony. He rode away at a slow pace so that his pony's hooves would not raise an alarm in case any of the white men were nearby.

He heard the rumble of hooves as the cattle began to run in thick columns away from the bone-dry pastures.

Black Feather widened the distance between him and the pasture where he had witnessed the branding and the gather for most of the night.

He kept shifting the horse's haunch from one side to the other as his arms tired. Soon he was riding all alone in the night, the sound of the herd lost in the distance.

When he approached the Cheyenne camp, a figure rose out of the darkness.

"It is you, Black Feather, and you stink."

"I have meat, Whining Dog," he said to the warrior who had been on watch.

"Did you kill a deer?"

"It is a horse I have. The White Eyes killed it."

"Ooh, that is good. Silver Bear will be happy."

Silver Bear was awake when Black Feather rode up to his lean-to. He sat on folded legs outside, puffing on a pipe. "What news do you bring, Black Feather?" he asked.

"I bring meat and the White Eyes are driving their cattle away."

"Meat?"

"The meat of a horse," Black Feather said.

"Good. So the White Eyes take the cattle away."

"Yes."

"Then we must go and start the fires."

"You will cook the cows on the hoof, then," Black Feather said.

"I will destroy the white man's ranch," Silver Bear said.

Silver Bear and Black Feather woke up the rest of the camp. The women scurried off to gather up the dried cattails, and some of the men picked up the brush from the piles. They walked and rode in a procession toward the Lazy B Ranch.

They did not speak. They kept silent and walked very fast.

When they reached the ranch, all who carried brush and the women who carried the cattails knew what to do. The men set the brush on the edge of the west pasture at intervals of thirty feet apart. The women came and laid the cattails down on the ground near the brush.

Two of the braves began striking their flints on horseshoes. This sent sparks into the brush and the brush ignited. Soon there was a row of fires and the women stuck the cattails into the flames until they caught fire.

Then the braves took the firebrands and hurled them into the dry grass. Smoke spiraled upward from the burning field and soon the blazes connected and began to race across the prairie.

The wind fanned the flames and blew the smoke in a southeasterly direction.

Louella smelled smoke and looked outside. To her horror, she could see a line of flames across the horizon. The fires were headed her way.

She grabbed a shawl and ran outside to the well. She began to draw water up from the well. When the bucket was full, she threw water on her front door, then on the wall.

She knew that she did not have much time and could not possibly save the house. But, she thought, perhaps she could save the front of it.

The grass fire drew closer and she looked off to the south, hoping Reese would come and save her. But there was no one in sight and she grew weary as she drew more water from the well.

To the south, one of the men riding drag turned and saw lights in the distance. Fiery lights.

The herd moved at a good pace and he wondered what he should do. The more he looked, the more he saw.

"Fire," he yelled, and the herd drowned out his words.

The flames lashed at the night and he knew, finally, that someone had set the west pasture on fire. And the fire was raging, rushing toward the ranch house.

Calvin spurred his horse and galloped to the front of the herd.

"Jimmy John," he yelled. "Look back

there." Calvin pointed.

Jimmy John swore when he saw the fire just barely visible to the north.

"Reese, Reese," he called.

Way off on the flank, Reese heard his name. "Yeah, what's up, Jimmy John?"

"Back there. Look. Fire."

Reese turned and saw the glimmers of fire on the horizon. His heart sank like a stone from a cliff. He could not believe his eyes. He turned his horse and, without a word, spurred the animal into a dead run.

The fire was moving fast before the wind and he knew that his home was right in its path.

The closer he got, the more flames he saw. The sounds of the herd faded and he was alone in the darkness.

He thought of Louella, all alone. Probably asleep.

And she was in mortal danger.

Chapter 9

Louella's crippled body gave out just as she turned to hear hoofbeats grow louder. Fear coursed through her heart because she could not see the rider. She froze and let the bucket drop through the tunnel of the well. The wooden pail hit the water with a loud splash.

"Louella."

She looked up to see Reese appear out of the darkness.

"Reese, thank goodness," she cried.

Reese swung off his horse and grabbed up his wife. His hands tangled in her nightgown as he stroked her hair and pressed his check against hers.

"Oh, darling," he murmured, "you shouldn't be doing this. And it's no good."

"I'm trying to save our home," she said. "The fire."

"Yes, yes, but you've got to go inside and

get dressed. Quickly. I'll saddle your horse. Hurry."

He helped her to the door and opened it. She limped inside and Reese dashed off to the barn. The fire blazed across the prairie, sending columns and curtains of smoke into the air. There was a line of fire across his land that seemed endless.

Inside the barn, he grabbed Louella's saddle, bridle, and blanket. Her horse was whinnying in terror as fumes of smoke drifted into the structure.

He calmed the horse down, put on its bridle, and then slapped her blanket over its back and lifted her saddle atop it. He pulled the single cinch under its belly and tightened it. Then he led the terrified horse, Rosalee, out of the barn and over to the house where he tied its reins to the hitch rail next to his horse.

He opened the front door and called out to Louella.

"Hurry, darling. We've got to get out of here."

"I'm coming," she called back from the bowels of the house. In a few minutes, she ran to the front door, carrying a winter coat in her arms. She was breathless as she went outside.

He helped her step into her stirrup and

boosted her up into the saddle. He took her coat from her and tied it in back of her cantle with leather thongs that dangled from the saddle. Then he climbed aboard his own horse.

They could hear the fire crackle now, and there was smoke all around them.

"Oh, Reese," she said. "We might lose our home."

"If we don't hightail it out of here, we'll lose more than that. Come on. Let's ride."

She followed him as he galloped his horse to the south.

The wind gusted and blew the fire closer to their house, the barn, and the corrals.

Reese saw a line where the fire did not burn and he halted his horse and looked back.

Cordwood stood piled next to the house, and he saw a tongue of fire lash into it. The dry wood caught fire and the stack began to tumble as the wood weakened. One of the flaming logs rolled over to the house and set the baseboards afire.

Flames attacked the barn and raced up the outer walls and into the loft.

He and Louella watched in shock and horror as the barn blazed like a giant torch, lighting up the night like a beacon. Then the house began to burn. Windows broke in a shattering of scorched glass. Flames shot through the roof and surrounded the outer walls.

Louella began to weep.

Reese leaned over and patted her on the shoulder.

"Oh, Reese," she wept, "our home, our beautiful home."

"I know, I know," he said.

"What are we going to do?"

"You're going to go on the drive with me, darling. We'll come back. We'll rebuild."

She could not stop crying as the two rode off into the night.

Behind them, the fire raged, burning down their corrals, the well housing, their home, the barn, the bunkhouse, and the cook shack. And on it raged, beyond the house and outbuildings.

That's when they saw a sight that would forever be seared in their memory.

A lame calf, with a broken leg, emerged from the darkness and tried to escape the encroaching flames. Its pitiful cries tore at their hearts as they watched the calf try to escape the onrushing flames. It could not move fast enough.

"She must have been crippled and left behind when we branded," Reese said.

"Poor thing. Is there anything we can do

to save her?"

Reese shook his head.

They had to watch as the flames caught up to the heifer and her hide caught fire. The calf screamed in terror as the fire rose and consumed her. She floundered for a few feet and then collapsed as the flames enveloped her.

Louella cried out in anguish at the terrible sight. Her sobs increased as Reese put an arm around her.

"Let's go," he said.

"That poor little thing," Louella said, and bowed her head. "How did this happen?" she cried as they rode away from the conflagration.

"I know who did this," Reese said.

"What? Who?"

"Silver Bear and his Cheyenne," Reese said. "He did it, I'm sure."

"That's terrible. What will you do?"

"For now, nothing. But I suspect we haven't heard the last from that redskin. He's out to get me and he won't quit. Until I kill him."

They rode on in silence, and the fires shrank from their sight except for a thin line across the horizon in their wake.

Reese thought of Silver Bear. He should have killed him when the man had asked for some cattle. He should have shot him down along with his braves and that would have been the end of it.

The question now was, how far would Silver Bear go to destroy him? Would he follow them south and try to steal cattle from the herd?

He might, Reese thought. He wouldn't put anything past that treacherous redskin.

It was a long way to Cheyenne, and Silver Bear knew the country better than he did.

He gritted his teeth in anger. He vowed that if he ever saw the Cheyenne again, he would kill him on sight. He wished now that he had Silver Bear's neck in his hands. He would wring it until the man's eyes exploded from their sockets, until he had squeezed all the breath out of him.

The rear of the herd came into sight. He waved to whoever was riding drag and rode on, Louella right beside him on Rosalee, her bay mare.

Finally they reached the head of the herd and saw Jimmy John riding point ahead of them.

"What you got there, Reese?" Jimmy John called out. "Afraid of bein' lonesome?"

"You just tend to your job, Jimmy John," Reese said. "I'll take care of Louella."

"I don't know if I can keep up with you,

Reese," she said. "My back is already killing me."

"Maybe Checkers can make a bed for you in the chuck wagon," he said as he slowed his horse to ride left flank.

"No, no. I don't want any special treatment," she said. "I'll get used to the pain."

Reese wasn't sure. His wife's hip might keep hurting on such a long trip.

But he was glad that she was safe. If he had not returned when he had, she might have been burned to death in that prairie fire.

Like the crippled heifer.

It was horrible for him to contemplate what might have happened.

And his hatred for Silver Bear grew like a monstrous mushroom in his mind.

While the north wind blew at his back, he watched the pale light of dawn seep onto the eastern horizon like a curtain opening up on a window.

And the first day of October breathed down his neck as the wind whispered in his ear. Winter was not far away.

CHAPTER 10

Silver Bear watched as the fire raced across the dry prairie. His eyes gleamed in the firelight.

That will teach the white dogs, he thought.

The Cheyenne all watched the fire eat up the prairie grasses. Smoke billowed up into the night sky and they saw the larger blazes consume the house, barn, wagons, corrals, bunkhouse, and cook shack. They raised their voices in jubilation. Their cries filled the night over the crackling of flames.

"The white man is gone," Yellow Horse said to Silver Bear. "He will not come back."

"I will wait for the Great Spirit to tell me what the white man will do," Silver Bear said. "The white man is gone and the land has been eaten by fire. But he took his cattle and his horses with him."

The men talked among themselves in both speech and sign. The women chattered and laughed as they marveled at the flames and the destruction.

Dawn's egg cracked open finally and painted the sky with cream and gold.

The flames died out at the two creeks and at other places as far as anyone there could see. The wind blew cold from the north, and there were smoldering hot spots in the prairie.

The women smelled the remains of the horse and the calf. Their bellies rumbled and contracted with hunger. The men too could smell the cooked meat of the horse and the calf.

Black Feather spoke of the horse. "There is still meat on the horse," he said. "It will be good to eat."

"When it is cool and the smoke is gone, I will send the women out to gather the cooked meat," Silver Bear said.

"That is good," Yellow Horse said, and the men grunted in agreement as they sniffed the morning air.

The smoke hung in the sky for a long time. When the land had cooled, the women, who had carried the bulrushes wrapped in saddle blankets, went to the creek, wet their blankets, and went out to find the dead horse and the dead calf. They stepped on wet blankets or beat the smoking ground with them. Some burned their feet and danced over the hottest places, giggling and laughing when one of them got burned.

Most of the meat on the horse had burned up, but the women nibbled on what was left and gathered up the leftover meat and placed the scraps in their blankets. The calf was mostly bone with some flesh clinging to the legs and spine. They harvested the leg bones and found meat clinging to other bones.

They carried their spoils to the men, who chewed on the charred meat and gnawed on some of the bones, sucking out the marrow.

Silver Bear told the women to forage through the burned buildings. "Go and see what you find," he told them.

To the men, he said, "We will return to our lodges and smoke the pipe. The smoke will tell us what we will do."

"That is good," Yellow Horse said.

The men returned to their lean-tos while the women returned to the pasture and ventured across it to the smoldering remains of the house and the other structures.

In the barn, they found plowshares and metal attachments to saddles, spurs, rakes, hoes, and other remnants of farm and ranch implements. They exclaimed joyously over every find and chatted about trinkets they would make from the O- and D-rings that they discovered among the ashes.

In the house, they found pots and pans, the metal lids from stoves that could be made into knives and arrowheads. They made several treks to the lean-tos and back with the objects they had plundered from the ruins of the ranch houses.

The men sat around the fire and smoked. They talked.

"Winter is coming," Silver Bear said. "We cannot live in the mountains. We must have food."

"What will we do?" Black Feather asked.

"There is nothing to hunt," Yellow Horse said. "There are no buffalo. The antelope run to the south and all the birds have flown away. We will starve here. We will all die."

"There are the cattle," Silver Bear said.

"Far away now," Black Feather said.

Speckled Hawk and White Duck agreed. Their faces were taut and their expressions grim.

"The man they call Reese is rich with cattle," Silver Bear said. "He drives them away, but that is to the good for us."

"What do you mean, Silver Bear?" Yellow Horse asked.

"There are many cattle and not many men to watch them as they all go to the south."

"That is true," White Duck said. "I have seen them drive cattle before when we hunted in the south."

"The cattle are in a long line," Speckled Hawk said. "There is one man in front of the cows, one on each side, and another at their tails. Men ride back and forth to keep the cattle bunched up."

"That is so," Silver Bear said. "The white men cannot watch every cow. If we go after them, we can steal some of the cows away. If the line of cattle is long, there will be a good chance for us to steal some cows."

The men grew more excited as they talked strategy and technique.

"We have enough of us to catch many cows," Yellow Horse said.

"Yes," Red Deer said, and he signed to the Lakota and the Crow who were there.

Whining Dog and Iron Knife both signed that they understood.

"We can fool the white man," Silver Bear said. "Some can ride in from one direction while others of us steal the cows from another side of the herd."

"It will be like the buffalo hunt," Yellow Horse said. "Except that we will not shoot the cows. We will steal them."

The men around the fire all laughed.

"Yes, that is so," Silver Bear said. "If we

81

steal the cows at night, we will have that dark to hide us. We can steal many cows and drive them back here. We will have food for the winter."

As the women returned and brought their plunder, the men prepared to leave their encampment.

Silver Bear did not want the herd to get too far away. Already he could feel winter's cold breath on the air.

They were all hungry and what little meat there was from the horse and the calf would not last long. And that meat was for the women. They would be busy with the bones and the trinkets they would make from the white man's things.

The white men would not move fast. There were many cows they had to watch and move.

The men rode from their camp as dusk shadowed the land and the stars began to appear in the fading blue sky.

Hunger drove them as the coming winter warned them.

CHAPTER 11

Louella was the first to spot Tommy Chadwick once it was daylight.

He rode all alone on the far side of the herd. He was hunched over in the saddle as if trying to hide.

"I wondered what happened to Tommy," she told Reese. "And there he is yonder. He was supposed to stay at the ranch to help me, didn't you say?"

"I did. And he was." Reese saw the boy too and scowled. He hadn't thought of him at all when he rode back to rescue Louella. He should have, he realized.

Now here he was, on the drive, without a word.

"I'll find out why he's here and wasn't back home trying to help you."

"Go easy on him, Reese," she said. "He's just a kid."

"A kid who neglected his duties. You stay here on this flank of the herd, Lou. I want to talk to that boy."

She watched her husband ride through the herd, dodging cattle and horns.

Tommy raised his head and looked at Reese. Then he shifted his gaze to Louella and turned away, as if in shame.

The cattle moved slowly under gray streamers of high clouds, and the glare of sunlight spread across the trail in gold and pink rays. The moaning of the cattle seemed to echo the mood of the sleepy hands that kept them all in formation.

"Tommy, what are you doing here?" Reese asked as he rode up to the young man.

Tommy was a slender, freckle-faced youth with brown eyes and hair, a wrinkle of a nose, and thin lips. Peach fuzz grew on his chin like spun cotton candy. His boots were scuffed and unshined, his shirt was rumpled, and his trousers hung on his frame like an afterthought of clothing.

"I didn't know where else to go," Tommy said, a slight quaver in his voice.

"You were supposed to look after my wife while I was gone."

"I know, but I heard this calf a-wailin' out in the pasture and I rode out to see what was wrong with it. Then I saw the fire a-comin' and I lit out so's I wouldn't get burned. I'm sorry. But I didn't know where to go, except after the herd. That fire was movin' so fast, and I like to have got caught up in it."

"Did you see the calf?"

"Nope, never did see it. Like I said, I just saw a whole lot of fire comin' at me like crazy and I lit out."

"You see my wife over there on the other side of the herd, don't you?"

"I seen her, sir, yes."

"She barely got out of there alive. And you weren't there."

"No, sir, I lit out when I saw that fire a-comin' acrost the prairie. I didn't think it would get to the house."

"Well, it did. You ought to get a whippin' for running off like you did."

"Heck, I didn't know what else to do. The fire come on real fast and I just barely got away from it."

"Well, you're here now, and you'll work like the rest of us."

"Yes, sir."

"You stay where you are and chase back any strays."

"I can do that, sir."

"See that you do," Reese said.

He rode back, parting the herd with his horse. Louella looked relieved when he joined her on the flank.

"What did he say?" she asked.

"He got caught in the fire. He heard that calf we saw and rode out to find it. He never did."

"Poor boy. He must have been scared out of his wits."

"He forgot his responsibility, Lou. That was to see after you."

"Don't be too harsh, Reese. I'm sure Tommy feels sorry for running away."

"Yeah, I'm sure he does. I just kick myself for ever taking him in."

"Kindhearted, Reese. That's what you are. And you did right to give the boy a home."

Tommy was an orphan who had run away from an orphanage in Denver. He wound up in Bismarck, where Reese found him begging on the street. He felt sorry for the boy and took him out to the ranch. To him, Tommy was like a stray dog, homeless and hungry, and he had taken pity on him.

The herd moved slowly that first day, and some of the cattle were restless and tried to turn back toward their home. The drovers had their hands full and had to change horses more than once as they chased cows back into the herd.

Checkers pulled up the chuck wagon next to a creek late in the afternoon. He gathered firewood and set rocks in a fire ring as he waited for the herd and cowhands. When he saw the first bunch of cattle approach, he lit his fire. All of his utensils and foodstuffs were laid out on the folding sideboard. There was a large expanse of land where the hands could bed down the herd and plenty of water for the cattle to drink.

Jimmy John let the cattle run to the creek. He had ridden point all day and was weary. His compass had brought him to that place where he knew Checkers would be waiting to cook supper for all hands.

Reese and Louella rode up from the right flank to see Checkers, and to let their horses drink.

"You picked a good spot, Checkers," Reese said.

"Perfect," Checkers said with a wide grin. His fire blazed in the pit and he set up the irons to skewer the meat. "I'm gonna have to kill a couple of cows," he told Reese. "You, or someone, can pick out two you don't care much about."

"I'll have George pick out a couple for you. He's been chasin' strays all day."

Checkers laughed. "George'll pick the orneriest ones."

"That he will," Reese said.

"Reese, I don't want to watch," Louella said. "I can't stand to see an animal suffer."

"They won't suffer none, ma'am," Checkers said. "I put a bullet under the boss and they drop plumb dead."

Louella shuddered at the thought as she watched her horse snuffle its nose as it drank at the stream.

"The thing is," Reese said to Lou, "it's not so bad if you don't name the animal."

"What?" Lou said.

"We raised rabbits when I was a kid back in Tennessee. And I named them. Gave 'em names like 'Fluffy,' 'Dolly,' 'Twinkle Nose.' "

"So?" Lou said.

"So, when it came time to take a hammer and knock their brains out so's Ma could cook them, I could hardly kill Fluffy."

"Oh, I see," she said.

"He's right," Checkers said. "I used to name our hogs and when it came time to butcher 'em, I just couldn't hardly take the ax to old Charlie or Humphrey. So you don't name what you're goin' to kill. Gives you a bad feeling when you have to —"

"That's enough," Lou said. "I don't want to think about it."

George picked out two head, roped them, and dragged them, one by one, over to the chuck wagon.

Checkers pulled out his .22-caliber rifle and proceeded to kill the two steers. He had

88

George skin and butcher the dead animals well away from the chuck wagon and Louella. George helped him hang the dead steers from a tree while Checkers gutted and carved up the meat. He kept the heart and liver in a wooden box inside the wagon and the cuts of meat in another.

"We'll let the meat cure for a few days," he told George.

"Them two gave me nothin' but trouble on the trail," George said. "I'm glad to be shut of 'em."

"You can't take cows too personal, George," Checkers said. "It's not like they have brains like a human."

"Them two had brains, and they were out to make my life miserable."

"They're just dumb animals," Checkers said.

"I ain't so sure about them bein' dumb," George said. "Seems to me they was deliberate when they kept boltin' from the herd and I had to chase 'em down."

Checkers laughed. He had heard cowhands talk about animal intelligence before. They assigned every human trait to every kind of animal when they were chewing the fat around a campfire.

He didn't put much stock in such stories until he remembered a goose that always chased him when he was a kid. The goose seemed to take a particular dislike to Checkers. He would chase the boy and bite him on the legs. Checkers hated that goose and he was sure that the goose hated him.

He cooked beans, beef, and potatoes that night and filled the plates of the hands as they came to eat in shifts.

Other hands made sure the herd was bedded down for the night.

Reese spoke to Roy and Johnny Whitfield during supper.

"I want you boys to trade off riding watch tonight," he said.

"What do you mean?" Roy asked. "I ain't supposed to get woke up until midnight to take my turn."

"Johnny, I want you to sit your horse well away from the herd and keep a lookout. You see anything suspicious, you let out a holler."

"You mean like a wolf or catamount?" Johnny said.

"I mean like a Cheyenne Injun," Reese said.

"Huh? You think them Cheyenne's gonna foller us?" Johnny said.

"They burned me out. I wouldn't put anything past them."

By then, the whole crew knew about the

prairie fire because Louella had given some of them a full account. And the word had spread to all hands.

"You think them Cheyenne will try to steal cattle at night, Reese?" Roy asked.

"I don't trust Silver Bear as far as I could throw that chuck wagon," Reese said. "He's treacherous and his bunch are starving."

"Why not give him a few cows and be rid of him?" Johnny said.

"It's the principle of it all," Reese said. "Let the Injuns farm or buy their own livestock."

"You can't expect that of no Injun," Roy said. "They don't know farm from hoopde-do. Bunch of dumb animals, you ask me."

"Oh, I wouldn't say that," Louella said. "They're not dumb. They're just used to a different sort of life."

Johnny snorted. So did some of the other men.

Louella drew herself up and expressed her indignation at the attitudes of the men.

"You have to be tolerant," she said. "A little tolerance makes all the difference."

"I don't know how you can tolerate a savage redskin," Roy said. "They got lice and eat snakes and stink to high heaven."

"We all stink if we don't bathe regularly,"

Louella said.

Reese gave her a look that told her she had gone too far.

Louella didn't back down. "I think we ought to give them a few head of our cattle," she said with a defiant look in her eyes.

Reese picked up a stick next to the fire and poked at the coals.

"The only good Injun is a dead one," he said.

And the other men who were scraping their plates grunted in agreement.

"You make sure you keep a good lookout, boys," Reese said to Roy and Johnny. "Shoot first and ask questions later."

Louella glared at her husband but said nothing.

They watched the sunset, and men began to lay out their bedrolls.

There was a definite chill in the air, and Reese noticed that the stars to the north were blotted out under a layer of black clouds.

His forehead wrinkled in worry.

Winter was the last thing they needed. If it snowed too much, he might lose some cattle. In fact, he thought, he might lose the entire herd in a blizzard.

He prayed that the good weather would hold as he laid out a bedroll for himself and

Louella.

They both fell asleep to the steady drone of the cattle lowing as they bedded down, and the night riders sang to them.

CHAPTER 12

Reese awoke during the night to the rumble of thunder. His first thought was that the herd might stampede, delaying the drive for hours or days. He crawled out of his bedroll at the sound of Louella's voice.

"What's the matter, Reese?" she mumbled.

"I heard thunder. Got to check on the herd."

"It's still dark," she said, half-asleep.

"I know. I'll be back."

He arose and walked over to his horse, which was tied to a tree. He looked up at the sky. It was dark, and the sound of thunder was still some distance away. He climbed into the saddle and rode until he saw one of his hands riding alongside the mass of bedded-down cattle.

"That you, boss?" the voice said.

It was Calvin Forbes on his dun horse. There was a rifle across his lap.

"I just wanted to check on the herd, Calvin," Reese said. "I heard thunder."

"It's far off."

"What's the rifle for?"

"Jimmy John told us all to be ready to shoot any Injuns in case he spotted them Cheyenne."

"Where is he?" Reese asked.

"Oh, he's way out yonder behind the herd. He comes up every now and then to check on us."

"You keep an eye on the cows. If they look like they're going to run, you get help."

"Oh, they're just fine. A little thunder ain't goin' to bother them none."

"Don't be too sure about that," Reese said. He rode beyond the herd and found Jimmy John standing watch next to the old buffalo trail they were all following.

"Anything, Jimmy John?"

"Nary a Cheyenne. Just that thunder up north. Makes it hard to hear anything every so often."

Reese looked into the darkness beyond where Jimmy John sat his horse. It was quiet and he could not see far. He stayed beside Jimmy John for several minutes, watching, listening. Jimmy John's rifle was resting on his leg, the barrel across the pommel. He had one hand on the stock near the trigger guard.

There was a rustling sound beyond their eyesight. Then the sound of rushing air. An arrow whooshed toward them and struck Jimmy John in the side, piercing through to his stomach. He groaned in pain and doubled up in agony. His rifle slipped from his grasp and struck the ground, barrel first.

Reese drew his pistol and wheeled his horse. More arrows arced all around him and he figured the shooters were some distance from him. He fired his pistol into the dark, once, twice, three times.

He heard no sound from where his bullets had gone.

He turned to see Jimmy John slumped over his saddle, an arrow sticking from his stomach. He rode over and put an arm around his chest and back.

"We'll get you some help, Jimmy John," he said. "Hold on."

Jimmy John swore an oath that was mostly breath.

Jimmy John's horse walked alongside Reese's as he led the wounded cowhand away from the flights of arrows. When they reached the nighthawk riding herd, Reese wondered if Jimmy John was still alive.

"Jimmy John," he said. "Are you with me?"

"Still here," Jimmy John groaned.

Lonnie Willets turned his horse and rode over to where Jimmy John and Reese were.

"What the hell . . . ?"

"Lonnie, you keep a close eye on the herd. There're Injuns out there and they shot Jimmy John."

"Oh God," Lonnie exclaimed. "Where are they?" He drew his rifle from its scabbard and levered a cartridge into the chamber.

"Somewhere behind me. I'm takin' Jimmy John to the chuck wagon."

"Yes, sir," Lonnie said, and turned his horse to face the darkness beyond the range of his vision. He gulped dry air and hunched over, peering into the blackness of night.

Reese roused Checkers at the chuck wagon.

"Get some blankets and boil some water, Checkers," Reese said to the cook. "We got a wounded man here."

Checkers dug out a blanket from the wagon and filled a small pot with water. He stirred the fire and put fresh wood on it. In the firelight, he looked at Jimmy John, who was lying on his side. The feathers on the arrow shaft were nestled against his back, while the flint arrowhead jutted from his stomach.

"You got to pull that arrer clean through,

Reese," Checkers said. "I got some alkyhol in the wagon to clean that wound."

"It hurts like hell," Jimmy John moaned.

"It's going to hurt more," Reese said.

At the trail end of the herd, they heard the crack of a rifle shot. Then the night erupted in a cacophony of whoops and chants.

More rifle fire.

The whoops died away, but the men could hear cattle rising from their beds and lowing in disgruntled protest at being disturbed.

Men rose from their bedrolls and grabbed their rifles. Others went for their horses under the trees that bordered the creek. Soon riders were racing to the rear of the herd.

The water boiled.

"Ready?" Checkers said to Reese.

"I'm ready," Reese said.

"I'll hold on to Jimmy John while you push that arrer through from the fletched end."

"You sound like you've done this before, Checkers," Reese said.

"I've plucked an arrow or two from soldiers when I cooked for the regiment under Crook," Checkers said.

"This is going to hurt some, Jimmy John," Reese said as he put his palm against the notched tip of the arrow, right behind the turkey feathers. He pushed as Checkers pulled on the business end of the arrow shaft, his hand just behind the chipped flint arrowhead.

The arrow pushed through and Checkers pulled it all the way out. The shaft was slick and wet with blood and slime. Checkers set the arrow down and reached for the bottle of alcohol.

Jimmy John moaned in pain.

Checkers rolled him over on his side and poured alcohol into the wound in Jimmy John's back. Jimmy John screamed.

"I'm gonna have to rig up a swab and get inside that wound," Checkers said. "Hold on to him right here, Reese."

Reese held Jimmy John in the same position. "Don't move, Jimmy John," he said.

"Ooh, ooh, it hurts so bad," Jimmy John said.

"I know, I know," Reese said.

Checkers brought some bandages from the wagon. He took his knife and cut off the arrowhead, then the fletching at the other end. He wrapped one end of the arrow with gauze and poured alcohol onto it until it was soaked.

"This is going to be like puttin' a firebrand inside you, Jimmy John," Checkers said as he held the gauzed end of the arrow close to the wound in his back.

"Do it," Jimmy John said, and closed his eyes. He gritted his teeth as Checkers shoved the soaked bandage through the wound. He twisted it as he pushed it out the other side of Jimmy John's stomach.

Jimmy John screamed.

Rifles cracked in the distance. Men shouted. Indians whooped their war cries.

"I should do this one more time with a fresh bandage," Checkers said. "But I don't know if Jimmy John can stand any more."

"Do what you have to do, Checkers," Reese said. "Maybe give Jimmy John something to bite on."

"Let's see," Checkers said. He felt the ground and pulled up a small stick next to the stack of kindling. "Here, Jimmy John, bite on this while I go in there again."

"Mmmmf," Jimmy John said as Checkers shoved the stick into his mouth.

Louella arose from her bedroll and came over, wrapped in a blanket.

"Oh dear," she said when she saw the blood oozing from Jimmy John's back.

Checkers removed the wet bandage and wrapped a fresh one on the shorn tip of the arrow.

"Anything I can do to help?" she asked.

"Just hold on to one of Jimmy John's hands," Reese said.

Louella gripped Jimmy John's left hand. She squeezed it and he squeezed back. He gripped the stick in his mouth as Checkers poured alcohol on the wrapped bandage. Then he swabbed the wound once again. This time, the bandage emerged from the stomach with less blood and less slime.

"Jimmy John, I got some iodine in the wagon. I'll pour some of it into the wound and bandage you up. You got to stay real still, but I don't think that arrer hit any vital parts. You'll live."

Jimmy John spat out the stick and let out a breath of air.

Checkers stood up and went to the wagon. After a few minutes he returned with a square bottle of iodine.

"Hold him right where he is," he told Reese.

Checkers poured a liberal amount of iodine into the hole in Jimmy John's back, then did the same with the exit wound in his belly.

"Let's hope it'll seep on through and get rid of any germs what was on that arrer," Checkers said. Then he wrapped a bandage around Jimmy John's waist and back, tied it off with a tight knot.

101

"You can let up now, Reese," Checkers said.

Reese let Jimmy John down until his body rested on the blanket.

Louella rubbed his forehead, felt his cheeks.

"He has a slight fever, I fear," she said.

"Likely he'll get a mite hotter before that wound has a chance to heal," Checkers said.

"Have you done some doctoring, Checkers?" she asked.

"When I was with Crook, a lot of us did doctorin'," Checkers said. "We had a surgeon, but when he was busy, well, a lot of us pitched in."

"At least you knew what to do for this man," she said.

"My name's Jimmy John," Jimmy John said, his voice weak.

"Sure, sure," she said. "I wasn't sure. I don't know all the hands, but I know who you are."

The gunfire stopped and a rider drifted into the firelight's glow.

"We didn't lose one head," Roy said as he dismounted and walked over to Reese.

"Did you get any Indians?" Reese asked.

"Nope, but we heard 'em hollerin' and might have clipped one or two."

"We'll have to double the guard duty,"

Reese said. "Silver Bear won't quit."

"They was pretty determined," Roy said. "One or two came after the cows and we chased 'em off."

"Good job," Reese said.

"I'll put all the men on nighthawkin'," Roy said. "Be light soon anyways."

"We'll get the herd moving as soon as the sun comes up," Reese said.

"I'll look after Jimmy John here," Checkers said. "Make room for him in the wagon."

Jimmy John squeezed Louella's hand in gratitude. She bent over and kissed him on the cheek.

"Thanks, ma'am," Jimmy John murmured.

"I'll give him some powders for the pain," Checkers said. "I got me a pretty good medical kit in my wagon."

Reese stood up. He could feel the dawn about to break.

The night seemed darkest just then, outside the ring of firelight. Mosquitoes and flies danced in the glow and in the east, the darkness faded to a pale gray.

He put his arms around Louella and walked her back to their bedroll.

"Thanks," he said.

"What for? I didn't do anything."

"You were a comfort to Jimmy John."

"Do you think he'll make it?" she asked.

"He might. Checkers will take good care of him, I think."

"I think so too," she said.

They lay down together but neither could sleep. The herd was getting to its collective feet and moving around. There was high grass to feed on, and most of it was still green. Reese knew it would get greener the farther south they went.

In the distance, they heard a coyote call and it sounded strangely like the keening of a Cheyenne warrior at the death of a fellow brave.

CHAPTER 13

Roy found traces of blood where the Indians had been. There were several arrows sticking out of the ground where they had landed. And one cow had an arrow in her rump. He pulled it out and the cow trotted off and joined the rest of the herd.

They forded the creek as the sun sprawled its light across the wide prairie. It had rained the night before, but only to the north of the herd.

Roy could smell the rain in the dawn air as he ate breakfast at the chuck wagon. Checkers had fixed cornmeal mush and thick slices of beef, sugar beets, and biscuits for all hands. They ate in shifts as the herd started moving across the creek in a slow procession.

Tommy rode into camp with George, who had been on drag that morning.

"Reese, Tommy's got somethin' to show you," George said. "What he done found back yonder."

"What have you got, Tommy?" Reese asked the boy.

Tommy opened his hand. "Looks like teeth," he said. "And I saw what looked like pieces of a man's brain lyin' near these bone chips."

Reese picked up a broken tooth, then a concave piece of bone that looked as if it had been part of a man's skull. There was blood on some of the teeth in Tommy's hand.

"Likely one of you got one of their braves," Reese said.

Others crowded around to look at the teeth and bone fragments.

"I found part of a bone breastplate too," George said. "Like a bullet went clean through an Injun's chest and cut the thong. I left it out there."

"Hmm," Reese murmured. "I wonder if that was enough to run Silver Bear off."

"Lots of tracks," Tommy said. "Mockersons. And flint arrerheads, a couple, and some turkey feathers. It must have been one whopper of a fight."

Checkers looked at the remnants in Tommy's hand as he set a fresh pot of coffee on the cook fire.

"Those are human teeth all right," he said.

"Looks like a bullet hit whoever square in the mouth, maybe blew out his brains."

"You should know," Reese said.

"That breastplate tells you somethin' too. The boys might have cut into a couple of them redskins with lead bullets."

The talk died down as the men drank coffee and Checkers cleaned up the plates and stowed the utensils in the wagon. He had made a bed for Jimmy John, fed him, and changed his bandage.

"Jimmy John's runnin' a high fever," Checkers told Reese in private. "He might not make it."

"You let me know, Checkers. Now you'd better hit the trail and find us a noon spot somewhere down the trail."

"Will do, pretty quick," Checkers said.

In fifteen minutes, the chuck wagon was splashing across the creek and passing the lead cattle in the herd.

Reese watched it disappear. He looked at the sky. The dark clouds had splintered up into gray streamers that drifted to the southeast. But there were thunderheads building to the northwest, and he too smelled the scent of fresh rain on grass that wafted on the morning wind.

George rode point. Roy took up drag and the other hands rode the flanks, including

Reese and Louella.

"How are you, darlin'?" Reese asked his wife.

"Tired," she said. "Sad about what we lost back home."

"We'll build it all back," he said.

"I know. It won't be the same, though."

"Nothing ever is," Reese said.

He knew that Louella was in pain. She never complained, but he had seen how hard it was for her to walk that morning. Just around the fire. Her limp seemed more pronounced and her face had looked haggard and drawn. Yet she rode her horse like a trouper, head held high, back straight, both legs draped over the side saddle. Her nightgown was rumpled and dirty.

"I'm going to see if one of the boys has a shirt and pants that will fit you," he told Lou after they had crossed the creek. "That nightgown won't last another day."

"I almost feel naked," she said, and he thought he detected a blush on her face.

"The gown covers you," he said. "Just barely."

Louella laughed.

"It's not what I would wear to Sunday meeting," she said.

They rode on as the herd picked up speed. The cattle would snatch up tufts of grass or chew their cuds, but Reese was pleased that they seemed to move faster than the day before.

He thought about the Cheyenne and what they might be doing or planning next. Likely his men had killed at least one of them. Those teeth and parts of a skull told a grim story.

The buffalo trail they followed was wide and long. The cattle seemed to take to it like ducks to water, Reese thought. His hands were doing a good job. They kept the herd moving and the strays in check. The farther they got from the home range, the less memory the cows seemed to have. That pleased Reese, but he was still worried that Silver Bear would try again to steal some of his cattle.

And, he thought, he might not wait until nightfall to do it.

CHAPTER 14

Silver Bear watched as the braves gathered rocks and covered the body of Whining Dog. One of the white man's bullets had struck him in the mouth and blown away part of his head. Limping Dog had been crouched and was putting another arrow to his bow when he was killed.

And they had not caught any cows.

Now the herd was moving again. Getting farther away.

He was hungry. So were the other braves.

The ground around the grave was still damp from the rain from the night before. The rain had stopped just short of where he and his men had been fighting. And it had not rained where he and his men had slept the rest of the night.

Now Yellow Horse and Black Feather were making fire to ward off the morning chill. In the distance, they could hear the rumble of cattle as the herd moved away in the morning sunlight.

Silver Bear took out his pipe from the pouch he wore. There was tobacco and he tamped the bowl when it was full. They did not have much tobacco left, and what little there was was precious.

"We will smoke," he said. "Make talk."

Yellow Horse and Black Feather looked up at him as the fire began to crackle.

"Yes. It will be good to make talk," Yellow Horse said.

The others finished covering Whining Dog's dead body with stones. It was all they could do. They had no scaffolding for the brave's body, and his face was almost gone. They knew that his soul had gone to the star path the night before, but his body would return to the earth.

The braves sat in a circle around the small fire. Silver Bear pulled a faggot from the fire and lit his pipe. He puffed and blew smoke to the four directions, then passed it to Yellow Horse, who sat next to him on his left.

Each man smoked, and then the pipe was returned to Silver Bear.

"We did not get any cattle last night," he said.

The men grunted in assent.

"That is because we did not do what we

should have done. I have given this much thought. We must change the way we go after the cattle and the way we attack the Long Knives."

"How do we change what we do with the white men?" Black Feather asked.

Silver Bear looked at each man before he answered the question.

"We attack the tail of the cattle herd," he said. "That is the most narrow part. We cut the tail in two. Some of us will ride fast from one side. The others will ride from the other side and shoot down the white men. We will get the rifles of the fallen men and we will take their pistols and their bullets."

"That is a good plan," Yellow Horse said.

"Those cattle that we cut off can be herded away from the others while we fight the Long Knives," Silver Bear said. "When we have finished the battle, those of us who fought the Long Knives will return to the cattle we drive off and help to herd them back to our camp."

"When do we do this, Silver Bear?" asked Speckled Hawk.

"When the sun is high," Silver Bear said.

"They will see us when we ride close," White Duck said.

"Yes, they will see some of us. We who go to do battle first will make them look at us.

That is when the others ride through the tail of the herd and cut it in two, like a knife on a snake."

The men all nodded in approval.

"We must all ride very fast. We must do our best with the horses." Silver Bear made sign with his fingers and hands so that all would understand.

"Who will attack and who will cut the tail of the herd?" asked Iron Knife.

"We will draw the pebbles from my hand, big ones and little ones," Silver Bear said. "Those with the big pebbles will attack the Long Knives. Those with the little pebbles will cut the tail of the herd."

"Hunh," grunted the men almost in unison.

"When the sun is high, we will ride," Silver Bear said. He pointed to the sky.

He started picking up different sizes of pebbles off the ground. These he held in the palm of one hand. When he had gathered the number of pebbles that corresponded to the number of braves, he closed his hand into a fist.

"Now," he said, "we will draw the little stones to see who cuts the tail of the herd and who attacks the Long Knives. Do not look into my hand. You must take one pebble each and we will measure them when they are all gone."

That's what the men did. Each closed his eyes as he reached for a pebble.

When they were all holding pebbles, Silver Bear examined them. He separated the men into two groups.

"You will cut the tail of the herd," he told Iron Knife. "And you must all ride fast. Those of you with the larger pebbles will attack with me from the other side of the herd."

The men grunted their approval of the plan and began to gather their bows and check their quivers.

Silver Bear was sure that his plan would work. There were enough braves in his band to cut the trail of the herd and keep the white men busy defending themselves. When the sun was high they would be able to see, and the white men would fall to their arrows.

When all his men were ready, they mounted their ponies.

Silver Bear led them to the south. The sun rose in the sky, heading for its zenith. The morning air was brisk and cool.

It was a good day to die.

CHAPTER 15

Reese put two men on drag, Calvin and Lonnie. He still did not trust Avery, and had him ride behind his point man, George. That way, he could keep an eye on him.

"If the Cheyenne come after us again," Reese told Calvin and Lonnie, "they'll likely come up behind us. You keep your eyes peeled real sharp and shoot at the first sign of Injuns. Keep your rifles in hand. They might ride up out of nowhere and try to catch you nappin'."

Calvin and Lonnie relieved Roy on drag and sent him to the right flank where the herd was more bunched near the center of the long line of cattle.

Louella rode ahead with Checkers and the chuck wagon so that she could look in on Jimmy John and try to bring down his fever. She and Reese kissed in an awkward embrace on horseback, and she rode off, following the wagon tracks.

Checkers was glad to see her when she rode up and spoke to him.

"We can tie your horse to the wagon," he said. "You can sit up here with me and look in on Jimmy John from the front seat."

And that is what Louella did. Soon she was sitting next to Checkers. She could see into the wagon. Jimmy John was asleep. She leaned in and touched a hand to his cheek.

"I think his fever's dropping some," she told Checkers.

"Fever burns out the poison," he said.

"I've heard that," she said. "From my grandmother back in Ohio."

"I'll try and pour some soup down his gullet when we make the noon stop," he said.

"How do you know when to stop and feed the boys?" she asked.

"I calculate it by the sun," he said. "When it's straight up overhead, I find a good wide spot and stop. Same with the evenin' meal."

"That makes sense," she said.

In the wagon bed, Jimmy John moaned as the wagon jounced over rough terrain. Louella leaned in to check on the wounded man.

"Do you need anything, Jimmy John?" she asked.

"More powder," he said.

She turned to Checkers with a questioning look.

"He's had enough," Checkers said. "He'll just have to bear up and tough it out."

"I'm sorry, Jimmy John. We can't give you any more medicine right now." Louella patted his head with a delicate touch.

"Pain all through me," Jimmy John said. "Like fire."

"I'm sorry," she said again.

Checkers cracked the reins across the backs of the horses. They picked up speed and the wagon bounced even more.

"Maybe if you slowed down, Checkers, it might make Jimmy John more comfortable."

"Tryin' to get to the noon stop a little quicker," he said, "so the boy can rest easier in that wagon bed."

Louella didn't say anything. Instead she held on to the side panel to keep from tumbling off the seat.

Eventually Checkers slowed the horses down and the wagon did not rock as much.

"Horses needed a breather," he told Louella.

Jimmy John stopped moaning and lay still, his face awash in sweat. But the bandage held tight and he was not bleeding.

As the sun rose higher in the sky, Checkers began to look for a good place to stop and set up for lunch. He scanned the trail ahead and saw a line of trees that marked a creek.

"We'll stop up yonder," he said. "See them trees? That means a creek or a stream."

"What's the difference?" she asked.

"None, I reckon. Just some people call a creek a stream and vice versa."

She laughed. What Checkers said was true. And nobody knew the difference.

They drove up on a small creek and Checkers wheeled the horses so that they were stopped in the shade of some cotton-woods. It was still cool and the wind was blowing from the northwest. In the distance, Louella saw large thunderheads and wondered if they would have rain before the day was over. The clouds did not seem to be moving, though, and the more she looked at them, they seemed impervious to the wind that washed against her face.

"We stopping?" Jimmy John asked.

"Yes, Jimmy John. Checkers found us a nice shady spot by a creek. Maybe now you won't have so much pain."

"I do feel some better," Jimmy John said.

They could not see the herd as both she and Checkers scanned their back trail looking for any sign that the herd was nearing them. They did not see any trail dust either.

"Herd's still a ways off," Checkers said.

"So we can tend to Jimmy John, maybe make him more comfortable."

"Can't you give him something for the pain?" she asked.

"He's over his limit now. Them are strong powders I give him. Right now he's better off just sleepin'."

She looked back into the wagon.

"How do you feel?" she asked Jimmy John.

"Pain's not so bad now," he said. "Just kind of a steady dull throbbin' in my back and gut."

"You'll feel better after a while," she said. "Hungry?"

"Nope, ma'am, and I'd be afraid to eat with that hole in my belly."

"Well, you rest easy," she said. "I'm going to walk around and stretch my legs."

Presently they saw dust in the sky on their back trail.

"Herd's a-comin'," Checkers said. "Be here in less'n an hour."

"I see the dust," Louella said, shading her eyes against the sun. "Still far off, though."

"They're movin', sure enough. Else we wouldn't see that dust a-risin' from the trail."

The dust dissipated in the stiff breeze, but it was there. The herd seemed to be moving at a good, steady pace.

Half an hour later, the point man came into view over the horizon. And behind him the herd rumbled on.

"Them cows smell water now," Checkers said. "They'll be here directly."

"I think I see Reese," she said.

She waved, but Reese, who was riding front flank, was too far off to see her. And he had his hands full as the herd swelled in the vanguard and some of the cattle tried to bolt out of the procession.

Whoever was riding point rode out of the path of the now charging cattle and let them stream by as they headed for the creek.

Checkers had a fire going in a ring of rocks and he was setting down fry pans and water-filled pots to make soup and to fry mush.

The cattle fanned out and drank from the creek as the riders on the flanks let them go while keeping watchful eyes for any that tried to stray from the creek or cross it.

"Well, here they are," Checkers said as he cut up potatoes and dried beef and let them fall into a large pot. "You can get some of them plates and set 'em on the tailgate. Bowls too, and spoons are in that side cabinet."

The coffeepot boiled and the aroma wafted to Louella's nostrils as she set out plates and bowls. Checkers stirred the stew pot and that scent was there too, stirring hunger pangs in her stomach.

Reese rode up and smiled at her.

"You're here early," he said. "I thought we were at least another hour away."

"Yes, Checkers wanted to set up so Jimmy John would get some rest without so much pain from the bouncing wagon."

Reese swung down from his horse.

"Smells good," he said. "We made good time too. Might do better'n ten miles before the day is done."

"Is that good?" she asked.

"Better'n yesterday," Reese said.

He looked up at the sky. The sun was nearing its zenith. He walked over behind the wagon to stand in the shade.

Louella walked over to stand beside him.

That's when they heard the first war cries and yelps from the tail end of the oncoming herd.

Then they heard a rifle shot in the distance.

"Uh-oh," Reese said. "Trouble."

"What is it?" Louella asked in confusion. The cries seemed far away and the gunshot just as distant.

"Cheyenne," Reese said. "The damn Cheyenne. They sound like they're tryin' to steal cattle from the rear of the herd."

Checkers stopped stirring and looked toward the herd, which had fanned out when the cattle went for water.

There were more rifle shots.

Reese went to his horse.

"Checkers, arm yourself. Louella, you get in the wagon and stay there."

"Where are you going?" she asked.

"To kill me some Cheyenne," he said.

Reese wheeled his horse and galloped off toward the rear of the herd. He yelled to the outriders as he pulled his rifle from its scabbard.

The herd was running toward the creek now as he rode past them and headed for the rear.

A feeling of dread rose in him as the rifle fire died down.

He rode on into a silence that was so deep, he could feel it like a cloak wrapped around him.

And the cloak felt a lot like fear.

CHAPTER 16

Silver Bear crawled through the grass on his belly. He held a sagebrush in one hand, his bow in the other. It was a slow, difficult process as he stirred up sand fleas, dust mites, ants, and other insects. The sun was low in the eastern sky when he and his men spotted the herd and took up their positions on the left flank.

Timing was everything, because Silver Bear wanted to be at the tail end of the herd when the sun was highest in the sky, the middle of the day.

With him, at thirty-yard intervals, were the two Lakota braves, the Crow warrior, Iron Knife, and Speckled Hawk.

Somewhere, on the other flank, he knew, Yellow Horse, Black Feather, and another Cheyenne brave, Water Snake, waited on their ponies to cut off the tail of the herd as it passed in front of Silver Bear and his braves.

When he reached a spot where he could see the passing herd, yet not be seen by any of the outriders, he stopped his crawl. He dug a hole and stuck the sage into it and tamped the earth to secure it. The sage was directly in front of him, affording him more cover.

He strung his bow, pulled an arrow from his quiver, and waited. Cattle streamed by him in a walk. His mouth watered at the sight of all that beef. His stomach rumbled and made noises.

He could not see the other braves, but he knew they were there.

He looked up at the sky. There was still time and the herd was still moving. Now and then, he heard one of the white men yell and watched as the flanker rode back and forth along the line of cattle, keeping them in line and holding them on the trail.

As the sun reached its midpoint in the sky, he heard the sound of hoofbeats. And he heard one of the white men yell out a warning.

Silver Bear rose from his hiding place and nocked his arrow on the bowstring.

As Yellow Horse and Black Feather rode into the herd, separating a dozen cows from the rear end, Silver Bear shot one of the men on drag. His arrow struck the man in the side of his chest with enough force to emerge on the other side. Silver Bear knew that the arrow had pierced both of the man's lungs. He would die within a few seconds.

George Billings fell from his horse as Roy Bledsoe opened fire with his rifle. Roy swung the barrel on a brave and squeezed the trigger. He saw the Indian throw up his arms and fall from his pony. The brave landed in front of some cows. The cows veered off to avoid running over the fallen brave.

One of the flankers started shooting at the marauding Indians, but he was too far away and his aim was lost.

Red Deer drove the separated bunch of cattle back along the trail, slapping their rumps with his bow to drive them well away from the herd.

More riders began to shoot at the Indians. But the Indians were expert horsemen and they zigzagged their ponies as they chased the cows backward along the trail.

Black Feather shot Roy at close range. Roy grabbed his chest as the arrow penetrated the breastbone and split it before poking out of his back. His rifle slid from his grasp and he slumped to his side before sliding off his saddle and landing on the hoof-scarred land, kicking up a small cloud of dust.

Men yelled and Indians whooped. Silver Bear ran toward one man and drove him off with arrows that came close. The rider turned back and galloped his horse to the south.

Then Silver Bear turned and ran to where he had tethered his horse. He saw the dozen head of cattle run from the main herd and knew that Red Deer and Black Feather had done their tasks.

The other braves rose and Silver Bear signed that they should retrieve their horses.

His one thought was to drive the cattle that Yellow Horse had taken. He and his braves could stand off any pursuit. He climbed onto his pony and rode off as the other braves came up to get their ponies.

The rifle fire died down and stopped.

Silver Bear caught up with Yellow Horse. Black Feather and the others came riding up.

"We have done it," Silver Bear said to Yellow Horse. "We have cows."

"Food for the winter," Yellow Horse said. He grinned with delight.

Silver Bear watched the humps of the cattle as they drove them north, well away from the main herd. When he looked back, the herd was on the run, drifting over the horizon and out of sight.

Only one brave dead, he thought, and at least two white men lying in the dust and turning cold.

He caught up to the cattle as they lumbered up the trail in a running walk. He joined the other braves who were driving the cattle. He counted them. He counted them twice.

There were thirteen head they had captured. This number gave him a good feeling. His band would have food to eat and the hides would make clothing and moccasins.

He silently thanked the Great Spirit for his good fortune. He looked up at the sky and felt the spiritual presence of his deity.

When he looked back, he saw no white men in pursuit. And around him were his own kind, brave warriors. He thanked them, in silence, as well.

They kept the cattle moving at a brisk pace, on into the night until, at last, they arrived back in camp with more than a dozen head of healthy white-faced cattle.

The women screeched with joy when the men rode up and they saw so many cows, heard them mooing and lowing.

Overhead, Silver Bear saw huge black

thunderheads blot out the stars. In the distance, he heard the drums of thunder and saw jagged streaks of lightning stitch silver ladders all along the north and west. And the wind blew cold and hard as he and his men bedded down their stolen cattle and stood watch over their sudden wealth.

The women killed one of the cows, skinned it, and cut off chunks of meat after offering the heart to Silver Bear and the liver to Yellow Horse and Black Feather.

The fire blazed bright as the women cooked the meat.

The Cheyenne would live on and the white man's ranch land lay in ashes.

It was a good night to live.

CHAPTER 17

Reese was struck with a pang of sadness when he saw the bloody body of George. He started to weep when some of the men pointed out the corpse of Roy.

Two good men lay dead on the hoof-roiled trail, with arrows sticking out of them like obscene markers.

Vernon Avery rode up. With him was Tommy Chadwick, wide-eyed with curiosity.

Reese looked at Avery, then at the fallen men.

"Vern. Get those arrows pulled from those men."

"Yeah, sure," Avery said, and dismounted.

Tommy looked at the body of Roy and vomited. He retched up his breakfast and turned away from the corpse.

Avery pulled the arrows from the two dead men. He jerked them viciously from their bodies and threw the arrows onto the ground.

"Anything else?" he asked.

"Find a low spot and lay them to rest."

"You ain't goin' to bury them?" Avery asked.

"No, we've got to keep the herd moving. The chuck wagon is too far ahead of us, and Checkers has the only shovels with him."

"What'll we do, then? Just lay the bodies in a low place?"

"Cover them with rocks to keep the critters off them."

"That won't keep the coyotes and the buzzards from eatin' their remains," Avery said.

"That's all we can do for them right now," Reese said.

He looked at Tommy, who was still doubled over and spewing out the contents of his stomach. "Tommy, when you get finished throwing up, you help Vern carry them bodies off to their graves."

Tommy looked up with tear-filled eyes. He nodded and swallowed. His face was drained of blood and had paled to chalk.

Reese knew that the other men were taking care of the herd and he didn't expect any more to ride back to see what had happened. They had all heard the rifle shots and probably suspected that the Cheyenne had attacked them.

When Vernon and Tommy carried Roy's body off the trail to a shallow depression, they both returned to pick up George. Color had returned to Tommy's face, but he still looked wan. His nose crinkled up when he lifted the feet of the dead man as Vern hefted him by the shoulders.

"Cover them good with rocks," Reese called out to them after they laid George's body next to Roy's. "Strip them of their pistols and any money they have in their pockets."

The dead men's horses stood on both sides of the trail, their reins drooping, their saddles empty. Reese rode over to Roy's horse and grabbed the reins. Then he rode to George's horse and gathered up his reins. The horses looked forlorn to him, dull-eyed and silent, as he led them back to the trampled trail.

Vernon and Tommy walked back. Both of them had pistol belts slung from their shoulders. Vern had a wad of bills and change in his hands.

"What do I do with what Roy had in his pockets?" he asked.

"We'll keep a kitty in the chuck wagon. At noon stop, you can put their pistols in the wagon and the money in the kitty. In the meantime, you can sling their gun belts from these saddle horns."

Tommy draped a gun belt from the saddle horn of George's horse. Avery slung Roy's from his horse's saddle. He stuffed the money into his pants pocket. Then the two climbed onto their own horses.

"You put plenty of rocks over those men, Vern?" Reese asked.

"We put all we could find that were right close," Vern said. "But there's already a buzzard up in the sky."

Reese looked up.

A lone buzzard was wheeling in the sky as if on an invisible carousel. In the distance, he saw two others flapping their wings and flying lazily to join the lone bird hovering over the makeshift graves of his two hands.

"Can't be helped," Reese said to no one as he turned his horse away from where the men were buried.

"Nature's way of cleanin' up the land," Avery said.

Reese shot him a look. "To hell with nature," he said.

Tommy stared at Reese with his mouth open as if surprised that his boss would say something like that.

"Nature wouldn't take kindly to you sayin'

that," Vern said.

Reese shot him a withering look. "You keep your thoughts to yourself, Avery," he said. "You're still on a short string in my book."

"What for?" Avery asked.

"You know," Reese said, and let it drop.

Avery scowled, but wisely said nothing.

Puzzled, Tommy wore a look of bewilderment on his face.

Reese noticed the empty rifle scabbards on the saddles of both horses. He felt a rush of alarm course through his body like liquid fire.

"Tommy, Vern," he said, "scout around here for the rifles of Roy and George. Look hard."

Tommy began to ride around the places where the men had fallen. He covered both sides of the trail.

A look of relief came over Vern's face, but he pulled the brim of his hat down to cover his elation. He thought of Silver Bear and his having two Winchesters. He knew that the Cheyenne were armed only with bows and arrows. Rifles could make them equal to any white man's firepower.

Reese looked for the missing rifles too. He tried to picture in his mind what had happened when the outriders were ambushed and the cattle stolen.

The men, Roy and George, would have dropped their rifles. Any Cheyenne close to them would have seen their rifles fall and gone after them.

The thought of Silver Bear having repeating rifles made Reese feel slightly sick.

"Anything?" he asked Avery.

Vern shook his head. "There are no rifles on the ground out here," he said.

"Tommy?" Reese asked.

"No, sir. I haven't found none. Redskins must've taken them."

"Stole them," Reese said as anger flared up in him.

"Stolen," Tommy said, and continued to look at the ground for one or both rifles.

Reese looked into the saddlebags on the horses of both men. Each had boxes of cartridges.

He breathed a short sigh of relief.

"Well, if the Cheyenne picked up those rifles, they didn't steal any ammunition from my men," he said. "All those redskins will have are the cartridges in the magazines."

Vern scowled. Reese was right, of course. But with rifles, the Cheyenne would gain an advantage. An arrow was lethal, but a rifle could even up the odds between a Cheyenne and a white man. The bullet could go farther and faster than an arrow.

Reese realized that they weren't going to find any rifles.

"Okay," he said. "That's it. The Cheyenne got two rifles and a little bit of ammunition. Let's pack it up and head back to take care of the herd."

Vern nodded, and Jimmy's face lit up. He glanced over at where they had taken the dead men and saw the buzzards dropping from the sky like autumn leaves. One of the birds was already at the piles of rocks, walking back and forth, its head cocked to look for an opening. Jimmy turned away with a feeling of sickness rising from his stomach.

"You boys take these reins. Put the horses with the remuda. Leave the saddles on until we get to the chuck wagon at sunset."

Tommy and Vern rode over. Each grabbed the reins that Reese held out for them.

The four rode away, down the cattle trail, over ground that was pockmarked with cattle hooves and horses' tracks.

Vern and Tommy were poor replacements for the two men who had died fighting off the Indians. Reese knew that it would be difficult to hold the herd with the men he still had left. And those who were still alive would have to work harder to keep the herd in line on the long drive to Cheyenne.

He would have to work harder too. He had to figure out the best way to use the hands he had left.

What he dreaded was a stampede.

And winter, which was not far off. Those black clouds in the north were an ominous sign that there might be a snowstorm only hours or days away.

He might lose most of his herd if it snowed before they reached Cheyenne.

Now, he thought, was the time for prayer. And speed.

CHAPTER 18

Sometime during that same afternoon, Checkers knew that Jimmy John was not going to make it. The man moaned and Checkers stopped the wagon.

"What's wrong?" Louella asked.

"Got to check on Jimmy John," he said. "I don't like the sounds he's makin'."

Checkers pulled the wagon off the trail. He set the brake and climbed into the wagon as Louella watched anxiously from her seat.

"Feelin' real bad, Checkers," Jimmy John moaned. "Burnin' up."

Checkers touched a hand to Jimmy John's cheek. His skin was flaming hot.

"You got a high fever, Jimmy John," Checkers said. "Maybe too high."

"I feel awful bad," Jimmy John said.

"Let's have a look at those wounds," Checkers said.

"Need any help?" Louella asked.

"Not yet," Checkers replied.

He unwrapped the bandage around Jimmy John's middle and looked at the wound in his stomach. The hole was filled with pus, and the skin around the wound was red and swollen.

"Let's have a look at your back," Checkers said. "You just lie still. I'm going to turn you over on your side."

"It hurts real bad, Checkers," Jimmy John said.

"I know, I know."

He rolled Jimmy John onto his side and examined the hole in his back. It looked the same as the one in his belly. The skin was red and there was pus oozing from the wound. He pushed to roll Jimmy John onto his back.

"You got an infection," he said.

"So?"

"So, it don't look good, Jimmy John. If I can't bring your fever down and heal up that infection, well, it's goin' to get worse."

"How much worse?" Jimmy John asked.

"I don't know. An infection in that wound might spread."

"Spread where?"

"All through your body."

"Meanin'?" Jimmy John's eyes widened and looked slightly bloodshot.

"Meaning you might not make it," Checkers said.

Louella gasped at his words.

"You mean I might cash in?"

"Yeah. Sorry. But it don't look good. I don't have medicine to bring down your fever or heal that infection. I guess you just have to ride it out."

"How do I ride it out?" Jimmy John asked, and there was a pleading tone in his voice.

"Unless that fever breaks and you start to heal inside, it's just going to get worse, Jimmy John. The infection will spread and you'll get real sick."

"I'm sick now," Jimmy John said.

"You'll likely get a lot sicker, son."

Jimmy John closed his eyes. His breathing was thready. There was a slight rasp in his throat every time he took in a breath.

Checkers climbed out of the wagon and back onto the seat. Louella looked into the wagon. Jimmy John looked as if he were asleep.

Checkers picked up the reins and took off the brake. He rattled the reins, and the horses stepped out. He steered them back to the trail and pulled out his compass. The needle spun and settled on a direction.

"Now we drive to the sunset," Checkers said.

The horses picked up speed and Louella was rocked back and forth on her seat. She held on to a side panel and looked at the horses. They strained against the leather harness but pulled the wagon along at a brisk pace.

"Is he going to make it?" she asked Checkers after he had slowed the horses.

He shook his head. "I doubt it."

"Is there anything we can do?" she asked.

"That infection looks pretty bad. It'll spread like all get out. I don't think he'll last the day."

"It's so sad. A fine young man like that."

"Way before his time, Louella, way before his time."

A feeling of sadness came over her. She looked back into the wagon. Jimmy John's eyes were closed. His face was pale. With no bandage, she could see his swollen stomach, the redness surrounding the wound. A few tears fled down her face. She wiped them away with a swipe of her arm.

"It's getting cold," she said as the wagon rumbled over the wide buffalo trail.

"Yep. Be some weather catch up to us by and by."

"What do you mean?" she asked.

"Storm comin'," he said. "Can't you feel it? Just take a look at that sky."

She looked up. The sky was leaden, with clouds stacked up like rolls of cotton batting. She shivered and wrapped her arms around her breasts and back.

The wind blew at their backs and the temperature began to drop.

There was a freshness to the chilly air. But when Louella looked at Jimmy John, there were flies swarming over the wound in his belly. The wagon was filled with the *zizz-zizz* of their wings. Flies crawled over the wounded man's clothes and face.

"There's a jacket of mine in the back," Checkers said. "A couple of them. You get too cold, you put one of them on and hand me the other one."

"I'm cold now," she said.

"Right up against the backboard," he said.

She reached in and felt a pile of cloth. She lifted one, a fleece-lined jacket that looked too large for her. The other one was heavier and also was lined with wool.

"I usually put on the lighter one, but you can use that one," he said.

"It is getting cold," she said.

She handed the heavier jacket to Checkers and slipped into the lighter one. The jacket was warm. She wrapped it around her as Checkers put on the other jacket.

"It's such a shame that Jimmy John has to

endure so much pain," she said as the wagon rolled along over dirt and grass. "Only to die so young."

"That's the way it is, ma'am," Checkers said. "I've seen a lot of good men die young out here in the West. It's something you never get over if you knew 'em. It seems like they leave a big hole in your life when they go like that."

"Yes. That was how I felt when my pa died. He left a big hole in my world."

"Your ma still alive?"

"She's alive, I think. But just barely. Poor thing lost her mind after Pa died and she just seemed to walk around in a daze. Her sister is taking care of her back in Ohio. But I haven't heard from Aunt Nellie since last Christmas."

"Jimmy John's folks booted him out of the house when he was still wet behind the ears. They were both drunks and didn't give a damn about their kid. He's been on his own since he was thirteen years old."

"I didn't know," she said.

"Everybody's got a story like that. The West is where they come. Some come out to die. Some come out to live."

"Yes, I think you're right," she said. "Reese came out west to live, but the Cheyenne were a problem."

142

"He should've left well enough alone," Checkers said. "He's made lasting enemies. And people forget that the Injuns was here first. It's their land we're on right now. We took it from 'em, but it wasn't right. Not the way we did it."

"You know, don't you, Checkers?"

"I know," he said.

They rode in silence for a long while. Checkers had started to look for a likely spot to make camp as they neared the sunset hour.

Louella looked in on Jimmy John every so often, but he didn't seem to be making any progress. When she touched his cheek, it was like touching a hot stove. He was burning up inside and often cried out in pain. Each time, his cries grew weaker, his voice softer.

The clouds thickened and thunderheads bloomed in the north. The breeze stiffened and grew colder. Louella looked up at the sky and wrapped Checkers's jacket around her more tightly.

As the sun dropped lower in the sky over the western horizon, Checkers sat up straight, his eyes fixed on a distant shimmer.

"There it is," he said. "Right where I expected it to be."

"What's that?" Louella asked.

"Our evening stop. That's a lake you see out there."

She looked in the direction Checkers pointed his arm and hand.

"Is that a lake?" she asked.

"Sure is. Spring fed. An oasis, you might say."

He veered the wagon in the direction of the lake, which was off to the right of the trail. It was not a large lake, and its surface was ruffled by the wind. Whitecaps rimmed the wavelets as they approached.

Checkers wheeled the chuck wagon onto a grassy spot near the water, and the wagon chugged to a stop. The horses whickered and cocked their heads toward the lake. They blew air through their noses in blustery equine snorts and pawed the ground with their front hooves.

"Well, here we are. Good place to bed down the cattle. Plenty of grass and water."

"It's ideal," she said.

"Jump down and stretch your legs, little lady. We're here for the night."

"My legs don't stretch much," she said, and Checkers suddenly remembered that she was a cripple.

"Sorry," he said. "Just a figure of speech."

"No need to apologize, Checkers. I'll

stretch what I can."

She looked into the wagon at Jimmy John. He was not moving. His eyes were closed and he looked at peace.

"Checkers," she said. "I think Jimmy John is . . ."

"Dead?"

"Yes. He's . . . he's . . ."

Checkers turned around and put a hand on Jimmy John's cheek. It was ice-cold. He climbed inside and put an ear to Jimmy John's mouth. He was not breathing. He shook him, but his body was already starting to stiffen.

"He's gone, Louella."

"Oh no," she cried, and covered her face with both hands.

"Nothing to do but bury him someplace out here," Checkers said. "I'll get a shovel."

She watched as Checkers dug a grave on the south side of the lake. Watched as he carried the young man's body over to the hole he had dug and placed him in the depression. She walked over and stood there as he folded Jimmy John's arms over his chest.

"He looks right peaceful, don't he?" Checkers said as he picked up the shovel.

"I'll pray for his soul," she said.

"If he has a soul, it's plumb gone," Checkers said. He began to shovel dirt over Jimmy John's corpse. Louella turned away, unable to witness the burial.

It began to mist over the lake. Then it began to rain.

Checkers finished piling dirt over Jimmy John's body and tamped the dirt down with the back of the shovel.

Louella had walked back to the wagon and was waiting for him.

"Best you get inside, ma'am," he said. "I'll try and get a fire goin'. This rain gets much heavier, the hands will have a cold supper."

"Yes, thanks, Checkers," she said as she pulled herself up over the tailgate and climbed into the wagon. She listened to the soft patter of rain and saw the prairie become veiled in the twilight with curtains of mist and rainfall.

She heard Checkers as he gathered dry brush and twigs to start a fire. She heard the clank of rocks as he built a pit.

Soon she felt the warmth of a fire and when she looked out, she saw the flames fight the rain, lashing up into the mist and sputtering as drops fell into the fire and onto the rocks.

She looked back at the trail from under the canvas and wondered how soon the herd would hove into sight. It was gloomy and wet as the rain increased. She heard the fire sputter and gasp as the rain fell faster and harder.

A few moments later, Checkers appeared at the tailgate. He was soaked. His hat dripped water from its brim.

"Fire's goin' out," he said. "And that rain is turnin' to sleet."

The point man, Calvin Forbes, rode into view, his head down, his slicker gleaming yellow in the dim light of dusk.

"Herd's comin'," Checkers said.

Louella looked out and saw Calvin. Behind him, starting to run, was the herd.

She did not see Reese.

And the rain turned to sleet as the first cattle lined up at the lake to drink. More and more cattle arrived and took up stations on the banks until the lake was surrounded by the curly brown bodies of cattle.

Reese came riding up. Relieved, Louella waved to him from inside the shelter of the wagon. The rattling sound of sleet was scratching at the canvas of the wagon.

"A hell of a night," Reese said. "And it's going to snow."

As he spoke, the sleet went silent and the first white flakes of snow began to fall. The fire went out and the shadowy land began to turn black as the night came on like a thief, stealing all the light.

CHAPTER 19

Silver Bear held up one of the Winchester rifles. He sighted down the barrel, swung it from right to left.

Yellow Horse examined the other rifle, turning it over in his hands, looking at the stock in admiration.

Silver Bear pulled on the lever and a cartridge ejected from the receiver. Another one, from the magazine, slid into place. He picked up the bullet and held it up to the sun. Its brass gleamed as he turned it over in his hand.

One of the Cheyenne women, Morning Doe, looked at the brass cartridge and made a sign to Silver Bear. She smiled. The sign she made was of a necklace.

Silver Bear shook his head.

"No, this is not for a necklace," he said. "It is for the fire stick. It makes a loud noise and kills from far away."

"I have many of those," she said. "What

do you call it?"

"The white man calls it a bullet. It is a death stone. It can tear a man open, tear his heart to pieces."

"Oh, I thought it would make a pretty necklace," she said.

"You have more of these, Morning Doe?"

"Yes. They were in an iron box. It was very heavy, but I carried it to camp. The fire did not burn inside the box."

"Bring me the box," he said, a flicker of delight on his copper face.

Morning Doe arose and walked away from the lean-to. She returned in a few moments with a strongbox in her arms. She set it down in front of Silver Bear.

The box was oblong and made of a strong metal. He lifted the lid and looked inside. There were boxes of .44-caliber cartridges and Colt .45 cartridges. There were some loose shells lying on the cartridge boxes.

"You did well to get this box," Silver Bear told Morning Doe.

"I was going to make a necklace out of those pretty metal things," she said.

"There is a black powder inside that would kill you like the thunder that comes from the sky," he said. "It would make a very loud noise and tear you to pieces."

"Oh. There is another box of those things.

Little Turtle has it. She wants to make a bracelet from some of them. They shine like the yellow stones in the river."

The other women were roasting beef over the cook fire, and the smell of food was strong. The wind blew harder and the skies were covered in gray clouds that bulged like snake bellies.

"Bring me the other box," Silver Bear said.

"I will do this," she replied, and rose from the blanket inside the lean-to.

The creek was whipped to a frenzy by the wind, and the women who were there to get water turned away from the water and carried their vessels back to camp.

The sun dipped low in the sky as Morning Doe carried another strongbox to Silver Bear. He opened it and saw the boxes of .44 cartridges. He could not read the words, but he knew what they meant. He picked up one box and shook it. It was full and did not rattle.

"This is good," he said to Morning Doe. "Now we have the fire stones to kill many white men."

"I am glad that we found these boxes," she said.

Silver Bear felt rich. His people had cattle and food. He had two rifles and plenty of ammunition. He knew how the white man's rifle worked and he was anxious to shoot them with it. He called for Yellow Horse and Black Feather to come to his shelter.

The two braves came to the lean-to and sat down.

"What do you have, Silver Bear?" Yellow Horse asked as he pointed to the two strongboxes.

Silver Bear held up a cartridge.

"There are many of these," he said. "They are the fire stones that kill from far away."

"Yes," Black Feather said. "I have seen these in the white man's camps. They are like the thunder and they kill from a long way."

"Now we can get as many cattle as we want," Silver Bear said. "We can kill the white men so that they will not come back to our land."

Yellow Horse and Black Feather both grunted in approval.

The cooking fire hissed in the gathering mist and when the sun fell off the edge of the earth, the first snowflakes began to fall from the gray sky.

Silver Bear went to the fire and held out both hands as the snow fell.

"This is a good sign," he said to all who were there. "This will stop the cattle and the white men from running away. We can catch up to them again and take what we want. We can shoot the white men like we would shoot blind buffalo. Then they will not return to our land."

They all tore off pieces of meat that was cooked and began to eat.

The snow continued to fall and stick to the ground like a blanket of ermine fur. The women and the braves all dressed in warm animal clothing.

The fire kept them all warm for a long time. Then the snowfall smothered it and the darkness settled on the camp.

And the white snow seemed to shine in the dark.

To Silver Bear, it was a good sign.

CHAPTER 20

Reese was worried.

He hugged Louella after he dismounted while Checkers stood by the fire.

"You might not have that fire going long," Reese said.

"I know. At least I can boil us some coffee. Be cold sandwiches for supper, I'm thinkin'," Checkers said.

"Reese, I'm so glad to see you. All day I had to watch a man die," Louella said.

"Jimmy John?"

Checkers nodded and added more brush to his fire.

"It was horrible, Reese," Louella said.

The snow began to fall thicker and faster as the herd streamed to the small lake and drank.

Checkers had told him where he had buried Jimmy John. Reese looked at the grave, which was visible from the chuck wagon.

One less man to make the drive, Reese thought.

Snow blew across the prairie. Flakes melted as they struck the lake. But some stuck on the hides of the cattle. These were slower to melt.

"It looks real bad, Checkers," Reese said to the cook.

"Sleet made the ground cold, so this snow's goin' to stick."

"How much snow do you think we'll get?"

"Couple inches," Checkers said. "Maybe more."

"Be hell drivin' cattle in this mess," Reese said.

"Well, you don't have to drive none tonight anyways. Maybe it'll stop snowing and melt off tomorrow."

"I hope so."

But it did not stop snowing. Nighthawks circled the restless herd as the wind blew snow into their eyes and swept over the horses, leaving a dusty patina on their coats. The horses blinked as snowflakes stung their eyes.

Reese and Louella shivered in their bedrolls beneath the wagon. Next to them Checkers pulled the blankets up around his neck. The horses rubbed against one another to ward off some of the cold.

It snowed all night. Slow, gentle flakes fell, but they did not melt. The wind blew drifts across the trail and up against the banks of the lake. The hands had to knock snow off some of the calves who were snuggled up next to their mothers, and a few times they had to brush snow off a steer that had gotten caught in a drift.

It was still snowing the next morning when the sky paled under blankets of cottony clouds.

Reese crawled from his bedroll beneath the wagon and stood next to the wagon. He saw the cattle all dusted with snow, looking strangely ghostly in the morning light.

There was at least two inches of snow that had fallen. But there were drifts that were much deeper. Reese felt a wave of disappointment envelop him as he looked over the snow-dusted herd and saw his men riding here and there around the cattle.

Men who had slept under the wagon stirred and crawled out of their bedrolls.

Calvin was the first to walk over to Reese. Checkers was wrestling with his blankets, grumbling at the cold as he tried to extricate himself and crawl from under the wagon. Louella lay locked in sleep under Reese's blanket that he had added to hers.

"I didn't get much sleep," Calvin said.

"Rode nighthawk most of the night." He rubbed his hands together for warmth. He wore a heavy jacket, and his bandanna covered the lower part of his face.

"I wonder how many calves froze to death last night," Reese said. He rubbed his hands together too.

"I didn't see none. But them drifts can raise hob with the little ones."

Both men saw their frosty breaths spew from their mouths as they breathed.

"Well, when you get warm enough to ride, you might check with the other hands. I expect we'll lose a few head. Especially if this damn snow keeps fallin'."

"We got caught — that's for sure," Calvin said. "Caught out in the open without even a prairie dog hole to crawl into."

Checkers emerged from beneath the wagon. He kicked at the snow that filled the fire ring. There was still brush piled up next to it, rimmed with thin lines of snow.

"Mornin', Reese," he said. He cupped his hands and blew on them. A frosty cloud of steam spewed from his mouth.

"Good mornin', Checkers. Think you can start us up a fire?"

"I can start one up," he said. "Just don't know how long it will burn. That snow is colder'n a witch's tit."

"Or a well digger's ass," Reese said.

Both men laughed as others stirred beneath the wagon. Snow had blown underneath, and all shook off the accumulated flakes as they tossed their blankets aside.

Lonnie and Tommy crawled from under the wagon as Checkers began to stack kindling in the snow-filled fire ring. Reese could hear his bones crack as he squatted.

"You sleep good, Tommy?" Reese asked.

"I wasn't warm, if that's what you mean. I slept some, but that wind blew snow on my face half the night."

"You have to cover your face with your hat," Johnny said.

"I tried that," Tommy said. "Hat blew off and I just now found it."

Johnny laughed and frosty air plumed from his mouth.

Checkers fumbled in his pocket and dug out a box of matches. He struck one and touched it to the thinnest branches of a dry bush. The wood caught fire and a feeble flame flickered. Its light bounced off the snow, and the snow beneath the kindling began to shrink as it melted.

"I'd better ride out and check the damage," Lonnie said. "I'll bet my saddle's stiff as a board."

"I'll go with you," Johnny said. "I ain't

gettin' no warmer just a-standin' here."

"Bring my horse over after you saddle up, Johnny," Reese said. "I want to check on the herd too. Saddle's still on him."

"Smart man," Johnny said.

He and Lonnie walked to where the remuda was quartered, near the lake, in the lee of the wind. They walked through falling snow, snow that swirled and clung to their jackets like cakes of white flour.

Checkers had the fire blazing and added more brush and chunks of wood.

As the fire grew higher, Reese and the others there warmed their hands. Snowflakes hissed as they fell into the flames. The wind fanned the fire and blew the flames in bright flares as it whipped across the prairie.

Tommy rubbed his hands over the fire. "Maybe I'd better get my horse," he said. "I just don't know what to do or where to go to help with the herd."

"You can ride around it and see if any of the cattle are in trouble," Reese said. "Look for cattle stuck in snowdrifts or floundering to get up from their beds."

"I'll do that," Tommy said. He rubbed his hands one last time and then walked over to the remuda. The wagon with the kegs of grain stood horseless nearby. Lonnie was feeding his horse with a coffee can full of corn and oats.

A fellow named Chuck Norcross drove the feed wagon, and his partner, Jeremy Coates, took care of the remuda while they were on the trail. But they were seldom seen, since they stayed well behind the herd and only showed themselves when the drive made camp.

The wrangler and the hauler were still inside the buckboard with its rigid canvas top, the side tarps pulled down to shield them against the wind and the snow.

"Go ahead and sleep, Jeremy," Lonnie said. "We can get our own horses."

Coates made a sound from inside the buckboard. Johnny laughed as he sought out his own horse. His was still under saddle too. He caught up his horse and then went after Reese's. "I'll get him, Lonnie," he said. "Reese don't care who brings him his horse."

"Thanks, but I'll do it," Lonnie said.

Tommy rode off to circle the herd with Johnny. Lonnie led Reese's horse to him.

By that time, Louella had awakened. She sat up sleepily and rubbed her eyes. "Is it morning already?" she asked Reese, who stood by the fire.

"Yep," he said. "And we'll be movin' out soon. Better get yourself some grub when

Checkers gets around to cookin' it."

"I'm settin' water for the grits on to boil now," Checkers said. "But that coffee's about ready to drink."

"I'll have a cup before I get the herd moving," Reese said.

"Better have two," Checkers said. "It'll be mighty cold on the trail. Even with that wind at your back."

"One's enough," Reese said as Louella humped out of her bedroll and crawled on all fours from under the wagon.

She stretched when she stood up, and yawned. "Ooh," she said. "It's cold and it's still snowing."

"Not a good day for a cattle drive," Reese said. "You stay in the wagon or you'll freeze to death."

"I will," she said.

Reese drank his coffee and hugged Louella. Then he rode off to the farthest point of the herd, where he saw Ben Macklin, one of the older hands, kicking snow from a drift that had pinned one of the yearling calves under its weight.

"Need any help, Ben?" Reese asked.

"Naw. This little critter just fell asleep in the wrong place. Third one I've hauled out from under a pile of snow this mornin'."

"I'm going to make one loop and then get

the herd movin'," Reese said. "You got time to get yourself a bowl of grits and some coffee."

"I could eat one of these beeves," Ben said. "If they was cooked."

Reese laughed. He beckoned to Johnny, who was riding up on the outer right flank. "Johnny, roust these cattle in about ten minutes, unless you want some grits and coffee."

"Naw, I'll get me a sandwich after the herd gets movin'," Johnny said.

Tommy rode some distance behind him, then cut into the herd.

Reese thought that was enterprising of the young lad.

He watched as Tommy got some of the cows up, then pulled on the horns of a steer that had its rump stuck in a snowbank.

"That kid might make a good cowhand one of these days," Ben said as he rode toward the head of the herd.

"He's green, but he's comin' along," Reese said.

Half an hour later, the entire herd was back on the trail. The snow kept falling and the wind blew at their backs.

Later, the chuck wagon passed them, and Louella leaned out to wave at Reese. He waved back and bent his head as he rode left flank along a line of white-faced cattle with brown bodies.

The sun was a washed-out glow in the morning sky. The sky was as gray as slate, the clouds low and lumbering like wallowing beasts.

Reese sighed. It was going to be a long, hard day without much progress. When, he wondered, would it stop snowing and the sun come out? There was no sign that it would ever stop, and the sun seemed to get dimmer every minute.

The cattle moaned and groaned like old men in an infirmary.

His horse blew jets of vapor into the air, and their hooves made no sound on the snow-flocked ground.

CHAPTER 21

Silver Bear handed one of the Winchester rifles to Yellow Horse.

"You have shot the fire stick before," he said.

"Yes. I shot one of these. It hurt my shoulder."

"You know how to make it bark," Silver Bear said.

"I can make it roar like the angry bear," Yellow Horse said.

"I too have made the fire stick talk," Iron Knife said. "It was called a 'Yellow Boy' by the soldiers at the fort. They laughed when I got knocked down the first time I pulled its little tail."

"Did you hit anything?" Silver Bear asked.

"I hit a pumpkin," Iron knife said. "I blew it to pieces at the fort, the one they call 'Laramie.' "

"Good, Iron Knife," Silver Bear said. "I give you the other rifle." Silver Bear picked

164

up the other rifle and gave it to Iron Knife.

"I will shoot many White Eyes with this fire stick," Iron Knife said.

"There are bullets in those iron boxes," Silver Bear said. He pointed to the strongboxes inside his lean-to. "Carry them in your pouch. I will use my bow to kill the White Eyes."

"Hunh," grunted Yellow Horse and Iron Knife.

"When do we go to kill the White Eyes?" Black Feather asked.

"We go now," Silver Bear said. "Tell the women to pack the camp and the food. Tell the braves to place the travois on the ponies."

"There is much snow," Iron Knife said.

"We drive the cattle in front of us. They will trample the snow."

"Why do we go after the white man now?" Yellow Horse asked.

"I have given this much thought," Silver Bear said. "If we kill the White Eyes their cattle will run away like the buffalo. And the cattle will cover the land like the buffalo. There will be many cows and they will be our buffalo. They will feed our people like the buffalo."

Yellow Horse thought of cattle roaming the prairie, making calves, multiplying like the buffalo. "That would be a good thing," he said.

"It would be what the Great Spirit would want for his people," Black Feather said. "And the white men would leave our land. They would dry up like the leaves that fall from the trees in the moon of falling leaves."

"Death to the White Eyes."

The women began to pack their goods and take down the lean-tos. They scurried like prairie dogs to load the travois after the men had attached them to some of the ponies.

Within hours, the Cheyenne and their friends, the Lakota and the Crow, left the deserted and empty camp. They drove the dozen head of cattle in front of them and headed south as the snow continued to fall.

The snow covered their tracks and there was no sign that they had ever been in that place.

None of them looked back.

Chapter 22

Reese could not see much through the heavy snowfall. The cattle were breaking the trail, but they struggled in the drifts. And he saw no sign that the snow would stop during those morning hours.

The land was cold and white. There was no longer any glimmer of a yellow sun. The land was bleak and peaceful.

He rode far off on the right flank of the lumbering, floundering herd that was curtained by falling snow. He could see the cattle, but their shapes were distorted and ghostly in the shroud of light and snow.

Calvin rode point some distance ahead of Reese, and Checkers was ahead of him, leaving wagon ruts in the snow as he and Louella rolled over an ermine carpet. Somewhere on the other side of the herd, the remuda was following the feed wagon, making its own trail on virgin snow.

Behind him on the rear flank, Lonnie was

holding the herd to the trail, while Johnny was on drag, with the easiest path of all as the herd trampled the snow into frozen mush.

Reese gnawed on a bone of hardtack biscuit mainly to keep his lips from freezing. The wind blew at his back and he could feel its chill through his coat. His face was raw and reddish from the cold and wind, and his eyes burned from the strain of staring at so much whiteness.

Reese was surprised half an hour later when he saw the dim outlines of a cabin. As he rode closer, he saw smoke rising from its chimney. There was a man outside with a shovel. And under a covered shelter, a horse whickered as he rode up.

The man who was shoveling snow away from the doorstep of the small log cabin looked up and waved to Reese.

Reese waved back. He reined up to talk to the man.

"Howdy," Reese said. "Didn't expect to see any folks out this way."

"Line shack," the man said. "Stuck here when it snowed."

"My name's Reese Balleen. That's my herd you see yonder."

"I heard 'em a while ago. Name's Kelso. Earl Kelso. Where you headed?"

"Cheyenne, the Flying U."

"Oh yeah, Chip's spread. Long way to go. How many head?"

"Near a thousand."

Kelso was a muscular man in his thirties, with long hair that was black as pitch. He had a three-day shadow of beard stubble stippling his jaw, and his eyes were a pale blue, close-set and straddling a nose that looked as if it had been broken more than once. He wore a mackinaw coat and Reese saw the tip of his pistol holster sticking out.

"You work for a ranch hereabouts?" Reese asked. "I mean you're in a line shack way out in the middle of nowhere."

"Yeah, I work for Jasper Mullins. He has a spread, the Crooked M."

"Cattle?"

"Horses, mostly. He's light on the cattle right now."

"Hard times?" Reese asked.

"Hard enough. Cattle all got sick and died on him. Pinkeye and black leg."

"Sorry to hear it," Reese said.

"That's the way it goes sometimes."

While the two were talking, Lonnie spotted them and rode over. A look of recognition flashed in his eyes when he saw Kelso.

"Howdy, Earl," Lonnie said.

"Lonnie. I see you got yourself a job."

169

"You workin', Earl?"

"If you call this work, yeah," Earl said.

Reese wondered if the two men were friends. He detected an air of hostility in Lonnie's tone and Kelso looked as if Lonnie was the last person he wanted to see.

"Didn't expect to see you way out here," Lonnie said.

"I didn't 'spect I'd be here neither," Earl said. "Damn snow. If I didn't shovel, I'd likely get locked into this godforsaken cabin."

"Yeah, well, I got work to do, Earl."

"That's a lot of beef," Earl said, and there was something in his eyes that ticked off warning alarms in Reese's brain.

But as Lonnie rode back to shepherd the herd, Earl slid his shovel into the lump of snow at his feet and tossed snow to one side.

"I'll be goin' too," Reese said.

"Luck on the drive," Earl said.

Reese touched fingers to the brim of his hat and turned his horse. There was something in Earl's tone that didn't sound right to him. Did the man mean good luck or bad? When Reese looked back, Earl was back to his shovel and seemingly without any further interest in Reese, Lonnie, or the herd.

A while later, Lonnie rode up to Reese on

the front flank.

"That feller you was talkin' to, Kelso," Lonnie said. "Know who he is?"

Reese shook his head. "He said he worked for Jasper Mullins. Never heard of him either," he said. "Said the ranch was the Crooked M."

"Crooked M is a good name for it. Mullins is no better'n Kelso. They're both horse thieves."

"He said they raised horses and some cattle."

"Ha," Lonnie exclaimed, "only horses they're raisin' are probably stolen. I wouldn't trust Earl Kelso as far as I could throw one of these steers."

"You know him from somewhere?"

"Denver. When I worked on the Lucky Day Ranch for Roy Davis. He and Mullins used to hang out at the Hitch Rail Saloon on Curtis Street. We'd go in there on a Saturday night and whoop it up. Them two had a gang that made everyone nervous."

"What do you mean?" Reese asked.

"Oh, just rumors, like they all was robbin' pilgrims on the road from Pueblo and had 'em a spread in the mountains where they kept the horses they stole. We'd see 'em at auction every now and then, and some of the brands on those horses looked like they had been altered with a runnin' iron."

"Any proof?" Reese asked.

"One of their gang was caught red-handed and hanged there in Denver. I forget the feller's name. But he was thick as a tick on a dog with Kelso and Mullins. I seen him in the saloon with them two."

"Well, thanks, Lonnie. I reckon we've seen the last of Kelso, though. Funny to stumble on him like that."

"Yeah. A big surprise to me too. I haven't thought about him or Jasper Mullins since I left Denver and come to work for you."

"Yeah, I heard Roy Davis was killed and his ranch sold for back taxes."

"Yeah. Roy was killed all right. Shot with a rifle from a long ways off, and his cattle herd stolen. Nobody ever caught the ones who killed Roy or knew what happened to all his cattle. But I have my suspicions."

"Mullins?" Reese said.

Lonnie nodded. "Mullins and his gang, four or five of the hardest cases you ever saw."

"Well, thanks, Lonnie. I haven't thought about Roy in a long while. I knew what happened to him because I bought cattle at the auction in Denver, the one they had at the stockyards. Roy was a decent man."

"And an honest one," Lonnie said. "Not

like Mullins. Or Kelso."

One or two of the cows drifted away from the herd and started to turn back.

Lonnie turned his horse. "Back to work," he said. "Them two cows want to get back to that lake, I reckon."

Reese watched him spur his horse into a run. Snow flew from the horse's hooves as it stomped its way through at least four inches of snow. More cows tried to turn from the herd. But Lonnie and his horse drove them back into line.

Reese thought about Earl Kelso and wondered why he had been in a line shack with no sign of any livestock anywhere near it.

And what, he wondered, was a hard case like Kelso doing so far from any town? Men like that were usually someplace where they could buy a drink or a woman and brawl on Saturday nights. He just didn't seem to fit in as a ranch hand.

He hoped he'd seen the last of Kelso. There was something about the man that made his skin crawl.

During the rest of the morning, Reese kept thinking about Roy Davis and how he had died. Someone had bushwhacked him, stolen his cattle, and left his widow penniless. It was not a typical story of the West, but it was one he knew well. He and Roy had shared many a drink at auction, and Reese knew him to be a man with a good eye for sound cattle.

Nobody had ever caught the rustlers or the man who had shot and killed Roy Davis.

So much for the law, he thought.

Town law, at that.

Out here, he mused, there was no law at all. And dangerous men like Earl Kelso hadn't a worry in the world.

And that was a worry as Reese rode on, alone with his thoughts and the bawling cattle that trudged through the snow that was still falling, still piling up on the trail as the wind blew in from the north like a banshee on the prowl.

And there was no sign that it would ever stop in that gaunt white world where a sea of cattle trampled through hock-high snow on an old buffalo trail.

Reese looked back once or twice. Back where he had been, at the little log cabin that served as a line shack on empty pasture.

He had the feeling that someone was following him.

But there was nobody there.

CHAPTER 23

Jasper Mullins was a giant of a man, with an appetite to match. When Earl rode up to the main house on the Crooked M, Jasper was gnawing on a shank of beef with two other men, Homer Parsons and Dave Riggs. Those two were playing cards at the same table while putting down shot glasses full of cheap whiskey. Neither was drunk, but they were well on their way.

Homer shuffled the worn and frayed deck of cards. "Five-card stud," he said. "Jokers wild."

"Deal 'em," Dave said. "It's quicker than seven-card."

"Don't you two ever get tired of playin' poker?" Mullins asked as he chewed his beefsteak.

"Hell, there ain't nothin' to do but play cards," Homer said as he dealt out two hands.

"I never been so bored in my life," Dave

said as he picked up his cards, one by one. "Same thing ever' day. Same cheap whiskey, same tiresome grub."

"Something will turn up," Mullins said. "Something always does."

"Hell, it's snowin' outside," Homer said. "And we're stuck out here with nothin' to do but put more wood on the fire." He glanced at the fireplace. The fire was burning and hissing as snowflakes descended the chimney and melted in the flames.

"You got anything planned, Jasper?" Dave asked.

Mullins swiped his sleeve across his wet mouth and swallowed the chewed chunk of meat.

"Nothin' right soon," Jasper said. "I'd like to get me to a town," Homer said, "where we can find a willing woman and eat some decent grub."

"Yeah, like Cheyenne," Dave said. "That's a town where we ain't known."

"Cheyenne is full of drifters and soldiers," Mullins said. "Denver's better."

"Yeah, but the law knows us in Denver," Homer said. "And I think there's a reward poster with my picture on it."

Mullins laughed. "We all got posters with our faces on 'em in Denver," he said. "Puny little rewards. Five hundred bucks. Nobody's goin' to come after us for that kind of money."

"What about Roger Collins?" Homer said. "Somebody shot him dead for two hunnert dollars. Money is money."

"Collins was sparkin' the man's wife," Mullins said. "He brought it on hisself."

"Yeah," Dave said. "Roger was a damn fool. But I'd like to get the bastard who killed him. I liked Roger."

"He was a fool," Homer said as he pushed poker chips into the center of the table. "I bet five dollars."

"I'll just call," Dave said, and pushed chips against the others. They made a clicking sound.

Homer looked up and across the table. Through the window and the falling snow, he saw a rider approaching at a slow, floundering pace.

"Somebody's comin'," he said. "Looks like Kelso."

"What the hell's he doin' comin' here?" Mullins asked. "I told him to stay in the line shack and watch for any cattle that might be on that old buffalo trail."

"Maybe he saw somethin'," Homer said.

"He'd better have seen cattle or horses," Mullins said. He got up from the table and walked to the window. He heard the whisper of cards and the click of chips from his two men at the table.

"Snow's driftin' in that wind," Mullins said.

Kelso was fighting his way through heavy drifts, slapping his horse's rump with his reins. The snow fell thick and fast, large flakes, and they made Kelso look shrouded in a curtain of white flakes.

"That damn snow is driftin' all over the place. Kelso's fighting it all the way."

The two stopped playing cards and walked to the window. They saw Kelso's horse shy from every hump in the snow and plunge into four-foot drifts. There was no sign of the trail leading to the house.

Presently Kelso reached the well, then the hitch rail. His hat and coat were white with snow and when he dismounted, snow fell from the horse like powder.

"Let him in," Mullins said.

Homer went to the door as Kelso tramped up the snow-flocked path. When he opened it, snowflakes flew through the door as Kelso walked in, his boots packed with snow. He took off his hat and shook it free of most of the flakes.

"Boy, it's good to be where it's warm," he said.

"Set down at the table, Earl," Mullins

said. "I expect you got a tale to tell."

The four men walked to the table in the center of the front room. They all scraped chairs on the hardwood floor and sat down. Mullins and the two others stared at Kelso in anticipation of what he had to say.

"Well, like you said, Jasper, somebody come down that old buffalo trail."

"Horses?" Mullins said.

"Cattle. A heap of 'em. Round a thousand head. Feller name of Reese Balleen is drivin' his herd down to Cheyenne."

Mullins pursed his lips and let out a long whistle.

"That's a lot of cattle," Homer said.

"Shut up," Mullins said. "Cows look okay?" he asked Kelso.

"Fat as pigs," Kelso answered. "And slow movin' in all this snow."

"Outriders? How many?" Mullins asked.

"Don't know. I just seen one flanker, and I knowed him."

"Who was it?" Mullins asked.

"Lonnie. Lonnie Willetts. You remember him from Denver, Jasper?"

"I don't have much of a recognition, but the name sounds a little familiar."

"He worked for Roy Davis on the Lucky Day Ranch," Kelso said.

"Oh yeah, that Lonnie. Smelled like cow shit."

The men at the table laughed. Mullins did not laugh.

"Can I have a shot of that whiskey?" Kelso asked.

"Have to swig it out of the bottle," Homer said. "I ain't gonna roust you up a whiskey glass."

"I'm plumb froze up inside," Kelso said. He uncorked the bottle and drank from it. His eyes teared up and he shuddered as the whiskey went down his throat.

"Feel better?" Mullins asked.

"I'm still half-froze," Kelso said.

"So, the herd is movin' real slow, you say," Mullins said.

"Real slow. It's snowin' like hell and there're drifts all across that buffalo trail. It'll take them a month of Sundays just to get out of North Dakota."

"Good," Mullins said. "That gives us a chance."

"Them two, Balleen and Lonnie, were packin' pistols and I saw rifles in their boots."

"Likely all the hands are totin' weapons," Mullins said. "No matter. We can pick 'em off one by one."

"You aim to keep the cattle we rustle, Jasper?" Homer asked. "Or sell 'em some-where?"

"We can't get all of the herd, so we won't be greedy on this. I'd say a couple hundred head ought to bring a fair price in Denver."

"Long drive, though," Riggs said. He swigged some of the whiskey and Mullins glared at him as he wiped his mouth.

"Maybe it'll quit snowin'," Homer said. "And it won't be so bad."

"Well, we need money," Riggs said. "Been a long while since we saw any greenbacks."

"Not so long," Mullins said. "Last horses we stole brought a pretty good price."

"Yeah, they did," Riggs said.

"Well, there're only four of us," Mullins said. "And a lot of cattle out there. You boys ready to ride?"

The three other men all nodded.

"One hour. We're goin' after them cattle in daylight."

"And in the snow," Kelso said.

"We drop those cowhands and we can take our sweet time," Mullins said.

"Be a pleasure," Homer said. Dave grinned and his eyes brightened.

"Dave, you pack us some grub. Leave the whiskey here."

"What if I get cold?" Riggs said.

"You can freeze your nuts off, for all I

care," Mullins said. "Now, let's get crackin'."

Kelso walked over to the fireplace and opened his jacket to let the heat in. He rubbed his hands to warm them. He shivered as the cold seeped from his body.

Mullins opened a gun case and took out a Winchester. From a drawer, he brought out a box of .44 cartridges. He set these on the table and from a wardrobe, he took out a heavy, fur-lined coat. Then he strapped on his gun belt from a clothes tree near the gun case. All the loops were filled with .45-caliber cartridges. He pulled the pistol and spun the cylinder. The magazine was full. He brought the hammer down to half-cock and slid the pistol back in its smooth leather holster. He walked over to the fireplace, carrying his coat under his huge arms.

"You did a good job out there," he said to Kelso.

"Thanks, Jasper," Kelso said. "You called it right. Somebody was bound to come down that old buffalo trail sooner or later."

"That's why I run the outfit," Mullins said. "Put that fire out before we go."

"I'll be ready," Kelso said. He thought of Lonnie, a man he did not know well. A man he might have to kill.

And he hoped he would have the chance

to drop Reese Balleen too. He had no use for cattle ranchers and their hired hands. As far as Kelso was concerned, they were all money-grubbing parasites who thought they were better than anybody else.

Well, he'd show them all right.

Their blood would look real pretty on the white snow.

CHAPTER 24

Checkers felt the wagon jolt and heard a horrible crunching sound. The wagon teetered and he felt the front of the wagon give way and drop. He knew that he had hit a hole in the trail. He had to hold on to the sideboard to keep from tumbling off the seat and falling to the ground.

Louella let out a loud cry of alarm as she swayed to the side. She reached out and grabbed the side panel to keep from sliding down toward Checkers.

"Checkers. What's going on? Did something break?"

"Wheel," he said. He set the brake since the horses were straining against their harness, struggling to pull the wagon out of the hole.

"Oh my," she said as she gripped the sideboard.

"Just hold on. I'll get her righted once I get off this dadgum seat."

The wagon lurched again as the horses stopped pulling and the wheel fell deeper into the depression.

A stab of pain jolted through Louella's hip and she cried out.

"You all right, ma'am?" Checkers asked. "Need some help?"

"I should get down," she said. "My hip is killing me in this position."

"I'll help you," he said. "Just let me get down. I got to fix that wheel or we'll be stuck here when the herd comes through. We're liable to get trampled to death if that happens."

"Oh my," she said again, and gritted her teeth against the surge of pain through her hip.

Checkers climbed down from the wagon. He looked at the wheel. There were at least two broken spokes. He shook his head and walked around the back of the wagon to the other side where Louella was holding on to the sideboard.

"Give me your hands," he said as he looked up at her.

She reached over and grasped his hands with hers.

"Can you stand up?" he asked.

"I — I think so. Give me a minute."

She struggled to turn and face Checkers.

Then she wobbled to her feet. She was shaky, but Checkers held on tight to her hands.

"Now step over, one foot only, and put your foot on my shoulder," he said.

She lifted one leg and stuck out her foot. The snow fell fast and the flakes were large. Checkers seemed to be in a white funnel with snow falling on and around him.

"Now I'm going to stoop some and you just foller me," he said. "Let your weight come down on me."

"I — I'll try," she said.

She felt his body sink as he bent his knees. She also felt the pressure in her foot increase as she put more of her weight on his shoulder.

"Now bring your other leg over the side and find my other shoulder," he said. He rose on his feet as she swung her other leg over. Her foot found his shoulder and then he pulled her.

"Ooh," she cried as she felt herself being jerked from the wagon.

"Hold on to my head," he told her. "I'll grab your waist when I squat and let you down easy."

She grabbed his temples beneath his hat and pulled on some hairs that were sticking out. She felt herself sink as Checkers squatted. Then his hands were around her waist. She squeezed her hands against his head.

A moment later he set her firmly on the ground. She was shaking inside, but glad to be on solid ground.

"Ooh, thank you, Checkers."

"Now, can you walk? I'll be a while fixin' that busted wheel."

"I'll be all right," she said. "There's so much snow."

"I know. I can lower the tailgate and lift you up so's you'll be under cover."

"No, I'll watch you fix that wheel and try to enjoy the falling snow." She was smiling, so he knew she was serious.

"Suit yourself," he said. "I'll help you walk around the wagon to the other side. He held on to Louella as she walked in her peculiar, disjointed gait around the back of the wagon to the other side.

"Wait here," Checkers said.

He walked a few feet away and found a somewhat flattened rock. He brushed away the snow with his hands and looked over at her.

"It'll be cold, but you can sit here and rest," he said.

"Thank you, Checkers. You're a dear." She limped over and Checkers helped her sit on the rock.

187

"It is cold," she said.

"Keep your toes moving in those boots and they might not freeze up on you. I'll be a while."

Checkers had spare spokes in the wagon. He brought those out, two of them, and then hunkered down to remove the broken ones from the wheel. He replaced those, twisting and working the replacements into their seats.

Then he took off the brake and walked in front of the horses and spoke to them. He pulled on their bridles and they stepped out, pulling the wagon. The wheel spun out of the hole and Checkers stopped pulling on the harness. He leaned over the sideboard and pulled on the brake.

Then he turned to Louella. "We're ready to roll," he said.

"I watched you work. You did a quick job on that wheel."

He reached out his arms and she took his hands. Checkers pulled Louella to her feet.

"Let's go around to the other side," he said. "Let me help you all I can."

"The snow," she said. "Hard to walk in it."

"You just take it easy," he said. "Let me take your weight. I'll walk real slow."

"Thank you," she said.

He walked her around to the other side of the wagon. Then he raised her foot up to the rest and put his hands on her waist. He lifted her up. She pushed on the footrest and then grabbed the sideboard. She climbed onto the seat without help.

Checkers came around and got into the wagon. He picked up the reins and took off the brake.

"Heeya," he yelled at the horses, and rattled the reins over their backs.

The horses plodded through the snow.

He kept them at a steady pace, and was able to stay on track.

Then Louella felt the wagon jolt to a stop. She had no idea where they were or why they were stopping.

Then she saw the water through the shawl of the falling snow.

"What's that?" she asked. "A lake? Or a big creek?"

He set the brake. "It's nigh noon," he said, "by my way of figurin', and that there is the Missouri River."

"Do we have to cross it?" she asked.

"Yep. We have to cross it. And it's a bear to cross."

She looked at the mighty stream and felt its power as it rushed down between its banks. She had never seen the Missouri

189

River before, but she had heard Reese talk about it.

"It's the longest river in the States," he told her.

Now she wondered how they, in the wagon, and Reese, with his cattle, would ever cross such a river.

It was frightening to think about it just then.

CHAPTER 25

The wind shifted and snow blew into the faces of the drovers and the cattle. Reese rode up to the head of the herd to find a cow fighting to take the lead. She swung her head and horns at the other cattle trying to take the lead.

Calvin Forbes had been riding point and now turned back to see what the ruckus was. Lonnie rode up on the flank behind Reese. He could see the turmoil at the head of the herd. Snow blew wet and cold against his face and he had to keep blinking his eyes to see.

"That cow has been causin' trouble for the last two miles," Cal said to Reese. "I don't know what to do about it. I keep havin' to ride back to break up the fights."

"Let her take the lead. They'll work it out." Reese kept the lead cattle from straying on his flank. They all seemed to want to avoid the fracas going on up front. The cow bellowed and struggled against the wind and snow to get ahead of all the other cattle. She was fat and heavy and seemed to have a belligerent nature.

"Need any help?" Lonnie called out.

Reese waved him away. "We're fine, Lonnie. Watch that flank."

"That wind shift has made all the cows nervous," Cal said. "They want to turn their butts and head back to home."

"You might have to shoot that ornery lead cow if she gets too rambunctious," Reese said.

"I'd hate to do that, Reese. She's prime beef on the hoof."

"I know. But she's a troublemaker."

Cal took off his hat and swatted at the cows around the bossy one. They swung away from the cow that wanted the lead and she forged ahead, seemingly impervious to the blowing snow. She held her head high and warded off any intruders that might make an attempt to question her leadership by passing her.

The fat cow warded off all the cows that came near. She wanted that front spot and meant to keep it.

Cal turned his horse and trotted off to take point again.

The dominant cow took that as a sign of

approval and jumped ahead of the other cows. Her hooves kicked up snow and she stormed on ahead of them all.

Reese smiled at the cow's determination to lead the herd. She was like a dog with a bone in her teeth as she braved wind and snow. And now she was all alone, up front. The other cows followed her blindly, seemingly content to have her as their leader.

A wave of sympathy suddenly engulfed Reese. He looked at the cattle and felt their misery. They were cold. Probably hungry. And they were being driven off their home range into a strange and foreign world.

He wished the drive had begun sooner. He longed for a blue sky and a hawk floating up high above gama grass. Instead he was cloaked in a white shroud, unable to see either the sky or very far ahead of the herd. Snow stuck to the cows' hides, and their hooves were caked with snow.

Even his horse was feeling the wind and the cold. But it was a brave horse, not stupid like the humans such as himself who ventured out in such miserable weather.

He missed being with Louella. He missed their home and a warm fire in the hearth. He missed the simple comforts she and their home had given them. It seemed an eternity ago, and now there was no home. It lay in ashes and Cheyenne were eating beef that he had raised.

Where was the fairness in all this? Reese wondered, and he pondered this and other questions as he rode and shivered, as the wind blasted his face until it was as raw as a skinned cat. They were not gaining miles in the snowstorm. They were gaining inches and feet. He felt as if he were in an icy hell. There was no shelter for miles and miles. No warm fire to warm his flesh and his bones. There was only the cold and the snow.

Would it never end?

Would he ever feel sunshine and smell prairie flowers again?

Suddenly Reese saw the herd bunch up ahead of him. Then all the cattle stopped moving, as if they had run into a barrier.

Moments later, Calvin rode up, emerging from the curtain of snow like some apparition.

"What's up?" Reese asked. "Why is the herd halted?"

"Somethin' I want you to see, Reese. Looks like Checkers run into some trouble."

"I'll follow you. But we've got to keep this herd movin'."

"I know, I know," Cal said. "This won't take long. Might be important."

Cal led him to the deep hole where the wagon tracks were still visible. They were fast filling with snow, but they told a story. Nearby, just barely covered with snow, were two splintered wagon wheel spokes. And a flat rock that was just now being covered with snow. There were boot tracks on both sides of the wagon tracks.

Reese recognized them as belonging to Checkers and Louella.

"Looks like he broke a wheel in that hole," Reese said.

"They were here long enough that the snow hasn't yet covered their tracks," Calvin said.

The herd bellowed and lowed. Some of the cattle stomped their feet.

That's when Johnny rode up.

"Why are we stoppin'?" he asked.

"Somethin' I wanted to show Reese," Cal said.

Johnny took it all in quickly. "Looks like Checkers run into a big old hole and busted a wheel," he said.

"Why are you here, Johnny?" Reese asked. "You should be riding drag or rear flank."

"Somethin' I found out this mornin', Reese. Somethin' that's been stuck in my craw since we left night camp."

Reese flapped a hand to clear away enough

snowfall to see Johnny's face. "Go ahead," he said. "Spit it out."

"We lost some cows overnight. I mean, they was lyin' dead in the snow this mornin'. Some of 'em dropped after we left, but they was half a dozen died durin' the night."

"Ah, not good," Reese said.

"This ain't no regular snowstorm," Johnny said. "It's a full-fledged blizzard." As if to emphasize his words, a gust of wind ripped into them, nearly blowing them out of their saddles. The cows protested with groans and moans.

"He's right," Cal said. "This is a bizzard, by damn, and them cattle ain't growed their winter coats yet."

"We're likely to lose more head if this keeps up," Johnny said. "Temperature's droppin' and it's snowin' like hell."

"The only thing I know to do," Reese said, "is to keep the herd moving. Keep them from freezing."

"Yep," Cal said. "You're right. I'll start 'em up again. Don't know what we're going to do tonight if this keeps up."

"I'll think of something," Reese said.

"I hope so," Cal said. He turned his horse and rode away, for the front of the herd.

"I'll be goin' back on drag," Johnny said. "The herd stretches near a mile, but we got to keep 'em movin'. It's way below freezin' and some of the cows just ain't ready for winter weather."

"Stay on it, Johnny," Reese said.

He watched Johnny disappear in a blinding mass as the wind picked up speed and blew snow over the herd.

How many cattle would he lose before the blizzard abated? Reese watched the herd slowly lumber on, their hides flocked with snow. They shook off some of the snow, but it was coming down too fast for them to shed all of it.

This was something he hadn't counted on when he left the home range. An early snowstorm. A blizzard.

And ahead, he thought, there was the Missouri River to cross.

He looked up at a nonexistent sky that funneled snowflakes down at him.

Would it ever stop snowing?

The answer was in the wind gust that blinded him with fresh snow.

This was a blizzard and it showed no signs of stopping.

CHAPTER 26

The women did not complain. They drove the dozen head of cattle through the heavy snowdrifts and cheerily called out to one another when one of them stumbled or fell. They were warm in their buffalo robes. Some of them walked in the ruts left by the travois poles.

A couple of the women rode the ponies that pulled the travois. The warriors rode their ponies or walked separately from the women. Mounted and following the women were Yellow Horse, Black Feather, and Silver Bear.

The snow hindered them all, slowed them down as the wind blasted them with strong gusts and furious crosscurrents.

Still, the snow kept falling. And no sign of the main herd of cattle.

"They go far, the cattle and the White Eyes," Yellow Horse said.

"Yes. But we will catch them," Silver Bear said.

"The fire stick I carry will speak to the White Eyes," Black Feather said.

Silver Bear and Yellow Horse both grunted in assent.

Suddenly the ponies pulling the travois stopped and the women broke ranks and ran ahead of them. Their excitement was contagious as all the women and the warriors on foot surged ahead of the halted ponies.

"What is it?" Yellow Horse asked.

"There is something ahead of us," Black Feather replied.

"We will see what the women have found," Silver Bear said.

He, Yellow Horse, and Black Feather rode their ponies up to where the women were crowded around something in the snow.

"What is that you have found?" Silver Bear asked Little Turtle, who was crooning with delight over her discovery.

"There is a cow here under the snow," she said.

"And look," Morning Doe said, pointing her arm in another direction, "there is another cow. We have meat to cook."

The women all spoke in high-pitched voices. They marveled over their discovery.

"We will eat again," Gray Dove said, and Little Turtle knelt down and drew a knife from the scabbard attached to one of her legs.

"Let us make camp here and make fire," Morning Doe said.

The women all voiced their approval of this and began hunting for a suitable place to pitch their shelters. There was a small butte some distance from the trail, an outcropping of rocks that sheltered the ground from much of the snow on one side.

The women all chattered and some began to cut up the dead cow, while others found more dead cows and cried out in joy.

Silver Bear rode up on them, followed by Yellow Horse and Black Feather.

"What are you doing?" he asked Morning Doe.

"There is much meat here. We are hungry. We will make camp and make fire to cook the meat."

"We will continue to hunt the White Eyes," he said. "Do you not want to be with us?"

"We are not warriors," Morning Doe said to Silver Bear. "We do not fight the White Eyes. We are just women. We make your moccasins and your clothes. We cook your meals. That is what we do."

"I cannot protect you if you stay here," Silver Bear said.

"We have knives and we will have fire," Morning Doe said. "You go and kill the White Eyes. We will make us a warm camp. We have wood and we have flint and iron."

Silver Bear snorted as he looked around and saw the women scurrying to the dead cows and over to the small butte. Some led the horses and dragged the travois over to their proposed shelter, while others dug in the snow for rocks and still others pulled brush from the ground and shook the snow from the leaves and branches.

"They are mad, these women," Black Feather said.

"They are crazy like the buffalo cow that eats the locoweed," Yellow Horse said.

"That is true," Silver Bear said. "The women have gone crazy over frozen cows."

Some of the other braves gathered around Silver Bear.

"We will stay with the women," Iron Knife said. "We are cold and we are hungry."

The other braves grunted in assent.

"You do not want to go with us and kill the White Eyes? We can steal more cows and have a bigger herd."

Some of the men signed in the negative.

Silver Bear looked at them with eyes

hooded by frozen lashes. "You are as crazy as the women," he said to them.

"We are tired and we are cold," Crooked Arrow said.

"We will stay with the women and warm our bodies at their fire," Broken Knife said. The others grunted their approval of his words.

"You are all women," Silver Bear said.

The warriors hung their heads in shame. But they did not walk back onto the trail. Instead they lifted their feet and stomped the snow where they stood.

Silver Bear turned to Black Feather and Yellow Horse.

"Do you want to stay with the women?" he asked.

"No. We will go with you," Yellow Horse said.

"We want to take the scalps of the White Eyes and steal more cattle from them," Black Feather said.

"Then we go," Silver Bear said. "Let the women and the cowards stay here."

"We should smoke the pipe first," Yellow Horse said. "Then paint our faces for war against the White Eyes."

"Yes, that would be good," Silver Bear said.

The three rode over to the butte where

most of the women were unloading the travois.

They had a fire started in a ring of wet stones.

Silver Bear spoke to Morning Doe. "We will smoke the pipe and paint our faces," he said.

"I will find the paints for you," Morning Doe said.

The three men dismounted.

Little Turtle brought the pipe and tobacco pouch to Silver Bear. Then she spread a buffalo robe over the snow near the fire pit.

Morning Doe brought the bowls of paints and set them out for the warriors.

Silver Bear filled the bowl of the pipe with tobacco. He offered tobacco to the four directions, then lit the pipe with a faggot from the fire.

The three men smoked. Then they painted their faces as was their custom when they went on the warpath. The women did not look at them but continued to make camp. Others came with fresh meat they had cut from the dead cows. They laid the meat in the snow near one of the lean-tos and went back to the trail for more.

When the men had finished their smoke, they arose.

The women all crooned in approval when

they saw the paint on the men's faces.

Silver Bear, Yellow Horse, and Black Feather mounted their ponies and cried out their battle whoops.

"May the Great Spirit watch over you, Silver Bear, and bring you many scalps from the White Eyes," Morning Doe said.

Silver Bear grunted and swung his pony away from the camp.

Yellow Horse and Black Feather caught up with him and flanked him on their ponies. They brandished their rifles and made little battle cries with soft voices.

They sang their song as they rode back to the trail.

"It is a good day to die," they sang, and their faces got wet with snow as they gazed skyward into the teeth of the blizzard.

They rode through the snow and the blowing wind like ghostly apparitions and disappeared from the view of the other warriors and the women.

Iron Knife spoke it. "It is a good day to die," he said again.

The women keened as they went about making camp.

And still the snow kept falling and the wind whipped the fire into a frenzy of flame, smoke, and golden fireflies.

CHAPTER 27

Earl Kelso put another horse under saddle and grained the one he had ridden from the line shack. But it didn't help much. It was still cold as a well digger's rump and he didn't like it.

"Damn snow," he said when he rode over to where Jasper Mullins was waiting, along with Homer Parsons and Dave Riggs. They were all wearing heavy winter jackets, but their gun belts were strapped on outside their coats.

"Yeah, yeah, it's a lot of snow," Mullins said. "Quit your bellyachin'."

"I just don't like winter," Kelso said.

"Apparently your horse don't neither," Homer said. "And likely that piebald won't neither."

Kelso patted the neck of the piebald gelding. The piebald whickered and tossed its head. "Old Skinface will do me just fine," he said. "He ain't got his winter coat yet, but he's got good lungs and sturdy legs."

"Yeah, like you," Homer said.

Dave laughed and Mullins gave him a scornful look.

"Let's head out," Mullins said. "You boys stick close. I don't want none of you to get lost in this blizzard."

"Can't snow forever," Dave said. "Too damn early for all this much snow."

"What in hell do you know, Dave?" Homer said as he rode up on Mullins's right flank. "You take all your weather inside a saloon."

"Good weather in there," Dave said.

"At least with all that flappin', your mouth won't likely freeze," Mullins said.

All three men chuckled and Mullins seemed satisfied.

They rode into the jaws of the storm and felt its windy teeth. Snow blew at them as if they were in a parade with gallons of confetti spewing down on them.

"How far is it that cattle trail anyway?" Homer asked as he hunched in the saddle in an attempt to keep some of the snow from blowing through the eyelets and seams of his heavy coat.

"Oh, it's a good three or four miles to that line shack," Kelso replied. "Seems a lot farther in this dang snow."

"Takes a long time to go a mile in this,"

Dave said.

"Look at how fast Earl's tracks are fillin' in," Homer said.

That was so. They could all see the tracks made by Kelso's horse. But they were nearly obliterated by the amount of snow that fell onto the ground.

As they rode, the horse tracks began to disappear. Finally there were only the faintest impressions of the hooves in the snow. The tracks became slightly lower than the surrounding accumulation of snow. And finally even those faint impressions were no longer visible.

"Where in hell are we?" Dave asked.

"Damned if I know," Homer said.

"Just keep ridin' straight," Earl said. "We only got about a mile or so to go."

"I hope to hell you've got your bearings, Earl," Mullins said. "It's like bein' in a room with all the walls painted white."

Kelso chuckled at the remark.

The other two men bowed their heads against the blowing wind, their humped forms aswirl with snowflakes. They rode on through a bewildering world of white. It was cold and the wind made it colder. When the line shack finally appeared, all of them were shivering in their heavy winter coats.

"There it is," Kelso cried out.

Beyond the line shack, the old buffalo trail was a mass of muddy snow. They all reined up and looked at the churned snow. Clods of mud and piles of offal littered the ground.

And there was not a cow in sight.

"Missed 'em," Mullins said. "I thought you said it was a big herd, Earl."

"It was, Jasper. It was a real big herd. I swear."

"Well, they've done passed on by," Dave said.

"Look how their tracks are disappearin'," Homer said.

"But you can see where they passed by here," Kelso said. "Plain as day."

"Well, if we aim to purloin us any of those cattle, we'd better start after 'em," Mullins said.

"Might not be so far at that," Homer said. "They're goin' to run right into the Missouri, they stay on this trail."

"That's right," Dave said. "Big old river."

"Hmm," Mullins said. "It'll take them hours to cross, won't it?"

"Damn sure will," Dave said. "I wouldn't want to cross it in this weather."

"Some places you can't cross," Homer said. "I had a hell of a time findin' a ford once't."

"Well, time's a-wastin'," Mullins said.

He rode onto the trail first. The others followed. Their horses' hooves came down on mud and snow, piles of offal, and yellowed streaks of urine that had burned furrows through the snow.

Not far behind them, three Cheyenne warriors on ponies followed the same track, their buffalo coats flocked with snow, their rifles held tight against their bodies.

Ahead of them, the cattle stood on the bank of the Missouri River, drinking the water with twitching nostrils and batting eyelashes.

And there was the smell of burning sage where men warmed their hands over the fire.

And still the snow kept falling, faster than before.

In the nearby buttes, the wind howled and there were eerie sounds from the mesas as the wind scoured the snow from their flat surfaces only to have them whitened again and again.

Not a creature was stirring on that vast plain. There were only the brown cattle with snow on their backs, slurping water through rubbery lips and yellow teeth.

And the remuda too, lined up on the riverbank, slaking their thirst, blowing snow away from their mouths and nostrils with heaving breaths that looked like steam.

Louella snuggled against Reese as they stood by the fire. Checkers passed out sandwiches with a cheery smile and a hat brim clogged with snow.

"We've got to find a ford," Reese said.

"Now?" Lonnie asked.

"The sooner, the better," Reese said. "While we still got daylight."

"That water's got to be freezin'," Lonnie said.

And no one said a word. They were all thinking about the river crossing and nearly a thousand head of cattle to drive onto the other side of the Missouri River.

Vernon Avery stared at the others. He wished they were all dead and that he was back with his people, or with the Cheyenne.

He thought about that and what he could do to slow down the river crossing.

Perhaps, he thought, Silver Bear was not far away.

He knew where they could ford the river, but he wasn't about to tell anyone. Let them drown a few head of cattle while they searched for just the right place.

Johnny was even then riding along the river, looking for a place where they could drive the cattle across.

There was no sun. There was only the

relentless snowfall and the lashing bullwhips of the brutal wind.

Only the river seemed impervious to the storm. As fast as the snow fell, the waters devoured the flakes. The hungry waters swelled ever so slightly and the river rolled on, swift and certain as time itself.

CHAPTER 28

It was Black Feather who first spotted the four white men.

The Cheyenne rode in single file, Black Feather in the lead, followed by Silver Bear and Yellow Horse at the rear.

Black Feather reined his pony to a halt and held up a hand to stop those behind him. He turned as the others rode up close to him and stopped.

"Why do you stop, Black Feather?" Silver Bear asked.

"I saw four white men on horses," Black Feather said.

"Where?" Silver Bear strained his eyes to see through the falling snow.

"There," Black Feather said. He pointed ahead of them on the muddied snow of the trail.

"I do not see them," Silver Bear said.

"I see nothing but the falling snow," Yellow Horse said.

"They are there. Four White Eyes."

"Let us see if we see them again," Silver Bear said. "Let us ride this path and see if the White Eyes appear to us."

"You will see them," Black Feather said.

They rode ahead with caution, until, through the streamers of snowflakes, they saw the four white men on horseback.

Silver Bear held up his hand to halt the other two braves.

"Did you see the White Eyes, Yellow Horse?" Silver Bear asked.

"I saw them," Yellow Horse replied.

"They do not look like the White Eyes who herd the cattle," Black Feather said.

"No," Silver Bear said. "These are strange white men."

"They follow the cattle herd," Yellow Horse said.

"Maybe they want to steal the cattle too," Black Feather said.

"Yes, I think they wish to steal cows from the white man, Reese."

"What do we do?" Yellow Horse asked.

"We follow them to see what they do," Silver Bear said.

"Do we let them steal some of the cattle?" Yellow Horse asked.

"No," Silver Bear said. "If they steal the cattle, we will fight them and take the cows away from them."

"That is good," Yellow Horse said. "Maybe they will steal many cattle and kill the White Eyes of the herd."

"Maybe there will be many White Eyes to die this day," Black Feather said.

"That is my wish," Silver Bear said. "Let us not let them see us. We will follow them to see what they do."

With that, he rode on.

The white men had disappeared ahead of them.

When they saw them again, they made their ponies match their speed so that the white men stayed in sight, but just on the fringe of the falling snow so that they could be seen.

The three Cheyenne were covered in snowflakes. They looked like the men the children made from piling up the snow.

CHAPTER 29

Once or twice, Mullins would look over his back trail. He wondered if someone was following them. He did not see anyone and he knew it was foolish of him to think such a thing.

He did not say anything to the others, but he noticed that Kelso also turned every now and then to look back. And soon the other two men who rode with him were doing the same thing.

"That herd has covered some ground since I left the line shack," Kelso said.

"They'll stop at the river," Mullins told him.

"Or go across," Kelso said.

"We'll find 'em," Mullins said. And he turned to look behind him once again.

"I see you got that feelin' too, Jasper," Kelso said.

"What feelin'?"

"Like somebody's on your hind end."

"I get that feelin' sometimes," Mullins said.

"Yeah, me too. You can feel someone's eyes on you and when you turn around, sure enough, somebody's starin' at you."

"It's just a feelin'," Mullins said.

"Maybe there is somebody follerin' us," Homer said. "I keep lookin', but all I see is snow."

Mullins suppressed a laugh. The laugh wound up as a snort. "Tell you what, boys. Let's just find out if there's anybody back there. Just to be on the safe side."

None of the men said anything.

"Riggs, you just ride on out in the snow where you can watch to see if we're bein' followed."

"Me?" Riggs said.

"Yeah, you. Just ride on out on my flank and stay put. You see anybody, you ride like hell to catch up with us."

"Oh, all right," Riggs said.

He halted his horse as the others rode on. Then he turned the horse and rode out into the snow. It was rough going for his horse, but when he was far enough from the trail, he stopped. He stared at the falling snow and watched Mullins and the other two disappear up the trail. He cursed and hunkered down over his saddle horn as the wind tore at his coat and scraped his face raw.

He could just make out the old buffalo trail. He knew where it was because of the moiled-up mud mixed with the snow. There was black among the white blanket of snow.

He wondered how long he would have to stay where he was before he could catch up to the others.

He also wondered if anyone was following them. It did not seem likely that anyone would be out in such weather.

He was about to ride back to the trail when he saw movement.

He rubbed his eyes in disbelief.

He saw ponies, three of them in single file. Then he saw three warriors. He glimpsed their painted faces and held his breath.

"Jesus," he said under his breath.

Slowly he grabbed the stock of his rifle and pulled it from its sheath.

The Cheyenne had not spotted him. But he felt a talon of fear claw at his stomach.

Would the Indians see him?

The warriors looked as if they were hiding something inside their buffalo coats.

What in hell were Indians doing way out here? And they were definitely following them. They could not fail to see the tracks of their horses. The tracks were fresh and the snow had not yet filled them in or covered them up.

Riggs brought his rifle up. He levered a cartridge into the firing chamber. The snick of the action seemed loud in his ears.

The Indians halted their ponies and looked in his direction.

Riggs took aim. His hands and arms shook with the cold. But his finger curled around the trigger as he lined up his sights on the Indian in the lead.

He took a breath and held it.

Then his finger tightened as he squeezed the trigger.

CHAPTER 30

Johnny rode up in a hurry.

"I found us a fordin' place," he said to Reese. "Just downriver a little ways."

"How far across?" Reese asked.

"Not too awful far. There's a sandbar that splits the river. The cattle might have to swim the deepest part. But they can make it across, I think."

"Then let's get the herd going before they all freeze to death," Reese said.

The men grumbled as they left the open fire. Reese gave Louella a squeeze. "Stay warm as long as you can," he said.

"I will," she said.

Then Reese turned to Checkers. "Think you can make it across?" he asked the cook.

"If we have to swim it, we'll get to the other side," Checkers said.

"Let's hope you don't have to swim that river," Reese said.

"Don't you worry about us, Cap'n. We'll

get across. I never let hell or high water stop me before."

Reese smiled and turned to his horse. He mounted and waved good-bye to Louella and Checkers, then rode up to the riverbank to help the others round up the cattle and get them moving downstream.

The hands began to drive the cattle. Johnny rode ahead to show them the way. When he stopped and pointed, the drovers turned the lead cattle toward the river.

The cattle balked. Men yelled at them and took off their hats to bat at the lead cattle. The lead cow was reluctant to step off the bank and into the river. Johnny splashed in with his horse and reached down to grab a horn. He gripped one horn and pulled on it. Reese rode in behind the cow, and his horse pushed on her rump.

The cow stepped into the river. Johnny turned loose of her horn and rode out to push the rest of the herd to follow the lead cow. He shouted and others shouted too.

Slowly the herd stepped into the river. Into the shallows. When the lead cow stepped out on the sandbank, she would go no farther.

"Get her goin', Johnny," Reese called out.

Johnny urged his horse across the shallows to the sandbank that split the stream.

There, he batted his hat on the cow's rump and let his horse sidle up to her and push her off the little island and into the water. The cow fell into the water. Her forelegs began to chop the water as she eyed the other shore. She swam toward it and floundered out of the water and up onto the bank.

Jimmy whacked his hat at the other cattle crowding onto the sandbar, and they all jumped in and began to swim.

Norcross found another place to ford the river. He drove the feed wagon across while Lonnie and Jeremy herded the remuda into the river. The horses did not have to swim, but the water was up to their bellies, even so.

Lonnie cried out in dismay as one cow was swept away by the current. It bawled and flailed at the water but was carried to deeper and swifter water. Lonnie's horse chased after the cow, but when the cow went under, he reined up before he too, along with his horse, got into trouble.

"Couldn't be helped, Lonnie," Reese told him.

"Damn. I hate to lose even one head," Lonnie said.

"We're bound to lose a few head. In any trail drive. And this one is a bitch willy."

"You can say that again, Reese," Lonnie said.

"I won't. Let's get back to the main herd. Get 'em across."

"I'll do my best," Lonnie said as his horse scrambled back up onto the bank. He rode to the center of the herd and made sure the cows all stayed in line and headed for the crossing.

As the herd thickened, the cattle in front were pushed into the river by those behind. The crossing seemed to go better and faster as the hands kept up the pressure to move the herd.

"Those cows can't see the river until they're in it," Lonnie told Reese.

"That's the idea," Reese said as he chased a straying steer back into the main herd.

The crossing took most of the afternoon, but Reese was pleased that they had lost only one or two head as near as he could figure.

"You picked a good place to ford the river," he told Johnny.

"Thanks, Reese. But I wouldn't like to do it again."

"I wouldn't either," Reese said.

Checkers crossed without incident and soon was way ahead of the herd. He used his compass because the buffalo trail was obliterated by snow. And the horses had to pull hard to roll the wagon through the heavier drifts.

The herd moved slowly.

Reese went to each of his cowhands and spoke to them.

"I want you to gather what brush and wood you can," he told each man.

"What for?"

"Tonight, we'll light fires to keep the cattle warm. I don't want to lose any more to the cold."

The hands made a sight as they gathered firewood and tied the bundles to their saddles. And firewood was difficult to find with all that snow on the ground.

"This brush will burn fast," Tommy said to one of the hands. "Not all night."

"Give Reese what he wants and you'll get along, kid," Johnny told him.

"Like a slave," Vernon remarked as he rode by, a bundle of twigs tied behind his cantle.

Reese did his share as well. Whenever he saw a bush sticking out of the snow, he rode to it and chopped branches to add to his pile.

The cattle struggled to make headway as the snow kept falling. The wind circled and blew. Finally the falling flakes began to thin and the clouds began to drift to the southeast. The skies began to clear to the northwest by late afternoon.

The wind died down.

The snow stopped falling by mid-afternoon. But there was still a lot of it on the trail. And even with the lessening of the wind, it was bitter cold.

Patches of blue began to appear in the sky. An encouraging sign, Reese thought. But he knew that as cold as it was then, it would be far colder once the sun went down.

He dreaded the end of that day when the skies would turn black and the temperature would plummet.

He did not know that the cold would be the least of his worries before that day was over.

CHAPTER 31

The minute he squeezed the trigger and heard the explosion from his rifle, Riggs knew that the bullet would miss.

For Black Feather saw Riggs at the same time. As Riggs brought the rifle to his shoulder, Black Feather opened his coat and freed his own rifle. He flattened himself on his pony's back just before Riggs squeezed the trigger.

Black Feather heard the *whiz-buzz* of the bullet as it passed over him. Out of the corner of his eye, he saw Silver Bear and Yellow Horse steer their ponies away from him.

Black Feather did not wait for Riggs to reload. He levered a cartridge into the firing chamber of his purloined rifle and took aim at the white man. He kicked his pony in the flanks and reined it on a path toward the white man. He charged straight at Riggs. He hugged his pony's bare back and aimed the rifle.

When he was within ten yards of Riggs, Black Feather squeezed the trigger. The rifle in his hands was aimed straight at Riggs. He reined to a halt after his rifle exploded and sent a bullet straight at the chest of the white man.

The bullet struck Riggs square in the chest. It split his breastbone and ripped through a lung. It exited out his back, blowing blood and bone out onto the snow.

Riggs's eyes went wide for a split second as his lungs expelled the last of his air. The hole in his chest spurted blood and he slumped in the saddle.

Black Feather rode in close and swung the butt of his rifle at the head of the white man. The stock struck Riggs and knocked him sideways.

He fell to the ground.

Black Feather jumped down and grabbed Riggs by the hair. He swept off his hat with a swipe of his hand. He whooped a war cry that carried to Silver Bear and Yellow Horse.

Black Feather set his rifle down in the snow and drew his knife. He slashed the throat of the man he had shot, then cut a circle on his head. He pulled the hair free with a strong jerk and held up Riggs's scalp. He uttered a yelp of triumph as Silver Bear and Yellow Horse rode up to look down at Black Feather and the dead white man.

"Good," Silver Bear said.

"You have a good scalp, Black Feather," Yellow Horse said. "And you struck coup on the white man."

Black Feather picked up his rifle. He stuck the bloody scalp in a small pouch attached to his sash. Then he beat his chest as a gesture of victory over an enemy.

He climbed back onto his horse.

"There are three more White Eyes," Silver Bear said. "They will fight us when they see us."

"Let us kill them too," Black Feather said.

"Yes, let us go after them and kill them," Yellow Horse said.

"We will find the three White Eyes and kill them," Silver Bear said.

The three Cheyenne rode away from Riggs, whose body was turning white with falling snow. They did not look back but followed the buffalo trail that was marked by clods of mud and disturbed snow. They saw the tracks of four horses that pressed their iron shoes into the mud and snow.

They were silent as they rode, and their eyes strained against the snowfall to see ahead of them.

Presently they saw only the tracks of three

horses. And after that, the tracks left the trail and split up. One set of tracks veered off to the right, while another veered to the left. One continued on a direct line for a few more yards and then it too left the trail on the left.

"They wait for us," Silver Bear said. "They know that we follow them."

"What do we do?" Yellow Horse asked.

"We each take a track and follow it," Silver Bear said.

"I will take the one that rides to my right," Black Feather said.

"I will track the horse that goes to the left," Yellow Bear said.

"I will go after the one who left the trail last," Silver Bear said.

They each disappeared through the curtains of snow. Each one followed a horse track that was filling up with snowflakes. They moved with caution. The unshod hooves of their ponies made no sound.

It was a silent world and each warrior knew that a white man was somewhere ahead of them, each waiting in ambush.

It was a question of which one was most ready to kill.

And which one was most ready to die.

CHAPTER 32

Mullins jerked hard on his reins to stop his horse. Homer and Kelso halted their horses too. They had heard one crack of a rifle. Then another.

"Uh-oh," Kelso said.

"Riggs must've seen something," Homer said.

"Two different rifles," Mullins said.

"Should we go back and check?" Kelso asked.

Mullins did not answer right away. Instead he waved the other two men to silence. Then he cupped a hand to his ear.

"Just two shots," Mullins said. "Two different rifles. That doesn't sound good."

"No, it doesn't," Homer said.

"We ought to ride back and see if Riggs is okay," Kelso said.

"No," Mullins said. "We don't know who in hell was follerin' us, how many, whether white or red."

"So, what do we do?" Homer asked. "It's awful quiet back there after them two shots."

"We'll split up and watch the trail," Mullins said. "Two of us will be on one side, one of you on the other. Pick your sides."

Homer and Earl looked at each other through the falling snow.

"I'll take the left side," Homer said.

"All right," Jasper said. "Earl and I will ride ahead a little ways and then we'll split up. That way we won't all be in a bunch."

"Who do you think is follerin' us, Jasper?" Earl asked.

"I don't know. Rustlers, maybe."

"Or maybe some of the hands who got left behind in all this snow," Homer said.

"Well, somebody with a rifle — that's for sure," Mullins said. "Pick your spot, Homer."

"Yeah. You hear me shoot, you come a-runnin', Jasper."

"There's no runnin' in this stuff," Mullins said.

He and Kelso rode on as Homer turned his horse and left the trail. He loosened his rifle in its scabbard and halted his horse about ten yards from the trail. There, he could still see the overturned mud the cattle had left when they came through. He hoped he was far enough away from the trail to see anyone ride up. Before they saw him. His stomach fluttered with wings of fear as he waited and shivered in the cold.

Mullins and Kelso rode for another fifty yards or so before Mullins reined up and halted.

"This suit you, Earl?" Mullins asked.

"It all looks the same to me. Just a lot of snow."

"You find yourself a spot where you can see who comes up the trail. I'll ride on a little farther and then stake me out a spot."

"Good luck, Jasper."

"Luck ain't got nothin' to do with it. You see anybody come down that trail, you put out their lamps right quick."

"Likely, it'll all depend on Homer and what he runs into back there."

"Humph," Mullins voiced.

Kelso rode away from the trail on the right side. Mullins rode another fifty yards and turned his horse off to the left of the trail. He pulled his rifle from his scabbard and levered a shell into the firing chamber. He rested the barrel across his pommel.

And waited.

As he stared up the trail, the snowfall began to diminish. A few moments later, the last flakes fell. And then the snow stopped falling.

Still, Mullins waited. The silence was nerve-racking.

Was there somebody following them? What happened to Riggs?

Who had fired the other rifle?

He was convinced that there was somebody following them. And he felt certain that Riggs was probably dead.

The wind died down to a breeze.

He looked up at the sky. It was still cloudy, and he could not see the glimmer of the sun. It was cold, but at least he could see some distance now that the snow had stopped falling.

Mullins was beginning to think that there was no longer anyone following them. It was too quiet. His horse whickered softly, and that made the silence even deeper.

He was about to ride back and check on Homer when the silence was shattered by the sound of a rifle crack.

Mullins stiffened. The explosion had come from a long way off. From Homer's position next to the cattle trail.

He tightened his pull on the reins, prepared to ride back and see what the shooting was about.

Then he heard a volley of shots from different rifles.

He thought he heard yelping. Human

voices, high pitched, almost screaming.

"What the hell . . . ?" he muttered to himself.

More shots. Whoops from unknown throats. Yelps.

War cries? He had never heard one, but the voices sounded strange to him. Almost inhuman.

And then they faded away and the silence rushed back in. Ominous. Deadly. Mysterious.

Mullins felt the silence descend on him like an iron door, shutting off all his senses, his ears straining to hear.

"Earl," he called out.

"Yeah. I'm here," Kelso shouted back.

"What in hell's goin' on back there?" Mullins yelled.

Kelso didn't answer. Instead Mullins heard the crack of still another rifle. Closer this time.

Too close.

He kicked spurs into his horse's flanks and turned him up the back trail.

Then he heard another rifle shot. From the same rifle.

But whose?

Mullins had to find out. He rode to where Kelso had stayed behind. His heart was in his throat. And the cold didn't matter anymore. There was damn sure something going on, and he had to find out. Even if it meant he was riding into a trap or an ambush.

Mullins had to know what was happening.

He was soon to find out.

CHAPTER 33

Homer saw the first Indian pony and his heart skipped a beat. Then there was another, and after that, a third pony. Three riders. His heart felt as if it froze shut when he saw their painted faces.

Were there more than these three? He didn't know.

But when he reached for his rifle, the movement must have caught the eye of at least one of the Indians.

As Homer pulled his rifle from its scabbard, one of the Indians turned his head and stared straight at him.

Homer levered a shell into the Winchester's chamber. In the silence, the action made a loud metallic snick.

The other two Indians turned their heads and he knew that they had seen him.

The first Indian threw open his bearskin coat and drew out a rifle similar to Homer's.

Homer's hands shook as he leveled the

front sight of his rifle on that first Indian. When it steadied, he drew in a breath and squeezed the trigger. He saw the bullet strike the Indian high on the shoulder. Snowflakes arose from the fur, and the Indian twitched.

Homer quickly levered another shell into the firing chamber of his rifle. Just then that first Indian recovered and aimed his rifle. He fired and Homer heard the sizzle of the bullet as it sped past his ear. He fired blindly at the warrior and then heard their blood-curdling cries. The other two opened their coats. One produced a rifle, the other a bow.

Homer's second shot was a total miss, and he levered still another cartridge into the firing chamber of his rifle.

The other Indian with the rifle shot at Homer. Homer ducked and heard the keening whine of the bullet as it blasted through snowflakes and carried to a spot behind him. It kicked up snow as it furrowed through the white blanket.

The Indians yelled and whooped and all three charged toward him.

Homer fired off another shot and saw the bullet kick up dust and snow on the first Indian's coat. Just above the Indian's belly.

The Indian kept coming.

In seconds, that first Indian was on him.

He saw the painted brave grab his rifle barrel and swing the stock toward him.

Homer ducked, but the stock dealt him a glancing blow. His hat flew off and he felt a stinging sensation on one side of his head. His brain danced with tiny lights and he grabbed the saddle horn with one hand to keep from falling off his horse.

The Indian rode on past him, then turned his pony.

Homer, out of the corner of his eye, saw the other two Indians, one with a rifle, one with a bow, riding through the snow straight at him.

The one with bow nocked an arrow on his gut string and loosed it.

Homer could no longer think. The raucous cries of the three Indians blotted out all thought.

Then he felt a jolt and what seemed like a fist blow in his right rib cage. He felt a hot rush of blood down his side. He looked down and saw the feathered arrow sticking out of his chest. A flood of pain engulfed him.

The Indians screamed their high-pitched war cries and surrounded him.

He tried to swing his rifle to bear on the other one with the rifle.

The first Indian grabbed the barrel of

Homer's rifle and jerked it from his hands.

The second Indian with a rifle fired at point-blank range and the bullet ripped into Homer's stomach. He felt the sledgehammer energy of the bullet as it ripped through his skin and tore up his intestines. There was a searing pain in his back where the bullet exited.

His brain grew cloudy and he felt his life slipping away.

Two of the Indians, the ones with rifles, were hitting him with the butts of their Winchesters. Blow after blow struck his face and his bare head. He hung on to his saddle horn, even as he felt his life flowing out of him in blood and oxygen. His lungs were on fire and each breath was torture.

Still, the Indians wouldn't let up. They hammered him with their rifle butts. They screamed in his ears.

The Indian with the bow drew his knife. He reached across his pony's head and swung his arm. The blade caught Homer in the side of the throat. It sliced deep across his Adam's apple. Blood gushed from the wound like a crimson waterfall.

Homer loosened his hold on his saddle horn. Sensation drained from his body and he could no longer breathe.

Then only blackness as he fell into the dark pit of death, all sound erased as if the Indian voices had been wiped away by a giant hand.

Homer fell from his horse and landed with a thump in the snow.

"I have a hole in me from the white man's fire stick," Black Feather said. He showed Silver Bear and Yellow Horse his shoulder when he peeled back his coat.

"Stuff the hole with snow," Yellow Horse said.

"You do it for me," Black Feather said. He slid off his pony's back and sat down in the snow.

Yellow Horse dismounted and laid his rifle on the lumpy carpet of snow.

Silver Bear looked on from atop his pony.

Yellow Horse scooped up a handful of snow and rubbed it on the wound.

"I think the lead stone is still inside you," he said as he felt the backside of Black Feather's shoulder. "I cannot find another hole."

"It should have passed through me," Black Feather said. "Maybe it glanced off a bone and went to another place on my body."

"I will touch more of you and see," Yellow Horse said.

He felt all over Black Feather's back, and

then his hand went over the other shoulder. There he found the other hole, the exit wound.

"I will put snow and mud in it," he said to Black Feather.

Yellow Horse walked back to the trail and dug in both hands. He brought up snow and mud, which he carried back to where Black Feather sat.

He rubbed the mud and snow into both wounds, pushing the mud in as far as he could.

"Take the scalp of the white man," Silver Bear said to Black Feather. "He is your coup."

"No, your arrow took away his breath, Silver Bear. It is your scalp to take."

"I will not take it," Silver Bear said.

"I will scalp the man and then you two can fight over it," Yellow Horse said.

Silver Bear and Black Feather both laughed.

Silver Bear slung his bow over his shoulder and held out his hand. "The snow is no more," he said.

"That is good," Yellow Horse said as he stood up. He extended a hand for Black Feather.

Black Feather grasped it and Yellow Horse pulled him to his feet. Both reached down and picked up their rifles.

Yellow Horse walked over to the body of the white man. He picked up his rifle and handed it to Silver Bear. "Now you have a fire stick, Silver Bear. I will get the pistol and wear its belt around my waist."

Silver Bear took the rifle from Yellow Horse. He felt of its cold metal, rubbing his hand across the flat of the receiver.

"I will kill many White Eyes with this fire stick," he said.

Yellow Horse unbuckled Homer's gun belt. He strapped it around his naked waist and drew his coat back over it. Then he drew his knife from its scabbard and made a circular cut into the hair and scalp of the dead white man. He jerked the fresh scalp free of the skull and stuffed it inside his beaded sash.

Black Feather climbed back onto his pony.

Yellow Horse found more ammunition in Homer's saddlebags. He gave the saddlebags to Silver Bear, who draped them over his pony's back and tied on the leather band that held them together.

He felt inside. "There is food for us too," he said.

"Do we ride on after the cattle and the white men?" Black Feather asked.

"Yes, we ride on," Silver Bear said.

"And soon the sun will be born again," Yellow Horse said.

But Silver Bear was already riding back to the trail, even as the wind died down and the ground began to freeze. His pony's hooves made crunching sounds when it reached the ground-up mud of the trail.

There were dead white men behind him, he thought. And more up ahead.

And the snow had stopped falling.

It was a good sign.

Chapter 34

Mullins saw them first. There was no time to grab his rifle and put it to his shoulder.

Three Indians in plain sight. Their faces were hideous with war paint. And they had Riggs under their guns, his rifle scabbard empty, his gun belt and pistol wrapped around the waist of one of the Cheyenne.

Mullins pulled the trigger of his cocked pistol. Fire and lead exploded from the barrel. One of the Indians, Black Feather, lurched with the impact of the bullet through his abdomen. His pony had started to turn away when Mullins fired again at the same warrior.

"Don't shoot," Riggs yelled.

Too late.

Yellow Horse fired his rifle. The barrel was only a few inches from Riggs's back. The bullet smashed into his backbone and he went rigid with paralysis.

Riggs fell out of his saddle and skidded in

the snow as his horse continued to move forward. He twitched several times, then lay still, his blood no longer spilling from his wounds.

Kelso and Mullins both fired their pistols, but Yellow Horse and Silver Bear made their ponies zigzag as they rode.

Kelso shot a bullet into Black Feather as the Indian kept coming toward him and Mullins. His bullet struck Black Feather in the neck, shredding the copper skin to pulp. The lead ball smashed the spine of the Cheyenne warrior. Black Feather's body went rigid and he fell sideways from his pony. He landed with a muffled clump in the snow and lay still, blood spurting from his throat.

Silver Bear and Yellow Horse rode off in different directions.

Mullins fired after them. So did Kelso. Their bullets never connected to the two Cheyenne as their ponies dashed right and left with superb skill and dexterity.

"Damn," Mullins said.

"We both missed," Kelso said, his pistol smoking.

"Those boys can ride," Mullins said.

"Should we chase after them?" Kelso asked.

"Hell no. Let 'em go, the rascals. Besides,

there may be others lurkin' about."

"Sorry about Riggs. Tough way to die."

"All ways to die are tough," Mullins said.

"But to get it in the back like that. He didn't have no chance."

"He let himself get caught by them redskins."

"Well, it could have been us," Kelso said.

"It wasn't."

"I wonder if Homer . . ."

"Oh, I'm sure Homer bought the farm too."

"That leaves only two of us. Can't round up many cattle without the other two."

"We can steal enough to make it worth our while, Earl," Mullins said.

"How many head? A dozen? Two dozen?"

"Maybe more. We'll have to see."

"I think them Injuns was thinkin' the same thing," Kelso said.

"Maybe. If so, they'll run into not only our guns, but the guns of those cowhands on the trail."

"And so will we, for that matter. I don't like it, Jasper. I don't like it none. Just you and me against a whole bunch of herders. And maybe some redskins to boot."

"You worry too much. There's plenty of time to catch up to that herd and cut out as many head as we can drive back to the spread. They won't foller us. They're thinkin' to drive that herd to Cheyenne and they can't stop for nothin'."

"What about Homer and Riggs? What should we do with 'em?"

"Let 'em lie. Hell, we can't bury nobody out here. We don't have no shovels and likely the ground is frozen solid."

"Yeah. It's a shame, though. Not to give those boys a decent burial."

"You're too sentimental, Kelso. Dead is dead. Puttin' them in the ground makes no difference to them. They're plumb gone."

Kelso thought about it a moment, then nodded in agreement. He just thought of those dead bodies lying in the snow, cold and forgotten. Men who were breathing just a short time ago now had their lives taken away from them. And it could have been him that was killed, not to mention Mullins as well. Such was fate, he thought. He was alive, and two men he had known were now dead.

"Let's get the hell out of here," Mullins said. "Them redskins might come back."

"Yeah, they might," Kelso said. He opened the gate to his pistol and used the plunger to eject the empty hulls of his cartridges. Then he stuffed fresh ones into the cylinders.

Mullins saw him and did the same with his pistol. He could still smell the burned powder as he filled his magazine with fresh cartridges.

Kelso holstered his pistol.

"I'm ready when you are, Jasper," he said.

Mullins slid his pistol back in his holster. His gun belt had empty loops now.

The two rode back on the track of the cattle herd. But they both kept looking back over their shoulders.

Just in case.

CHAPTER 35

Lonnie rode drag once the herd had crossed the river. With him was the kid, Tommy, shivering like a dog spitting out peach seeds from its hind end.

"You hear anything?" Lonnie asked Tommy.

"Nope. Why?"

"I thought I heard gunfire. Way off. Way down our back trail."

"I didn't hear nothin'," Tommy said.

"Well, just the same, you keep your eyes peeled. We could have Injuns comin' after the herd again."

Tommy looked behind, the river a thin ribbon on the horizon. Snow everywhere.

"I don't see nobody behind us," he said.

"Kid, you go find Reese and tell him I thought I heard gunshots on our back trail."

"Okay."

"Hurry," Lonnie said. "They were far off, but that can't be a good sign."

"I'm on my way," Tommy said.

He rode off, but the heavy snow slowed his horse. The cattle were having a rough time making progress on the churned-up mud and snow. He passed them and the other outriders on the flanks. They did not wave or acknowledge him.

At the head of the herd, he found Johnny and Reese flanking the lead cow. The cow was struggling to break a path through the virgin snow and kept wanting to turn back. He was out of breath by the time he rode up to Reese.

"Thought you was ridin' drag with Lonnie," Reese said. "What's all the hurry?"

"I — I was," Tommy stammered. "I got somethin' to tell you. Lonnie told me to tell you."

"Well, spit it out," Reese said. "What did Lonnie want you to tell me?"

"He said — he said he heard gunshots. Or thinks he did. Way far off on our back trail."

"That right? But he wasn't sure?"

"Pretty sure, Mr. Balleen."

Reese looked at Johnny. Johnny shrugged and continued to rag the lead cow to stay on the trail.

"Maybe I'd better see what this is all about," Reese said.

"You go on, Reese," Johnny said. "I can

handle it from here on out."

"I'll take a flanker or two with me just in case," Reese said.

"The herd's movin' pretty good now. I don't reckon there'll be any strays for a while," Johnny said.

"It could be Lonnie's imagination."

"Or he could have heard something," Johnny said.

"Yeah. Well, it won't hurt to take a look on our back trail," Reese said.

"What do you want me to do?" Tommy asked.

"You stay here and help Johnny," Reese said.

"Yes, sir," Tommy said.

Johnny snorted but did not say anything. His expression was one of disdain, but Tommy didn't see it. He was trying to stay ahead of the herd and stay out of Johnny's way at the same time.

Reese rode toward the tail end of the herd. On the left flank was Calvin. Reese rode up to him.

"What's up, boss?" Calvin said.

"Ride on back to where Lonnie's ridin' drag, Calvin," Reese said.

"What's up?"

"I don't know. Did you hear any shots a while ago?"

Calvin shook his head. "Nope. Just the cattle mushin' through the snow, the usual grunts and groans."

"Ride on back with me, just in case."

"What? Lonnie heard gunshots?"

"That's what Tommy said."

"I saw the kid ride by in a hurry. I wondered what was goin' on."

"Might be nothing."

"Well, Lonnie's got good ears. But ridin' drag like that, you can hear a lot of things in your head."

"I know," Reese said. "But let's check it out."

"I reckon there won't be no strays just now," Calvin said.

"If there are, they won't stray far in this snow," Reese said.

"Good point," Calvin said. He rode alongside Reese to the rear end of the herd. There, Lonnie was doing his job, keeping the cows moving ahead of him.

"Oh, glad you're here, Reese," Lonnie said.

"You said you heard gunshots?" Reese asked.

"I thought I heard somebody shooting. Long way off, though."

"Who do you think might be shooting? A hunter? Hunters?"

Lonnie shook his head. "Didn't sound like hunters to me. Hard to tell."

"Well, we can't be too careful. We'll just wait it out and see if anyone comes down that trail. The Cheyenne now have a couple of rifles they took off of dead white men."

"I know. But what would they be shooting at way back there?"

"That's a hard question," Reese said. "And I don't have an answer."

"So, what do we do?"

"We'll just have to wait and see if anyone rides up on us."

"Rustlers, maybe?" Lonnie said.

"Maybe," Reese replied. "If you really heard gunshots, that is."

"I'm almost sure of it. Far off, but I know a gunshot when I hear one."

"Rifle or pistol?"

"Pistol maybe. Close together. Bang, bang."

"Well, it's stopped snowing. We should be able to tell if anyone comes up to rustle our cattle. White or red."

"Yeah, we should," Lonnie said.

They rode along behind the herd for a few moments. Then a rider appeared and called out to them.

"Hold it right there, Lonnie," Kelso shouted.

Lonnie reined up. So did Reese and Calvin. They all stared at the stranger riding to them from the right of the trail.

"That's Kelso," Lonnie said to Reese. "Wonder what he's doing here."

"I don't know," Reese said, "but he looks like a damn rustler to me."

Lonnie's hand darted for his pistol.

Kelso beat him to it.

"Leave it holstered, Lonnie," Kelso said as he drew his pistol.

Calvin, Reese, and Lonnie heard Kelso thumb the hammer back to full cock.

"What in hell are you doing, Kelso?" Lonnie asked.

"You'll see," Kelso said as he rode closer. He was still forty or fifty yards away when they heard another horse ride up behind them from the left side of the herd.

"Just hold steady," Mullins said. "I'm going to cut out a few head and we'll be on our way."

"Like hell," Reese said.

Mullins drew his pistol as he and his cutting horse sliced into the herd, separating some twenty head from the rest of the cattle.

"Best to do what he says," Kelso said. He held up his horse about thirty yards from the cattlemen.

Reese drew his pistol. He cocked it on the

rise and aimed it at Kelso.

Kelso fired at him, his .45 spewing golden sparks and smoke from the barrel. The lead projectile whizzed over Reese's head as he ducked and fired.

Missed.

Kelso fired again. But his horse twisted sideways and his shot went wild.

Lonnie drew his pistol.

Mullins fired a shot at Calvin. Calvin was slow to draw, but finally he too had his pistol in hand. Cocked and ready to fire. He tried to get a bead on Mullins, but the rustler reined his horse into a zigzag. Mullins fired off another shot, which whizzed past Calvin's face.

Calvin fired his pistol at Mullins.

Kelso fired again, but his horse acted up and his shot was wide of its target, Lonnie.

Lonnie spurred his horse to charge at Kelso.

Kelso cocked his pistol and raised his arm to shoot at Lonnie.

Lonnie fired from ten yards away and his bullet smashed into Kelso's chest with the force of a sledgehammer.

Kelso caved in but held on to his saddle horn. Blood spurted from his chest and bubbled up out of his mouth.

Lonnie cocked his pistol again and reined

up his horse about five feet from Kelso. He took aim and shot Kelso in the throat.

Kelso made a gurgling sound. His pistol slipped from his hand. Then he fell backward and tumbled from his saddle. He landed in the snow with a crunch, blood still spurting from his neck.

Lonnie whirled his horse to go after Mullins.

Calvin fired his pistol at Mullins.

Mullins was a superb horseman and he twisted the animal through the herd with precision.

Calvin's shot seared the air behind Mullins.

Mullins twisted in the saddle and fired blindly at the three cowmen.

Reese tracked the outlaw with his pistol. He led him just enough and squeezed the trigger. The .45 bucked in his hand, but his aim was true.

His bullet plowed into Mullins's left arm and ripped into a lung. Blood spurted from his arm and lung.

Reese fired again from twenty feet away.

Mullins turned to look at him, a surprised expression on his face. Then his features contorted in pain as Reese fired again and the bullet smashed into Mullins's neck. Blood spurted from the wound and Mullins jerked from the impact. His pistol slipped from his grip and tumbled into the snow and mud. He fell out of the saddle and landed with a loud thump in the snow.

Reese whirled around to scan both sides of the herd.

"Any more like them?" he asked Lonnie.

"Them's all I seen," Lonnie said.

Calvin looked around for any more cattle rustlers too.

"Just them two," he said. "Looks like anyways."

Reese sucked in a deep breath.

"That's odd," he said. "Just two rustlers. Fools."

"Maybe there was more of 'em," Lonnie said as he ejected the empty shells from the cylinder of his pistol.

"What do you mean?" Reese asked.

"Them shots I heard. Maybe there was more of 'em and somebody thinned 'em out."

"But who?" Calvin asked as he reloaded his pistol.

"Maybe Injuns," Lonnie said.

Reese looked at him sharply.

"By damn, you may be right, Lonnie," Reese said. "I don't think these are the only men looking to steal my cattle. There're still Silver Bear and his band."

"Well, if so, then we still have more trouble on the way," Lonnie said. He inserted fresh cartridges into his pistol.

"Damn," Calvin uttered.

Reese reloaded his Colt .45 and looked down their back trail. Wondering. He wondered if there had been more cattle rustlers and they had run into the Cheyenne.

Right now it was the only thing that made sense.

He spoke to Lonnie and Calvin.

"Get their rifles and pistols," he said. "No need to hand over more firepower and ammunition to the redskins in case they are still after my cattle."

He watched as both Lonnie and Calvin dismounted, walked to the two dead men, and stripped them of their gun belts.

"Calvin, you lead their horses up to the feed wagon. We'll add them to the remuda."

"Yes, sir," Calvin said. "Boy, that was some shoot-out, Reese."

"It was. We were lucky. Those two meant business."

"I'll say they did," Lonnie said. "We were damn lucky. Kelso was a killer. I don't know about the other feller, but he was probably the boss of a gang of thieves."

"You're probably right, Lonnie. That one knew what he was doing."

Lonnie rifled through Mullins's pockets. He pulled out a piece of paper.

"His name was Jasper Mullins," he said to Reese. "I've heard the name, back in Denver. He was a bad one."

"What you got there, Lonnie?" Reese asked.

"Bill of sale for the property."

"Keep it," Reese said. "It won't do him any good now."

"Might make one of us a pretty good spread," Lonnie said.

Calvin caught up the two horses that were ridden by Mullins and Kelso.

"I'll stay here with Lonnie, Calvin," Reese said. "When you deliver those two horses to the boys with the remuda, you hightail it back here. We might need your gun again."

"Yes, sir, Cap," Calvin said as he led the two horses along a line flanking the herd.

"It's a wonder they didn't stampede," Lonnie said.

"Yeah. Like I said," Reese said, "we were lucky."

"This time," Lonnie said, and his words hung in the air like an omen.

Reese stared off at the snowy land. He wondered if the Cheyenne were out there somewhere. Just waiting for a chance to steal more cattle and exact revenge for what he'd done to them.

For now, the land appeared empty, deserted.

And the cattle were moving down the trail, the snow-covered trail.

Chapter 36

Silver Bear and Yellow Horse halted their ponies when they heard the pistol shots. They looked at each other wordlessly and waited.

Yellow Horse signed that the white men must be fighting.

They waited until it was quiet again. Then they rode up on the bodies of the two dead white men, Jasper Mullins and Earl Kelso.

"The White Eyes feed on one another like wolves," Yellow Horse said.

"And they take all the fire sticks," Silver Bear said.

"And the horses."

"They leave the boots and the clothes."

"Do you want to wear the white man's clothes or his boots, Yellow Horse?"

"No, I do not want to wear the clothes of the dead men."

"Do you want their scalps?"

"I did not strike coup, so I do not wish to

take their hair."

"That is good," Silver Bear said.

"It is good that these White Eyes are dead. Now we have only those who drive the cattle."

"They are few and are scattered like the leaves in the mountains."

"They will fight if we take more of their cattle," Yellow Horse said.

"We must be like the owl or the puma," Silver Bear said. "We must sneak up on those who ride at the sides of the cattle and use our knives so that we make no noise."

"Yes, that is the best way, I think," Yellow Horse said.

"The night will be our friend. Our ally."

"Yes. We can see the White Eyes, but they will not see us."

"One by one, we cut them with our knives. They will bleed onto the snow and their spirits will be gone from their bodies."

"It is a good way. Then we can take the cows from them and go back to our people."

"Let us find them now and wait far away," Silver Bear said.

They rode away from the dead men. They followed the tracks of the cows and the horses.

"Do not forget that the half-blood called Avery is with the White Eyes," Silver Bear said as they rode slowly over the snow and mud.

"If we see him, we will make the sign for him to join us?" Yellow bear asked.

"I do not know. If we do not get the cows, Avery will be the enemy under the coat. He can cut with his knife and make us strong in our small numbers."

"Yes," Yellow Bear said. "The half-breed is good to have in the camp of the White Eyes."

"Let us try to talk to him," Silver Bear said.

"Our hands will speak to him," Yellow Horse said.

They rode on until they heard the lowing of the cattle on the trail. Then they reined in their ponies until the sounds of the herd faded.

They started riding again when it was dead quiet. And that was the way they followed the herd of cattle and dreamed of killing white men.

They were patient, and there was no hurry. They would perform their deeds at night, in the dark. They would take more cattle from the white men and go back to their camp.

They were only two, but they both felt strong.

They would be panthers in the darkness.

CHAPTER 37

By prearrangement, the herd began to angle to the west, toward Montana.

Reese knew that Checkers would follow the prearranged route, and so would the wranglers with the feed wagon and the remuda.

In fact, the wagon tracks through the snow had veered off to the south-southwest. A check of his compass showed him that Checkers and Chuck Norcross were right on target for Montana.

Reese rode left flank with Ben Macklin, who was beginning to show signs of extreme weariness. He was the oldest of Reese's hands, but Reese knew he was as tough as a boot.

"Tired?" he asked Ben.

"I've seen better days, Reese," Ben replied. "It's the damn cold. It kicks up my rheumatiz. My old bones are like a dadgum weather vane. Any change, hot or cold, and my knees feel like they got the mumps."

Reese chuckled. "I'm feelin' a twinge or two myself, Ben."

"Oh, you got years before you feel it like I do. My knees are sore as a boil. Dang the snow anyway."

"Well, we're heading for new prairie. Down in Montana. Likely the snow didn't spread that far to the southwest."

"I'll be glad to see grass again," Ben said.

"Me too," Reese said.

"Okay if I ride drag for a while?" Ben asked. "I ain't much for chasin' cows what want to leave the herd."

The two of them had been keeping the herd together, despite the fact that some cattle were trying to run off from behind the leader. Reese thought they must have snow blindness and were seeing green pastures instead of snow. The herd was restless and skittery, though.

"Sure. Tell Lonnie to ride up here," Reese said.

"Sure will," Ben said. He turned his horse and started the long ride to the tail end of the herd.

Reese moved his horse in close when he saw a couple of cows edging away from the herd. The cows filed back in line and he began to breathe easier.

Presently Lonnie rode up and joined him on the flank.

"All quiet back there," he said. "Didn't see anybody follerin' us."

"Good. Can old Ben handle the drag, you think?"

"Yeah. The herd's movin' slow, but none are tryin' to turn back. Leastwise when I was back there."

"The cattle up here are jumpy as Mexican beans. Some of 'em want to run off. Ben and I have had a time with 'em."

"They get that way sometimes," Lonnie said.

There was less snow on the ground now that they had altered their passage along the trail. Gradually, the snow shrank so that they reached a point where it had not snowed. The ground was firm and the herd moved more quickly than before.

By late afternoon, near dusk, the herd reached the Little Missouri River. There, the chuck wagon was parked on the other side of the small stream. So too was the remuda and the feed wagon. The herd moved onto the river and drank.

"Do we bed down on this side of the Little Missouri?" Johnny asked Reese.

"No. That'll only hold us up in the morning. When the cattle have drunk enough water, let's get 'em across and bed 'em down a mile or so from the river."

"It's still mighty cold, but I'm glad we're out of the snow," Johnny said.

"You and me too," Reese said. He watched as the cattle spread out and populated the riverbank, slaking their thirst. It was still very cold, near freezing, Reese figured, and he had a plan for that night.

As dusk fell, the herders drove the cattle across two or three fording places, then continued on for another mile.

"Make places for the wood you've gathered," Reese told Johnny.

"What do you aim to do, Reese?" he asked.

"Light fires to keep the cattle warm," Reese said. "I don't want to lose any more cows to the cold."

"Might be a good idea," Lonnie said. He had a bundle tied behind his cantle. So did all the other hands, including Tommy.

Reese watched as the men placed their bundles at strategic places among the herd.

"We'll light those fires after supper," Reese said. "Now, let's some of us go and get grub so you can spell those who stay with the herd."

Johnny divided up the men. Some rode back to the chuck wagon where they warmed themselves at Checkers's cook fire and filled their plates with beans and beef, turnips, and canned pears.

"Been savin' them pears for an evenin' like this, with no snow," Checkers said. "They're mighty tasty."

"Delicious," Louella said.

She and Reese sat together on kegs that Checkers had set out. They were filled with rice and flour in separate barrels.

"I'm glad we left the snow behind us," Louella said. "And this is a pretty spot."

"Yes. It'll still be below freezing tonight, though," Reese said.

"Will you keep me warm?" she asked. "Or will you be up all night?"

"I'll try to get back for some shut-eye," he said.

She squeezed his arm at the elbow.

"Is that all?" she asked coyly. "Just some shut-eye?"

"That depends," he said.

"On what?"

"On how many ears and eyes are around us when we take to our bedrolls."

"Oh. Maybe we can get off by ourselves."

"Not a good idea," he said.

She looked startled. "Why?"

Reese looked back down the trail. "We may have visitors tonight," he said.

"Visitors?"

"Injuns, darling."

"Oh, they wouldn't follow us this far," she said.

"I wouldn't be too sure about that, Lou. Silver Bear has a grudge against me and I wouldn't put anything past him."

"Seems to me there's been enough bloodshed on this awful trail." Firelight painted her face, shifted shadows from her fair skin, brightened her eyes.

Reese scraped his plate with his fork, stabbed a last chunk of beef, and put it in his mouth. The second round of cowhands came up to eat. Tommy, Ben, and Calvin all got in line and filled their plates as Checkers doled out the grub.

"Well, I hope you're wrong, Reese," she said. "I hope the killing is over and the Indians have given up trying to steal more of our cattle."

"I hope so too," he said, but just knowing that Silver Bear was alive made him apprehensive. He could not forget the look in the Cheyenne's eyes when Reese had refused to give him any of his cattle.

It was a look of pure hatred.

And hate could carry a man a good long way.

CHAPTER 38

Reese rode through the milling herd. He barked orders to every cowhand there.

"Bunch 'em up," he shouted, just loud enough for the intended listener to hear. "Bunch 'em up tight."

Vernon Avery hid his dark look by lowering his head so that his hat brim covered part of his face. His hatred of white men in general, and Reese in particular, had grown like a poisonous mushroom since the drive began. They were on Indian lands, stolen lands, his people's lands. He thought of his mother in Canada and all the other Lakotas who had been driven from their land, their food supply, the buffalo, slaughtered for money, not hunger, and his blood ran hot.

He watched as Reese rode up to the other men and showed them where to drop their bundles of firewood. Reese rode through the herd and pointed to various places. Avery waited for him to approach and tell him where he should put the firewood he had collected.

The man was plumb crazy, he thought. There was no snow on the ground. It was cold, yes, and the ground was frozen hard as a rock. But a few fires weren't going to do much good. Even though he was a half-breed, he did not understand the white man. He hated that part of him that was like Reese, or the others. His own father had been no better than these men. They were all greedy and heartless.

He longed for the simple life he had once known, among the bronze-skinned men and women and children of the Lakota, the Minneconjou. There, his childhood had been a learning experience. He had learned to hunt and fish and to survive on plants and animals with nothing but a bow and a quiver of arrows.

Life had been simpler back then. There was harmony among the tribe members, and his mother's love had kept him warm at night. They lived in teepees, and their lodges went with them when they traveled. They followed the great buffalo herds and there was always plenty of meat and good clothing to wear.

And then the white men had come. They trapped the streams in the mountains for beaver, marten, mink, anything that had fur. They had cleaned out the beaver dams and shot the buffalo just for their hides, leaving the meat to rot.

He had seen all these things and heard the men and women talk of the changes. He had seen his mother weep at night, and he grew to hate the white interlopers who were destroying not only the land and the game but his own people.

"The white man wants to own the land. The land that the Great Spirit gave to us, his people." That was what his mother told him, and he believed her.

"Avery, you take your firewood over yonder and drop it. Gather as much more as you can."

Reese jarred him out of his hateful and sorrowful reverie. Avery nodded but did not reply. He rode to the spot that Reese had indicated. He untied the thongs around his bundle of firewood and threw the assortment of sticks and twigs to the ground.

Reese rode off to talk to another cowhand, weaving his way through the herd. The cattle seemed to be wondering what they were supposed to do. They eyed Reese as he passed through them, and some moved out of his way.

Vernon dismounted and began to look for

more firewood. He pulled a sage from the ground and added it the pile that he had dropped. He found several twigs and picked those up. Even with the added firewood, the fire would not be big enough to warm the cattle, he thought.

Reese was crazy. All white men were crazy. And thoughtless.

"Vernon, you're going to need more firewood," Lonnie called out to him as he rode by. "You may have to look harder."

"It's gettin' dark, Lonnie. Hard to see," Avery said.

"Go look for cow pies," Lonnie cracked. "You don't have to see 'em. You can smell 'em."

"Go to hell," Vernon said.

"Be a lot warmer there, I bet," Lonnie said, and rode on.

Avery continued to look for anything that would burn, but his heart wasn't in it.

It was growing darker and the cattle were still nervous. They were not bedding down, because they were still grazing on drying grass, tearing off tufts of gama and munching on them as they roamed around.

He added more twigs to his pile, then led his horse away from the herd. He stood at the edge and watched the other men, now no more than dark shadows, gather fire-wood.

"Do we light 'em?" Calvin called out to Reese.

"Not yet," Reese answered. "More toward midnight when it's coldest."

"Okay," Calvin shouted.

"Be a chore," Lonnie said to Reese. "A dark, dark night."

"Just remember where those piles are. When they're lit you'll have light."

"Sure enough," Lonnie said, and rode out of the herd to make his rounds.

"I want all you nighthawks to sing to these cattle," Reese said in a loud voice. "Sing 'em to sleep like they were your babies."

Some of the men laughed. Others snorted in derision.

Avery climbed into his saddle. He did not feel like singing. He would ride nighthawk, but he wasn't going to sing. He did not know any of the cowboy songs. He only knew the songs of the Minneconjou the Lakota. And he wasn't about to sing any lullabies to a herd of cattle.

As he rode around the edge of the herd, he heard something. A hissing sound from some distance. He knew the sound and he stiffened. He turned slowly and peered into the darkness.

There it was again. A soft hissing sound. He rode toward it.

His senses were on full alert.

"Who's there?" he asked in English.

Then he saw a shape arise from the ground just a few yards from him.

"Come close, brother," Silver Bear said, his voice barely audible.

Avery rode close and saw that it was Silver Bear. He held a bow in his hand.

A moment later, Yellow Horse rose from the ground and walked up to stand beside Silver Bear.

"What do you do here, Silver Bear?" Avery asked in sign.

"We come to steal the cattle," Yellow Horse said. "Will you help us?"

Avery read the sign. There was just enough light to see the hands of both men.

"What do you wish me to do?" Avery asked, his hands like flying birds in the darkness.

"Show us where we might run off some cows and keep the white men away," Silver Bear said.

"I know where some of the cattle are bunched," Avery signed. "It would be a good place."

"Show us," Silver Bear said.

"Follow me," Avery said. He turned his

horse and rode slowly to where the tail end of the herd was gathered. He stopped and pointed.

"There," he signed.

There was no rider there at the moment, but out of the corner of his eye, Avery saw the first nighthawk start on his rounds. He was some distance away.

When he turned his head back to Sliver Bear and Yellow Horse, they were gone. The two Cheyenne had melted into the night as soundlessly as a pair of panthers.

They would be back, he knew. The next time he would see them, they would be on their ponies.

And maybe, he thought, he would have to kill his first white man that night. He would kill to protect his brothers, Silver Bear and Yellow Horse.

He touched the handle of the knife on his belt. He loosened his pistol in its holster.

He waited in the shadows, nearly invisible to the nighthawks, who were not looking in his direction.

Then he heard one of the men, Ben, he thought, begin to croon to the cattle.

The cattle began to crumple and bed down.

"Oh, I come from Alabama with a banjo on my knee," sang Ben.

And it was the loneliest sound in the world that night.

CHAPTER 39

Well before midnight, Reese woke up Checkers with a gentle hand on his forehead.

"Checkers," Reese said, "I need some paper to start those fires."

Checkers rubbed his eyes and sat up.

"Gawd, it's cold," he said.

"You got on your long johns, don't you?" Reese asked.

"Yeah, and they itch like hell."

"Well, I won't keep you up long. I just need paper to start those fires so the cattle won't freeze to death."

"I've got what you need," Checkers said. He crawled out of his bedroll and went to the wagon. He rummaged around inside as Reese waited, shivering, outside. Reese knew the temperature had to be below freezing. He knew the cattle had to be feeling it. They were all close together in clusters, their bodies touching, to keep warm.

There was a rattle of papers and Checkers emerged from the wagon with a handful of old newspapers.

"Been savin' these," Checkers said. "Use 'em sometimes to start my fires. They're dry and if you twist 'em up, touch them with a match, they will make miniature torches."

"That's just the thing," Reese said. He took the papers. All except one.

"I'll show you what I mean," Checkers said. He rolled up the sheet of newspaper he had kept and twisted it. Twisted it to a tight spiral. One end sprouted the thin paper.

"You light it where the flaps are thin. Torch will last a few minutes twisted up like this," he said.

"Yeah, I get it."

"You'll have fun twistin' up all them newspapers. Got 'em in Bismarck."

"I've done this before, Checkers," Reese said. "At home. When I started fires in the fireplace."

"Twist 'em tight," Checkers said.

"I ought to make you come with me and twist all these up," Reese said.

"If I did go with you, I'd burn you with the first torch I made."

Reese laughed.

He heard Louella, under the wagon, stir. He thought she was turning over, but he couldn't see her in the darkness.

"Go back to sleep, Checkers," Reese said. "And thanks."

"You're mighty welcome, Reese. Just don't wake me no more tonight."

Reese mounted his horse and rode toward the bedded-down herd. He began to twist his first newspaper page. The other ones he tucked under his crotch so that they wouldn't blow away.

He found Ben first. Ben was circling the herd at a slow pace, still singing Stephen Foster songs in his gravelly voice.

"What you got there, Reese?" Ben asked as Reese handed him a twisted news page.

"Fire starter. You light the thin end and touch it to the firewood. Should catch pretty quick."

Ben took the twist, held it close to his eyes so that he could see it. "Yeah, this should work. Goin' to be hard to find one of them woodpiles, though. Cows have probably trampled all over 'em."

"Well, do the best you can, Ben. I'll look for your fire."

"Sure enough. I know where I put my brush. It's just so damn dark I don't know

279

if I can find it."

"You'll find it."

"I gotta wade through a lot of slumberin' cattle before I can even look," Ben said.

"I'm counting on you. So is the herd."

Reese rode off to the next man and twisted another sheet of newspaper before he reached him. It was Johnny.

Johnny griped about the dark and the difficulty in finding a woodpile in the middle of such a big herd.

"You'll do fine, Johnny," Reese said, and rode off to encounter Lonnie.

He did the same thing with each man, finally coming upon Tommy.

"Think you can light one of these twists and set fire to a pile of brush?" Reese asked.

"Sure."

"The dark doesn't bother you, Tommy?"

"No, sir. I got eyes like a owl's. I can sure see a brush pile."

"Even with that herd here? Some of the cattle may have bedded down right on top of the brush."

"I'll find one," he said.

They both looked at the first fire. The one Ben had set at long last.

"Golly," Tommy said. "It's a-workin'."

Then they saw another fire blazing. And then another.

Where the fires had been set, the cattle rose from their beds, bellowing and lowing. But they did not run off or stampede, because the hands were still talking to them and singing to them as they rode through the herd to circle them on horseback.

"Good luck, Tommy," Reese said. "Stay warm."

"Yes, sir," Tommy said. He rode into the packed herd and started looking for a brush pile.

Reese saw him disappear among the hulks of cattle still sprawled on the cold grass. He rode back to the chuck wagon and dismounted. He tied his reins to a wagon post. He looked out at the cattle and saw several fires blazing. The fires would keep them warm if they wanted to stay close to the blazes. The fires would not last all night, but maybe they would provide warmth for the coldest part.

"That you, Reese?" Louella said from underneath the wagon.

"Yeah. I'm back."

"Get your fires lit?"

"I reckon we got enough lit to do some good."

"I feel sorry for the cattle," she said as he crawled beneath the chuck wagon and found his bedroll. "Poor things."

"Our cattle are pretty hardy," he said.

"But it's so cold, Reese."

"That's why I wanted the fires lit."

He crawled into his bedroll, took off his hat, and set it beside him. He unstrapped his gun belt, rolled it up, and laid it close by, within reach.

"Good night," she said.

"Good night, Lou." He closed his eyes.

An hour later, he was jolted out of sleep by the unmistakable sound of a rifle shot. It sounded fairly close and was loud enough to awaken Louella. She reached over and grabbed his arm.

"Was that a shot?" she whispered.

"Yeah, I think so." Before he could get out from under his blanket, he heard more shots. And he heard men shouting in alarm.

He grabbed his hat and gun belt and crawled from under the wagon.

The cattle were making loud noises and there was a flurry of gunfire from the tail end of the herd.

He unwrapped his reins and climbed into the saddle. He saw flashes of light as pistols and guns boomed and crackled at the far end of the herd.

The fires had burned low, but he could see their glowing embers as the herd milled around, back and forth, up from their beds, startled by the sounds of gunshots.

Reese rode toward the last flash he had seen. His throat was constricted. Not from fear, but from apprehension.

Somebody was after his cattle.

And he had a pretty good idea of who it might be.

"Damn Cheyenne," he muttered as he saw riders, like galloping shadows, silhouetted by the faint firelight.

His biggest worry was that the cattle might stampede. It would be hell rounding them all back up again.

He prayed that the cattle would just mill around in confusion and not dash off in all directions. But his mouth went bone dry, and the worry was a ball of nettles in his brain.

And how many of his men would die that night? That cold, cold night on the Montana prairie.

CHAPTER 40

Vernon Avery rode to the back of the herd that was bedded down.

Calvin was watching the tail end of the herd. He rode near a fire that was outside the bedded-down herd.

That was a surprise to Avery.

"You make your own fire?" Avery asked.

"Yeah. There's a dry wash I stumbled over. Looks like some flash floods cut through it. Lots of dry driftwood in there. So I started my own little fire. Keeps me and my horse warm."

"Calvin," he said, "you can go on. I'll take over guarding this end of the herd."

"I lit a fire, like Reese said, but I don't think it will do much good."

"No matter, Calvin. You get some shut-eye or make yourself useful somewhere else," Avery said.

"Yeah, some shut-eye would be good about now," Calvin said. "Reese tell you to spell me?"

"Yeah, he sent me back here," Avery lied.

"He's a decent man."

"Yeah," Avery said.

The fire crackled and spewed orange sparks into the air.

Avery watched until Calvin was out of sight. Then he rode his horse until he was on the far side of the fire. He made sign with his hands and waited.

He did not wait long. They came on foot. Their moccasins made no sound as they emerged into the firelight. Yellow Horse carried a rifle. Silver Bear carried his bow. They looked like woolly bears in their buffalo coats.

Silver Bear spoke a greeting to Avery.

"We see you, my brother," Silver Bear said.

"Where are your ponies?" Avery asked.

"They are near," Silver Bear said.

"Good. Here are the cattle," Avery said. "Yours for the taking."

"We will count twenty cows and drive them away. You hold them until we get our ponies. Then we will drive them out of this place to our camp."

Avery understood the sign language Silver Bear used. He nodded in agreement.

"You go there," Silver Bear said. He pointed to a place where the herd was bunched.

Avery rode into the herd.

"Awaken them," Silver Bear commanded.

Avery prodded the cattle to rise from the ground.

Yellow Horse and Silver Bear began to drive several head away from the others. They picked the largest and heaviest. They chased them out of the herd.

Silver Bear counted them. When he and Yellow Horse had rounded up twenty head, Silver Bear beckoned to Avery.

Avery rode out to await further orders from Silver Bear.

"Hold the cattle here," Silver Bear said. "Yellow Horse and I will catch up our ponies and meet you."

"I will do this," Avery said.

The cattle the Cheyenne had separated tried to head back into the herd. Avery rode back and forth to keep them at bay. His horse performed well, prancing and pawing the ground as he chased the cows back into the isolated bunch.

Soon Silver Bear and Yellow Horse appeared out of the darkness and rode into the firelight.

"You have done well, half-breed," Silver Bear said. "Now Yellow Horse and I will take the cattle away from this place."

Silver Bear dropped his hands and signed farewell as he did so.

Avery watched the two warriors drive the stolen cattle away from the firelight. Just then he heard hoofbeats. He turned to see Calvin gallop up.

"I forgot and left my sougan in that wash," Calvin said. He halted his horse and turned it to ride to the dry wash. That's when he saw the paint ponies and two Indians with part of the herd.

"What in hell's goin' on here?" he asked.

"None of your business, Calvin," Avery said.

"The hell it isn't. Them redskins is stealing our cattle."

"Just you forget about it, Calvin," Avery said.

"Like hell."

Calvin drew his pistol. A split second later, Avery drew his pistol.

Calvin fired first.

A second later, Avery fired his pistol.

Yellow Horse turned and saw the two white men shooting at each other.

"I will help the half-breed," he said. He turned his pony and rode back to the fire. He cocked his rifle with the lever action.

Avery felt a raw pain in his arm. He knew

he had been hit by a bullet from Calvin's pistol.

Calvin fired again.

So did Avery, blood in his eye, hatred in his veins.

Yellow Horse rode up, took aim at Calvin after he put his rifle to his shoulder. He squeezed the trigger and saw sparks and smoke spew from the rifle's snout.

Calvin felt the hammer blow of the bullet as it smashed into his belly. Pain shot through him as he felt part of his back tear away from the exit wound.

He grunted and held on. He tried to focus on Yellow Horse. His pistol waved as he brought it up. When he thought he had the Indian in his gun sight, he squeezed the trigger.

His brain grew cloudy. He felt a dizziness assail him. Blood gushed from his stomach and spilled onto the leather of his saddle.

He could not tell if he had hit the Cheyenne brave or not.

His eyesight blurred. Darkness crept into his brain.

Avery rode in close and shot Calvin in the chest.

The bullet smashed through a lung and ripped into Calvin's heart. He had only a tiny fraction of a second to know that he was a dead man.

He fell from the saddle, and his pistol struck the ground at the same time as his body hit. Calvin was dead before he reached the dirt.

Other riders appeared out of the darkness. They started shooting at Yellow Horse.

Avery shot at them.

Johnny and Tommy saw in an instant what was happening. Tommy fired his rifle and the bullet smashed into Avery's chest just below his neck. Blood spurted from his mouth. He reached up and gurgled as blood bubbled from the wound.

Johnny ducked as Yellow Horse fired off a round from his rifle. The bullet whistled over Johnny's head. He took aim at Yellow Horse and squeezed the trigger.

Yellow Horse jerked into a rigid paralysis as the bullet from Johnny's rifle smacked into his right lung, ripping through tissue and air sacs before blowing a cup-sized hole out through his back.

Yellow Horse fell from his pony.

Just as Silver Bear rode up to join the fray.

Tommy saw the bow in Silver Bear's hands. He fired off his rifle at the approaching Cheyenne.

Missed.

Silver Bear nocked an arrow to his bowstring and aimed at Johnny. He loosed his arrow within ten yards of the cowhand.

Johnny swung his rifle and squeezed the trigger. The shot missed Silver Bear. But Johnny felt something sharp enter his body and felt a force like a hammering fist just below his breastplate. He reached down and felt the shaft of the arrow that was sticking out of his body.

Tommy saw Silver Bear nocking a second arrow to his bow. He took aim and pulled the trigger.

Silver Bear was lit by the firelight. He stood out like a sore thumb, Tommy thought.

He fired again at close range.

Silver Bear's bow dropped from his hands as he clutched his side.

Tommy fired again, this time from less than ten feet from the Cheyenne warrior.

Silver Bear flew from his saddle as if jerked by a rope. The bullet from Tommy's rifle had blasted through his side, knocking him from his pony's back.

Tommy rode up close and aimed his rifle down at Silver Bear.

"Die, you damn redskin," Tommy muttered, and he fired another round.

The bullet smacked into Silver Bear's forehead and turned his brain to mush. The body twitched once and then was still.

Johnny's rifle went off again, but he wasn't aiming it at anyone. He was groggy with pain and his innards were on fire.

Other hands rode up and saw the carnage. They also saw the separated cattle, which were streaming back to rejoin the main herd.

Ben rode up first, rifle in hand. He saw the dead Cheyenne and the cattle. Then he looked at Johnny, whose hand gripped the arrow sticking out of his belly.

Ben swore.

Reese rode up a few seconds later, along with Lonnie. He swore too.

Johnny turned sideways and opened his mouth to speak. He fell from his saddle and they all heard the arrow crack as it broke in two.

"My God," Ben said.

Reese dismounted and knelt over Johnny. He bent down to put an ear to the man's mouth. There was no air coming in or going out.

Reese stood up. "Johnny's dead," he said to Lonnie and Ben. "Damn it all."

"Looks like he took a couple of them redskins with him," Lonnie said.

"I shot the one with the bow," Tommy said.

The other men looked at him in astonishment.

"Looks like you finally growed up, kid," Ben said.

Reese and the others drove the twenty head back into the herd. They did not speak. But they all looked at the body of Johnny on the ground.

Reese felt a wave of sadness wash over and engulf him. He had liked Johnny. Johnny was about to be named foreman of the outfit. Now he was gone. Gone with all his hopes and dreams.

Reese looked at the bodies of Yellow Horse and Silver Bear. There was bitterness in his heart. He shook his head at the madness of it all.

Silver Bear had not given up. Now he was dead too. Was that the end of it, then?

Reese didn't know, but as he turned to ride back to the chuck wagon, he hoped he had seen the last of the Cheyenne.

"Give him a good burial, men," Reese said as he pointed to Johnny. "I'll say a few words over him."

"Mighty sad," Ben said.

Tommy drew a deep breath and tears stung his eyes.

Lonnie's jaw hardened.

The fire dwindled to ash. But it had

thawed the ground so that when Ben and Tommy returned with shovels, they dug a grave with comparative ease.

In the morning, Reese said a final farewell to Johnny over a mound of fresh earth where wranglers, Checkers, and Louella were gathered.

"Rest in peace, Johnny," he intoned. But he felt his words were hollow. A good man lay under that mound of earth.

And there was no bringing him back.

CHAPTER 41

Tommy approached Reese after Johnny's burial.

"Mr. Balleen," he said, "I got somethin' to tell you. It's been eatin' at me all night."

"Yes, what is it, Tommy?"

"That Vernon Avery. I think he was in cahoots with them Injuns. He was helpin' them."

"I know."

"You know?"

"Avery didn't know who he was. He was a breed, half Injun, half white."

"I didn't know that," Tommy said.

"I guess he made his choice. He could have lived as a white man, but he chose to throw in with those Cheyenne."

"That why you didn't bury him or them other Injuns?"

"They didn't deserve a proper burial, Tommy. Let 'em rot or get eaten by buzzards and wolves."

"That seems kind of cruel to me," Tommy said.

"Life is cruel sometimes, Tommy."

Tommy shuffled his feet and looked down at the ground.

Reese patted him on one shoulder. "See you on point, Tommy. All you have to do is scout ahead. Follow the compass settings Johnny gave you."

"I will."

"See you," Reese said. He watched as Tommy climbed into his saddle and rode off. He saw him take out his compass and begin to figure out the route.

Luckily, he had ridden point with Johnny, so Tommy knew what to do. But Reese vowed to check on him once the herd got moving again.

They had already lost time and Reese was concerned that bad weather would overtake them by the time they got to Wyoming Territory. He looked at the sky and saw only white clouds floating in a blue bowl. Perfect.

He and Louella rode back to the chuck wagon. When Checkers pulled out, he waved good-bye and she waved back.

Reese was short of hands now. He just hoped those few he had left could control the herd. He didn't want any more mishaps or attacks.

Soon the herd was on the move again. Like some rolling river, the cattle streamed across that far southeastern corner of Montana. Mostly prairie, it was scarred by arroyos, dry creek beds that threatened to become raging rivers in heavy rain when flash floods flourished all over the country.

"Rough country," Lonnie said to Reese as they rode right flank. "One bolt of lightning could scatter this herd all over creation."

"Don't tempt God, Lonnie. We've got blue skies and fair weather."

"Yeah, right now we do."

"And from the looks of those skies, for many days to come."

"You trust that kid on point, Reese?" Lonnie asked. "It's a pretty big responsibility."

"It isn't a matter of trust. Tommy has a compass and he's been on the drive long enough to know how we run things."

"I don't know. A kid like that. He gets to daydreamin' and might lead us into a box canyon."

Reese laughed. "I'll ride up and check on him a little later," he said. "He's big enough to wear britches, he's big enough to ride point."

"If you say so, Reese. That's a mighty big responsibility. Kid's still wet behind the ears, you ask me."

"Tommy got baptized last night, Lonnie. Baptized in blood. That's a heavy weight for a kid to carry. Killing a man."

"Hell, it was only a Injun. That don't hardly count."

"A man is a man, no matter if his skin is white or red."

"Funny to hear you say that, Reese. You hate Injuns as much as I do."

"That doesn't mean I don't see their worth, Lonnie. Look, the Cheyenne were on the same land where I set my ranch. We whites took it away from them. I'm not sayin' it's right. I'm just sayin' it's the natural course of things."

"You have a funny way of looking at what happened to the Injun," Lonnie said.

"Well, when Silver Bear asked me to give him some of my cattle, I was stingy and mean to him. That's somethin' in my craw that don't taste real good. If I had given him some cattle, he might not have caused me so much trouble. Caused me to lose some good men."

"Yeah, but I wouldn't have given them redskins the time of day."

"They were starving, Lonnie. I could see their ribs. I was heartless and cruel."

"Sounds like you've had a change of heart, Reese."

"Maybe. I certainly got a lot to think about. Seein' Silver Bear dead like that got me to thinkin'. Thinkin' real hard about what was right and what was wrong."

"And do you think you were wrong to turn Silver Bear down when he begged for free cattle?"

"I don't know. It's not an easy question to answer. I could have shown him some human kindness."

"But the Injuns is our enemy," Lonnie said.

"Yes. And we white men made them so."

Lonnie was quiet for a while. Reese could sense that he was thinking about their conversation. So was he.

When he saw Silver Bear lying dead in the firelight the night before, he had thought of the kind of life the warrior had left behind. Reese had never thought of the Indian except as some kind of pest, like a weed that had to be jerked out of the ground and stomped back into it.

Now he thought of a proud man with copper skin who must have been a family man. He must have been a hunter, a provider of food for his family. And then, over time, his main source of food, the buffalo, had been taken from him. He had been reduced to some kind of beggar, no longer able to provide food for his family.

Still, Silver Bear had stolen some of his cattle. Now he hoped they would provide food for his family in the remaining months of winter. Perhaps that would help compensate for Silver Bear's death in some way. He hoped that it would, because no matter how much he hated Indians, he saw their worth and respected their dignity in the face of adversity.

He wondered how he would feel if people from another land and another culture invaded his land and took it away from him.

He knew how he would feel. And he would fight to the death to defend what he claimed was his.

That was all Silver Bear had done, but not as he might have. He stole cattle, yes, but Reese was convinced that he only killed white men in self-defense.

He could not fault a man for defending his life. Except Silver Bear was in the act of taking things that did not rightly belong to him.

There was just no answering all the questions in Reese's mind. And the more he muddled over Silver Bear and his tribe, the more uncertain he became. It was no longer a question of who was right and who was wrong, but who was alive and who was dead.

Reese was glad he was alive. But he was not glad that Silver Bear was dead. It was as if something important had been taken from the land. Like, perhaps, the last buffalo. If someone came along and killed it, there would be an emptiness that could never be recovered.

That was how he felt about Silver Bear now that he thought of that starving Cheyenne warrior. In a way, Silver Bear was among the last of a dying breed. Reese hadn't killed them off, but his fellow man had taken away everything the Cheyenne cherished, the land, the buffalo, the mountains with their beaver streams, the rivers with their fish.

Reese felt a strong sense of guilt, and more than that, he felt a deep shame for what his people had done to the Cheyenne, the Sioux, the Arapaho, the Ute, and the Kiowa.

He looked over at Lonnie, who seemed to be ruminating about something, just as he was.

"What're you thinkin', Lonnie?" Reese asked.

"Oh, nothin'."

"Yeah, me too."

Both men knew that this wasn't the truth.

Something had happened last night, and both men were deeply affected by it.

Now they faced a long stretch on the trail. The buffalo trail was no longer there to guide them. There was only a compass and the stars and a lot of lonesome land.

Reese felt the loss of something. Something important. But he did not yet know what it was. Still, he carried that loss with him as the herd trampled through a corner of Montana, headed for Wyoming Territory.

He rode along almost in a stupor with his thoughts and his ultimate confusion.

Life was a wonder. But it was also a tough school that was not for sissies.

"I guess I'll ride up to see how Tommy's doin' on point," Reese said after a while.

"You can't run away from your thoughts, can you, Reese?"

Startled, Reese looked sharply at Lonnie. "No, I guess you can't. But I'm goin' to try."

"Tommy can't help you, Reese. It's somethin' you got to work out yourself."

"I know." He touched a finger to the brim of his hat in farewell to Lonnie. He rode to the head of the herd and beyond, to where Tommy was on point.

His stomach, by then, had knotted up like a starched clump of manila rope.

"So long, Silver Bear," he said to himself. And his words were like a prayer.

CHAPTER 42

Tommy turned in the saddle to see Reese approaching. He raised his hand in greeting. "Howdy, Mr. Balleen," he said.

"Tommy, why don't you just call me Reese? When I hear Mr. Balleen, I think people are talkin' to my old pap."

"Yes, sir, Mr., uh, Reese."

"How's it goin', Tommy?"

"All right, sir. At least it's gettin' warmer. Warmer than it was."

"Yes. We should have fair weather ahead."

"I hope so," Tommy said. He looked up at the sky. Then he pulled out his compass again. He watched the needle swing and then settle on numbers in a quadrant. Satisfied with the reading, he put the small brass compass back in his pocket.

"How do you like riding point?" Reese asked.

"It's all right. Kind of lonely, though. I wonder how the herd is doin'."

"It's going just fine. What you want to watch for when you're out in front like this is any riders on the horizon, any dangerous places, like gully washouts and such. Then you let the lead man know what's ahead."

"I saw a bunch of antelope a while ago. They looked at me, then ran off. Pretty sight."

"You'll probably see more pronghorns in the days ahead," Reese said.

"I hope so. The way they run off, graceful and all, got my blood to pumpin'."

"You're liable to see a lot of wild animals out here, Tommy."

"Boy, them antelope were a sight to see, I tell you."

The two were silent for a few moments as they rode along through high grass and over broken land full of wrinkles and humps.

"I been thinkin'," Tommy said. " 'Bout Johnny and them Injuns."

"Yes?"

"Why do men die like that? Or why does anybody have to die?"

"Good questions," Reese said. "Some men die because they made a mistake. Johnny was in the wrong place at the wrong time. So were the Cheyenne."

"I know they all died, but I was wonderin' why other people die. They get sick and die, or somebody murders them. It seems a cryin' shame."

"Yeah, it is. Sickness claims people. That's life. People are born and they die. In fact, nobody lives very long. Our time is short and there's no explaining it."

"It just don't make no sense to me. Why people have to die."

"That's the way of the world, Tommy. That's why you live each moment as if it were your last. You never know when the Grim Reaper is going to come for you."

"Whew. It's a caution."

"Don't worry about it. Chances are you've got a long life ahead of you. You're still young and have a lot of living yet to do."

"I hope so," Tommy said.

They rode until the sun was midway across the sky, and that's when they saw Checkers and the chuck wagon. He was parked on the rim of a deep arroyo.

Louella limped over to the fire and waved as Reese and Tommy rode up.

"Thought I'd better stop here," Checkers said. "Don't know if you want to drive them cows through that arroyo."

"I'll take a look," Reese said.

He rode over to the rim and looked down into the arroyo. It was choked with brush and rocks. It looked like so many he had seen that were gouged out by flash floods. He rode back to the wagon and dismounted.

"We can go around it, I reckon," Reese said. "Might lose a few head if we run 'em in there."

"That's what I was thinkin'," Checkers said.

Louella limped over to Reese and put an arm around his waist. He hugged her and kissed her on the forehead.

Tommy, who had also dismounted, blushed.

"Missed you," she said. "And it's such a beautiful day. Got warm enough for me to take off my coat."

"Yeah, it's a dandy day," Reese said.

Checkers put more brush on the fire and set out his pots atop a grill he had set on top of some strategically placed stones.

In the distance, they heard the rumble of cattle as they traversed the rough ground and waded through tall grass.

"How come the cattle didn't stampede last night with all the gunfire?" Tommy asked as he stood by the fire and took off his heavy jacket.

"I suppose because most of them were asleep," Reese said. "They could have stampeded, but I'm mighty glad they didn't."

"What makes a herd stampede anyway?" Tommy asked.

"Depends on their mood, I guess. A rifle shot at the wrong time can send a herd off in all directions. Sometimes thunder. Or something they see that scares 'em. There's no certain reason for a herd to stampede."

"Remember, Reese," Louella said, "one night when there was lightning and thunder and the cows got scared and started running around in circles? Took you and your men two days to round them all up, and some of them you never found."

"I remember," he said. "Something spooked those cattle that night. And they scattered far and wide like dead leaves blown by the wind."

"I nearly got kilt in a stampede once," Checkers said. "Warn't pullin' no wagon, but leading a herd from one place to another and a rattlesnake come after me. I drew my pistol and shot at it. Herd took off like a pair of bridegroom pants on weddin' night. Took me a good day and a half to find all of 'em. But find 'em we did."

"Yeah, there's no tellin' what will spook cattle," Reese said.

Over the horizon, the lead cow appeared. Then more cows followed until all they could see were the approaching cattle.

"Here they come," Louella said.

"Yeah, and we have to stop 'em before they run down into that arroyo. I'd better tell Lonnie to hold 'em up." He got on his horse and rode out to meet Lonnie, who was riding alongside the leaders.

As he rode, he wondered how he and Lonnie were going to stop an entire herd from running down into that dangerous arroyo. They'd have to turn the herd back onto itself. And it would not be easy. The cattle were moving at a pretty good clip.

It might become a longer day than Reese intended. For Lonnie was struggling to hold back his horse and maintain control over the herd.

Reese took off his hat and waved it at Lonnie.

But Lonnie was too busy to wave back.

Then the lead cow bolted away from Lonnie and took a different tack. The herd followed blindly and Reese knew they were in trouble. He had to head off that lead cow and turn her back onto the herd.

Lonnie didn't move fast enough. The cattle turned on him and he was rocked nearly out of his saddle.

A moment later, Lonnie was surrounded by a sea of cattle.

Reese saw that he was trapped and would

308

not be able to help him. He spurred his horse to head off the lead cow, and his horse stepped into a gopher hole.

Reese heard the snap of a leg bone as it broke. Suddenly he was tossed from the saddle, and his horse lay on its side, its eyes wide and bright with pain.

There were lights in his head after it struck the ground. The world and the sky spun out of control as the herd rumbled toward him with their cloven hooves as sharp as knives.

CHAPTER 43

Lonnie fought to control his horse. The horse reared up and neighed. Its neigh was high-pitched, like a woman's scream. It clawed the air with his front hooves as cattle brushed past, gouging his sides with their horns.

He heard the bone snap on Reese's horse and knew it had probably broken a leg. He saw the horse go down and Reese get thrown from the saddle.

And Reese didn't get up.

"Damn you, hoss," Lonnie yelled as he jerked his reins back and forth. He tried to gain control and ride out of the herd before he got into more trouble. He knew how dangerous cattle were, and that lead cow had spooked at something she saw ahead or around her. She had bolted and the herd had followed her like blind lemmings.

"Hold on, Reese," Lonnie shouted. "I'll get out of this mess in a minute."

Reese heard Lonnie, but he was temporarily dazed and unable to move. His horse was moaning in pain and kicking its hind legs. Reese sensed that his horse was attempting to rise and stand up. But he knew that if the horse did manage to stand, it would be on only three legs.

Lonnie's horse fought its way out of the herd. It whinnied and kicked both hind feet to rid itself of cattle pressing it from behind. The cattle in front of the horse began to separate. But they all still followed the cantankerous lead cow as she bolted away from the main herd.

Reese struggled to rise. He was groggy and dizzy. He pushed against the saddle and slid away from his downed horse. He managed to roll over on his stomach. Then he pushed himself up with both hands and pushed backward until his feet were planted. Slowly he pushed up and stood on wobbly legs.

Lonnie rode up a few seconds later.

"Looks like your horse broke a leg, Reese," he said.

"Yeah. Lonnie. Get them cows rounded up before they run too far. I'll get me another horse to ride."

"What about this one?" Lonnie asked.

Reese drew his pistol. He cocked the hammer back and placed the muzzle just behind the horse's ear.

"Sorry, old buddy," he said.

He pulled the trigger. There was a loud report as the pistol spat a bullet into the horse's brain. The horse's body jerked and its hind legs kicked out.

The horse was dead in seconds.

Lonnie winced when the gun went off. His entire body twitched.

Tears flowed from Reese's eyes as the smoke spiraled up from the barrel of his pistol. He set the hammer to half-cock with his thumb and holstered it.

Then he turned away as cattle flowed around him.

Lonnie rode off with a "heeya," waving his hat as he chased down the lead cow.

Groggy, Reese made his slow way to the chuck wagon where Checkers had the cook fire blazing.

"What happened, Reese?" Louella asked. "We heard a shot. Where's your horse?"

Checkers looked at Reese, his eyebrows raised.

"Had to put my horse down," Reese said.

He hugged Louella. She reached up and wiped tears from his face.

"Reese, I'm so sorry," she said. "What happened?"

"Gopher hole. Horse stepped in it and broke its leg."

"How awful," she said.

"A crying shame, Reese," Checkers said.

"Checkers, go tell Chuck to bring me another horse, will you? I'll ride Rambler, the sorrel gelding. And have him and Jeremy go get my saddle and bridle off the horse I had to put down."

"Sure will. Him and Jeremy just put out feed for the remuda. See 'em yonder?" He pointed down the rim of the arroyo. Reese saw the feed wagon parked on a thick patch of grass and his two wranglers setting out feed for the horses. "And tell them to help Lonnie get a handle on those cows."

"Will do," Checkers said. He walked toward the feed wagon.

"I'm so sorry you had to shoot that horse, Reese," Louella said. She put an arm around her husband's waist. "It's a pity."

"There was no saving him, Lou. Broke my heart. Damn gophers anyway."

"You always liked Rambler, though."

"Rambler's a good horse. They're all good at this point."

Presently Reese saw Chuck and Jeremy saddle up two horses. They put a halter on Rambler and led him over to the chuck wagon.

"We'll get your saddle and bridle, Reese," Chuck said. "Just point us in the right direction."

"You may have to wade through a passel of cattle to get to it."

"We'll find your gear," Chuck said.

"Jeremy, you help Lonnie round up that herd and get the cows back on track. Chuck, after you bring me my saddle, you can help them."

"Them cows just don't want to go into that arroyo," Chuck said.

"And neither do I want them to go in there," Reese said.

He watched the two men ride away in the direction he had pointed. The herd was still following the lead cow, and Reese knew that Lonnie had his hands full. But help was on the way. And once he was saddled up on Rambler, he'd join the men in turning back the herd.

"What're you goin' to do about this damn arroyo?" Checkers asked.

"We'll have to go around it," Reese said. "I'm not going to risk losing cattle in that tangle of brush."

"Looks like them cows are headed in the right direction," Checkers said. "And that ditch stretches quite a long ways."

"Maybe they are," Reese said. "But we've

got to control the herd. No matter what."

"Right enough," Checkers said.

Reese patted Rambler on the neck and the sorrel whinnied.

"Pretty horse," Louella said.

"And he's only four years old," Reese said.

Soon Chuck rode back with Reese's saddle, bridle, and rifle. "A damn shame," he said.

"Yeah. But my horse broke its leg. There was no saving it on the trail."

"I know, Reese. That was a good horse too."

"He was."

"Well, I'm ridin' back to help Lonnie and Jeremy."

"Good luck," Reese said.

"We'll get them cows back on track." Chuck waved and then rode off at a gallop.

Reese threw the blanket on Rambler's back, then hoisted the saddle and positioned it on top of the blanket. He slipped on the bridle and removed the halter. He handed the halter to Louella.

"See you, hon," he said as he climbed into the saddle.

"Be careful, Reese," she said.

"Lunch when you get through," Checkers said. "Sandwiches and corn on the cob."

"Sounds good," Reese said. He turned

Rambler and rode off to join the other men.

Then abruptly he stopped and rode back.

He looked down at Checkers, who was laying out the vittles on a one-by-twelve board he carried in the wagon and had set atop three stones.

"Forget something?" Checkers asked.

"Next cow you butcher," Reese said, "it's going to be that lead cow. She's just too headstrong to suit me."

"I know the cow," Checkers said. "You sure?"

"I'm sure. Butcher her next time you need meat."

Louella gasped but said nothing. She watched him ride away, then turned to help Checkers.

"I hope Reese is doing the right thing," she said.

"He is," Checkers said. "You got an outlaw cow like that, you could be in big trouble the rest of the drive."

That lead cow would give me a lot of meat, he thought.

He would sharpen his knives that very day. They'd be needing more meat soon. And that lead cow would certainly fit the bill.

CHAPTER 44

Lonnie gained headway against the rogue lead cow. He turned her back into the herd. She fought all the way. She moaned and kicked.

He thought something had sure spooked her. Or maybe she had second sight and knew that menacing arroyo was just ahead.

The lead cow was turning and twisting as Lonnie chased after her. He thought about breaking out his lariat and throwing it around her neck to bring her to a jarring halt. But there were other cows running right along with her, and the way she was running would make it a difficult catch.

Jeremy Coates rode up and made his way through the herd.

"Need some help, Lonnie?" he asked.

"If you can get ahead of that cow and turn her toward me, that would be a help," Lonnie replied.

"Nothing to it," Jeremy said, and he put

the spurs to his horse's flanks.

He rode fast until he got ahead of the cows in front of the herd. The lead cow charged at him, her head down, her horns aimed at his horse.

"Whoa!" Jeremy shouted, and steered his horse away from those dangerous horns. "She's got a mad on for sure," he said to Lonnie.

"Somethin's gotten into that cow. I ought to shoot her."

"Hold on. I'll try and turn her back."

Jeremy took off his hat and rode in front of the lead cow. He swatted the air in front of her nose with it, and she jerked her head up to impale the foreign object.

Jeremy's horse danced away, out of harm's way. The cow charged after him.

She seemed determined to hold to her path. She snorted and swung her head back and forth, tracking Jeremy on his horse.

"Can you turn her back, Jeremy?" Lonnie called from a point some yards away on the cow's flank.

"I'm tryin', Lonnie. Damn cow don't want to turn back."

"I know. I think she's plumb crazy."

Jeremy rode past the cow again, batting his hat on her nose. She tossed her head and horns, trying to impale the hat.

But she slowed down.

So too did the rest of the herd.

Lonnie rode in alongside the cow and kicked her in the side.

She turned on him then, and Jeremy rode in close on her other side.

"Maybe we can box her in," Jeremy said. "You keep her busy on your side and I'll nudge her on this side with my horse."

And that's what the two did.

They held their horses just in back of her head. They jostled her with their horses.

Just then Chuck Norcross galloped up and saw what was happening.

"I'll get ahead of her and see if she'll stop," he said.

"Be careful," Jeremy said. "She wants to gore anything in her path with them horns."

Chuck rode in front of the snorting, head-tossing cow and kicked her square in the nose.

The cow stabbed at him with her horns. But Chuck and his horse sidled away, just out of reach.

Jeremy and Lonnie pressed her on both sides with their horses, staying just out of reach of the cow's horns.

Chuck turned his horse and rode across the cow's path. He kicked her again in the snout and she lowered her head and twisted it to try to gore his horse.

Then she stopped and stood spraddled as the herd swarmed past her before they stopped too. They all looked back at their leader and mooed.

Chuck rode up and leaned down in front of the ornery cow. He grabbed one horn and twisted it.

"She needs to be bulldogged," he said.

"I'd like to put a damn bullet in her brain," Lonnie said. "She's run this herd way off course."

It was then that Reese rode up and saw the milling herd, the defiant cow. She was hemmed in by three horsemen.

"Hold 'em right there," Reese said.

"We're way off our trail, Reese," Lonnie said.

"No, we're not," Reese said. "I was going to drive them to the end of this here arroyo, then turn back on our track once we got past it."

Lonnie lifted his hat and scratched his head.

"What for?" he asked.

"I'm not goin' to drive the herd into that arroyo," Reese said. "We'll hold the herd here while one of us rides to the end of this arroyo and finds us a place flat enough to get the herd into Wyoming."

"We that close?" Chuck asked.

"We're pretty close," Reese said.

"I'll scout out the end of this blamed arroyo," Chuck said. "Can't be too far before it peters out."

Reese looked at the deep gouge in the land. He could see no end to the arroyo. There was a lot of sagebrush and grass along its border. Dead wildflowers too, withered and tangled in grass. So far, the weather was holding and he was grateful for that. And it was getting warmer.

"You boys are probably as hungry as bears," Reese said. "But let's see what Chuck finds out and then I'll let two of you boys ride over to the chuck wagon for grub. Two of us will stay here and hold the herd."

"I guess me and Lonnie can wait awhile for our chuck," Jeremy said.

"You'll wait on Chuck for your chuck, right, Jeremy?" Chuck said.

"Or I can wait on Grub for my grub."

"Very funny," Chuck said.

"Better get to it, Chuck," Reese said. "Find us a new trail."

"You mean a detour," Jeremy said.

"Yeah, a detour around this dad-blamed gulley," Reese said.

"I'm off like a herd of turtles," Chuck said, and he turned his horse to the south.

He rode away and disappeared.

"I want you and Jeremy to put ropes on that lead cow," Reese said to Lonnie. "I want her tied up tight so she can't run off like a wild cow."

Both men untied their lariats. They shook out loops.

"Ready?" Lonnie asked.

"You go first, Lonnie," Jeremy said as he twirled the loop over his head.

Lonnie wound up and threw his rope at the lead cow's head.

The loop encircled the cow's neck. Lonnie pulled the rope tight.

Jeremy threw his rope and it landed over Lonnie's. He took up the slack and the cow was secured on both sides.

"What do we do now, Reese?" Lonnie asked.

"Just both of you keep those ropes tight. When you go to the chuck wagon, you'll drag her with you and tie her to the chuck wagon."

"You going to keep her tied to that wagon all the way to Cheyenne?" Jeremy asked.

"I have other plans for Boss Lady," Reese said.

Lonnie and Jeremy rolled and lit cigarettes as they all waited for Chuck to return. The cow stopped struggling and stood in a defiant stance, two ropes holding her in check.

Chuck returned at a gallop. He was drenched in sweat. He reined up and mopped his forehead with his bandanna.

"Find the end of the arroyo, Chuck?" Reese asked.

"Boy, did I!" Chuck said.

"How far?" Reese asked.

" 'Bout two mile, maybe less. Arroyo peters out all right, but we got to go around a lake."

"A lake?" Reese said.

"Yep. There's a five-acre lake at the end of this big old ditch."

"And beyond the lake?" Reese asked.

"Flat as a flapjack," Chuck said. "Lots of land just a-rollin' on like a green carpet."

Reese let out an exhalation of relief.

His shirt was sweat-stained under his armpits and on his back.

It was getting hotter as the sun crawled across the sky.

Just then Ben rode up from the rear of the herd.

"What's the holdup?" he asked. "Cattle are bunched up like they was in the loading docks at the slaughterhouse."

"See that arroyo there, Ben?" Lonnie asked.

Ben looked past them at the arroyo. "So?"

"So it's a tangle of brush and stuff," Lonnie said. "Cattle can't go in there without gettin' worn down to a nub."

"Well, shoot. Them cows back there been fartin' like thunder and gassin' me half to death. It seems deliberate."

The others laughed, including Reese.

"Cows have four stomachs, Ben," Reese said. "And each one of 'em produces gas. It's got to come out at one end or the other."

The men laughed again.

"Well, shoot," Ben said. "If I'da knowed that I would have brought along a gas mask."

Reese explained to him what Chuck had learned.

"Who's watching the tail of the herd, Ben?" he asked.

"I got Tommy on it. Herd's bunched up. They ain't goin' nowhere."

"Get yourself some grub, then relieve Tommy," Reese said. "We'll move the herd down past that lake after lunch."

"That suits me just fine," Ben said.

"Lonnie, you and Jeremy drag that bull-headed cow over to the chuck wagon and get yourselves some grub. After you tie her up, come back here and Chuck and I will go eat."

"Fair enough," Lonnie said.

Reese looked over at Jeremy. "Ready, Jeremy?"

"Ready as a bride on weddin' night," Jeremy said.

They followed Ben as he rode toward the chuck wagon.

"Ben's right about them cows. When they fart, they like to choke a man to death. That's why I like horses better'n cows."

"Horses fart too," Reese said.

"I know. But horses smell better'n cows."

"What about people?" Reese asked.

"Out in the open air, it ain't so bad. But in a closed room, that's the worst."

Reese laughed. He looked at the herd. They were restless and lowing. They seemed to sense that water was not far away. Well, they would drink and then be back on the trail.

And they'd be in Wyoming very soon.

CHAPTER 45

The cattle crowded on the bank of the small lake as Checkers rolled past in the chuck wagon. Tied to the wagon was the lead cow, and she was acting up like a prima donna in chains.

Lonnie was riding left flank, along with Jeremy. Jeremy was ordered by Reese to ride with Lonnie and learn how to handle cattle. Jeremy was a horse wrangler and did not know much about cattle.

The herd moved into Wyoming.

Broken land, low hills, arroyos, and gulches greeted the herders and the herd.

"This don't seem like much of a tough job," Jeremy said as they rode alongside the herd.

"So far, so good," Lonnie said.

"Cows are so dumb," Jeremy said. "Compared to horses."

"They're not dumb, Jeremy. Cows are herd animals and when they're following a leader, they look like dumb animals."

"They sure do. I never thought I'd be wrangling a bunch of cows. Especially in country like this."

"Where do you hail from?" Lonnie asked.

"Missouri."

"What did you do back there?"

Jeremy laughed.

"I guess I was kind of a prospector," he replied.

"Gold?" Lonnie said.

"Nope. Silver."

"Silver. I didn't know there was silver in Missouri."

Jeremy laughed again. "Well, there's a story behind my prospectin', I tell you. It all started with a silver dollar."

"Yeah? What do you mean?" Lonnie asked.

"I was in a saloon up in Springfield. It was just after the war. Barkeep gave me change for a double sawbuck. A bunch of silver dollars. One of 'em looked funny and I picked it up. I read what was writ on the dollar."

"What did it say?"

"It was a Yocum dollar. A Yocum silver dollar."

"Never heard of it," Lonnie said.

"Me neither. So I asked the barkeep, a man named Artie Ayers. Artie said he got the silver dollar down in the river bottoms around a town he called Branson. White River runs down through there."

"And?"

"He said there was a man down there who had a hidden silver mine. Man name of Yocum. Yocum, I think was German. Spelled his name different at one time."

"So, did you go down there?" Lonnie asked.

"Sure did. I had that Yocum silver dollar in my pocket, and I wanted to find that secret mine of Yocum's. Or one near it."

"Did you find it?"

"Nope. Never did. Nobody else did either. I think old Yocum died and never told nobody about his silver mine. There were men diggin' all over the place and none of them found no silver."

"So, what did you do?"

"I took up with a man who raised horses, man named Fred Pfister. He taught me the wranglin' business. Then I went out west and run into Reese, who hired me on."

"Do you still have that whatchamacallit silver dollar?" Lonnie asked.

"Sure do. Wouldn't part with it. It might be worth a pile of money someday."

Jeremy slid a hand into his pants pocket and pulled out a silver dollar. He handed it to Lonnie.

Lonnie turned the coin over and over in his hand. He read the legend. It was, he saw, a Yocum silver dollar. The name was plainly stamped onto the ninety-nine percent silver dollar.

"Boy, you got somethin' here, all right. It looks odd to see that name on a silver dollar." Lonnie handed the coin back to Jeremy.

"Yeah, I know."

"So, where do you think that old Yocum silver mine might be?" Lonnie asked.

"Beats me," Jeremy said. "Me and a bunch more looked all over for it. Never could find it."

"Will you ever go back there to look for it?"

"I doubt it. Yocum was mighty careful. And secretive. He never let on where that mine might be. But he stamped out a bunch of coins to prove he'd found silver in the ground. We, none of us, ever knew where. Even Artie Ayers went down there to look for that silver mine. Last I heard he was still lookin'."

Lonnie laughed.

"Sounds like a wild-goose chase," he said.

"Well, we were a lot of gooses all right," Jeremy said.

He slid the coin back in his pocket.

Jeremy and Lonnie drifted along with the slow, lumbering herd. They traversed broken ground and passed buttes that rose like ancient monuments or fortresslike structures made of stone. The cattle navigated the rugged terrain as if they had traveled there before.

They entered an open plain.

Just then, slightly to their left, a large jackrabbit bolted from cover.

A bull in the herd reacted. It broke from the herd and chased after the jackrabbit.

"Uh-oh," Lonnie said.

The jackrabbit bounded away and streaked across the plain in a zigzag.

Other cattle broke from the herd and began to stream after the bull.

"You stay here and hold any more cows from breaking away," Lonnie told Jeremy.

"What are you gon' to do?" Jeremy asked.

"I got to get that bull turned back into the herd. You hold 'em until I get 'er done."

"Sure thing," Jeremy said.

He watched as Lonnie put his horse into a gallop and went after the runaway bull.

Lonnie gained ground on the bull, which was also beginning to zigzag. The jackrabbit leaped out of sight and stopped behind a clump of sagebrush. It froze there for safety and concealment.

The bull became confused and swung its head back and forth as it sought to see the jackrabbit that had startled it.

"Ho, bull," Lonnie yelled.

The bull swung its head to eye the oncoming horseman.

It stood rigid for a moment or two, then changed direction and began to run away from Lonnie.

"Ho, boy," Lonnie called, and overtook the bull. His horse, responding to its reined commands, turned back on the bull.

The bull turned away from the horse.

Lonnie pressed his horse to chop off the bull's flight.

For a moment, the two animals squared off like two human pugilists. The bull turned right and the horse parried its rush by cutting it off. Then the bull turned to the left and, without any urging from Lonnie, the horse switched its direction and cut off the bull once again.

"Git, boy," Lonnie yelled at the bull.

He took off his hat and waved it in front of the bull's snout.

The bull tossed its head and turned a full hundred and eighty degrees.

It ran toward the herd. The other cattle turned as if on wires and followed after.

Lonnie stayed on the bull's rump. He

yelled and slapped his hat across the bull's rump. The animal picked up speed as it angled back toward the main herd.

Jeremy watched in admiration as Lonnie's horse matched every move of the bull. The horse turned one way, then the other, right on the bull's tail. It chased the bull back into the herd several yards in front of Jeremy.

Lonnie hauled in on the reins to let the other cattle pass him and join the bull on the side of the herd.

Jeremy watched in fascination and admiration as all of the strayed cows blended in with the herd. They followed the trail as if nothing unusual had happened.

Lonnie slowed his horse and waited for Jeremy to catch up to him.

"That was some horsemanship," Jeremy said.

"Thanks. Horse is a cutter. It's trained to chase cows and cut them off when he sees them run off like that."

"Amazing," Jeremy said. "I didn't know a horse could do that. And so expertly."

"This horse don't stand for no orneriness from cattle," Lonnie said. "It can herd cattle better'n any man."

"I see that," Jeremy said.

"Let's hope the cattle stay in line the rest

of the day," Lonnie said.

"Well, it don't look easy over this rough ground," Jeremy said. "It's full of little washes and gullies."

"And buttes and mesas," Lonnie said. "But we should have smoother ground ahead. Somewheres."

Jeremy laughed.

"This has got to be hard on the cattle," he said. "And I see little hills ahead, off in the distance."

"And very little grass to tempt the cows to stop and graze."

"Will they do that if they see a lot of grass?" Jeremy asked.

"Some of them will want to, but the point man will keep that lead cow to the trail. The herd will follow."

"Blindly," Jeremy said.

Lonnie chuckled as he jogged and rocked in the saddle, his gaze ever steady on the cattle. "Oh, them cows want to stay in the herd. That's where they feel safe. They don't have to think as long as the whole bunch of them is movin' on ahead of them."

"I'm beginning to see how this all works," Jeremy said.

"Well, you'll learn more as we head down the trail."

"Is there a trail? I don't see none," Jeremy said.

"If not, the cattle will make one," Lonnie said. "We're following a compass to Cheyenne. Reese knows what he's doin'."

"Yeah. He's pretty smart."

"Smarter'n any of us," Lonnie said. "You can bet your Yocum dollar on that."

Jeremy laughed and patted his pocket.

"I'm beginning to think that Yocum dollar is my lucky piece," he said.

"Keep thinkin' it," Lonnie said. "And it might turn out to be your lucky dollar."

The two rode on, and the herd flowed across the broken land.

The sun was beginning to set above the mountains in the hazy distance when the herd began to stop and bunch up.

"Well," Lonnie said, "here's where we bed 'em down for the night. Probably at some water hole we can't see ahead of us."

"How does anyone know when to stop?"

"It'll be dark right soon. Suppertime. I just hope Checkers has us a good meal. I'm plumb tuckered out."

"Me too," Jeremy said.

The herd stopped completely and the cattle began to nibble on the few tufts of grass.

The clouds in the west shimmered gold

on their edges and turned pink, then blue, then a deep purple.

The sun sank over the snowy peaks of the Rocky Mountains, and a kind of solemnity seemed to settle over the land.

The kind of peace that comes to the end of a day during a long cattle drive.

And all seemed well in the herders' world.

CHAPTER 46

Leo Chippendale was worried.

His tanks were low and drying up. The fall seemed unusually warm with blazing heat. But the grass was dying and he wondered when he would have to put out alfalfa hay for his small herd.

He was in the barn, feeding and watering his horses, when his wife, Carlene, called to him from the house.

"They're coming, Chip."

"Oh, all right, Carlene. I'll be right there."

"Hurry. You ought to wash up before they get here."

He poured oats and corn into a small trough in one of the stalls. His horse neighed and began to nibble at the fodder.

He stepped outside and looked down the lane. He saw a sulky approaching with two men in it. Both wore dark suits and one of them had on a derby hat, while the other sported a stiff new Stetson such as Chip himself wore. His was not in such a pristine condition, however.

"Bankers," he muttered to himself. "Wolves."

He walked into the house and Carlene, a petite woman with dazzling green eyes and naturally curly hair the color of copper, grabbed his hand and led him to the kitchen, where she had a porcelain bowl of warm water on the counter. She dabbed a washcloth into the water and wiped his face. Then she dried it with another towel.

"Your hands are clean enough," she said, "but you've got dirt under your nails."

"That's ranch dirt, darlin', and is come by honestly."

"Oh, you," she said, with a twinkle in her eye.

"I've made coffee," she said, "and set out a box of cigars for Mr. Alsworthy and whoever's with him."

"That's probably Ned Hamilton ridin' in the sulky with Alsworthy. I know what he wants."

"Oh, Chip, don't be so harsh. They're just tryin' to help you through hard times."

"Little do you know, Carlene," he said as he turned away from the sink and his wife's ministrations.

Chip was not tall, but he had a symmetry

to him with his square, broad shoulders, chiseled, cleanly shaven face, brown eyes, and lean, strong, muscular arms, freckled hands, and a tinge of gray threading his short sideburns.

"What's Ned Hamilton doing with Mr. Alsworthy?" she asked.

"You know why he's here," Chip said.

"I thought you told him you weren't interested," she said.

"I did. In no uncertain terms. The man's a bulldog. He bites and holds on."

"Well, you just tell him you're not selling the Flying U."

"I've told him," Chip said. "He's like a shark that smells blood in the water."

"Well, I hope you tell him you're not interested, Chip. I don't like that man. He makes my skin crawl."

"Mine too," Chip said.

The banker and his companion pulled up at the hitch rail in front of the log and stone home. They climbed out of the buggy and walked under the lattice arbor and up the walk.

Carlene went to the door and opened it.

"Why, Mr. Alsworthy," she said, "what brings you this far out to the Flying U?"

"I need to see Mr. Chippendale," Alsworthy said.

"And, Ned, whatever brings you out here?" There was more than a hint of cattiness in her voice. Her green eyes flashed an emerald fire as she stared at Hamilton.

"Ma'am, I'm here to save your lives, yours and Chip's."

"Why, do come in, won't you? I'm sorry the house is in such a mess. You're both so unexpected."

Alsworthy knew that Carlene's house was spick-and-span.

She stood to one side and the two men walked in. They removed their hats out of politeness.

"Won't you gentlemen sit down?" she said. "I've made fresh coffee and set out sugar and cream."

She escorted the two visitors into the front room, where they both took a seat on the divan. On the small table, there were three cups and saucers, a sugar bowl and small pitcher of cream, and a steaming pot of freshly brewed coffee in a pewter pot.

She bent over and poured coffee into the three cups as her husband sat down in his easy chair, covered with cowhide.

The three men sipped their coffee as Carlene took a chair in front of a small desk.

At first, no one spoke. Alsworthy cleared his throat after swallowing a mouthful of hot coffee that burned his tongue.

"You got something to say, Alsworthy, go ahead," Chip said. He blew on his cup and took a sip of his coffee.

"Yes, well, uh, what brings me here, Chippendale, is the matter of your mortgage. As you know, the bank advanced you a sum of money so that you could complete the building of your home and barn, along with some pole corrals and digging a water well."

"Yes, I know," Chip said. "Very generous and kind of you and your bank, Alsworthy."

"I've brought Mr. Hamilton with me in order to save you embarrassment and a dead loss."

"What has Hamilton got to do with my bank loan?" Chip asked.

"Nothing at the moment," Alsworthy said. "But I'll let Ned explain his presence at this meeting."

Ned Hamilton fixed hazel eyes on Chip's face and began to speak slowly.

"Chip, I made you an offer for your five thousand acres, not once, but three times. I thought my offer was generous and I'm willing to stand by the original figure. If you agree right away."

Chip leaned back in his chair. He put his hands behind his neck and looked at the two men seated across from him.

"I've put a lot of work into the Flying U," Chip said. "Since your first offer, I mean. So your offer is way low. However, I'm not of a mind to sell my ranch. I've got too much of me invested."

Alsworthy cleared his throat of phlegm. He made a steeple of his fingers, and his face took on a serious mien. "Chippendale, the way I see it, you have little choice at this point. Your cattle herd is depleted because of the drought, and the grass has dried up in this unusual spell of heat we've had here. Mr. Hamilton has made you a generous offer and should you accept, you would ward off certain foreclosure by my bank."

"You don't have to foreclose, Alsworthy," Chip said. "You could very easily grant me an extension of my loan."

"On what basis would I do that?" Alsworthy asked.

"I've got a fresh herd coming down from North Dakota. A thousand head. They should be here sometime before my loan comes due."

"We're prepared to foreclose on the Flying U around the middle of November," Alsworthy said.

Hamilton took another swallow of his coffee and looked at Chip with a baleful eye.

"Let's see," Chip said. "Mid-November.

That's about the time of the beaver moon."

"Beaver moon?" Alsworthy said. "What do you mean?"

"Mountain man trappers call that last full moon in November a 'beaver moon.' That's when they set their last traps before the rivers freeze over."

"It's a suitable image," Alsworthy said. "That means when that moon is full again, your time has run out to pay off your mortgage."

"Alsworthy, I just need a little more time," Chip said. "When I get that herd in, I'm going to drive them to Kansas where I can make a profit."

"All that takes time, Chippendale," Alsworthy said. "Time is money. And the bank is not willing to extend your loan."

"I'm making you an offer, Chippendale," Hamilton said. "A buck fifty an acre. More'n you paid when you got this here ranch."

"The ranch is worth more than when I bought it," Chip said. "A lot more."

"You paid a dollar an acre," Hamilton said. "It's not worth a whole lot more. I'll throw in a hundred bucks extra for the house."

Chip's anger rose in him like the mercury in a thermometer on a hot day.

"That's insulting, Hamilton," Chip said.

"We've got more'n a hundred bucks in this here home."

"Well, if the bank forecloses on you, Chippendale, you'll wind up with nothin'. I'm makin' you a fair offer. One way or another, I'm going to buy this property."

"Or steal it," Chip said.

"Now, now, gentlemen," Alsworthy cut in, "that's enough bickering. Let's keep this conversation on a civilized level."

He paused and looked at Chippendale with his swollen neck and reddened face.

"Mr. Chippendale," Alsworthy continued, "you have until that beaver moon to pay off your mortgage. That's final. And if Mr. Hamilton wants to pick up the mortgage, he gets the Flying U for what amounts to a song."

"That's damn mean-spirited of you and your bank, Alsworthy," Chip said. "All I need is more time and I'll pay off the mortgage."

"That's enough," Carlene interrupted as she rose to her feet. "You've gone over all this and I can see that Mr. Alsworthy is not willing to give us more time. Gentlemen, please leave my house this instant."

Both Alsworthy and Hamilton rose from their seats. They marched to the door and, once outside, donned their hats and walked to the sulky.

"Good riddance," Carlene said as she watched the two men leave.

"Honey, I'm sorry," Chip said to her as she closed the door.

"Nothing to be sorry about," she said. "The bank just has no heart."

"I don't trust Hamilton at all. He's wanted the Flying U for a long while now. I wouldn't put it past him to mess up my deal with Balleen on the cattle he's driving down."

"You think Hamilton will resort to stealing?" she asked. "You practically accused him of that when he was here."

"Hamilton is a snake," he said. "He got the little ranch he has by running off a sodbuster at gunpoint."

"I didn't know that," she said. "How do you know about that?"

"Fellow in town told me," he said. "Man name of Elves had a small spread west of Cheyenne. He was tryin' to grow winter wheat and make a livin'. Hamilton run him off with some hired guns, and just took over his property."

"How awful."

"That's why I don't trust Hamilton to play fair. He might want to see me foreclosed on. Or he might just shoot the both of us and grab the deed from the bank for peanuts."

"You can't let that happen, Chip," she said.

"No, I can't," he said. "And I won't. When those cattle get here, I'm going to try and sell some of them in Fort Laramie. That way I can pay off this mortgage."

"But what if Hamilton still wants to get the Flying U?"

"Fire with fire," Chip said. "We'll fight for this ranch, me and my hands. He'll never get the Flying U. Not even over my dead body."

"Let's pray that won't happen. And pray that the herd from up north gets here soon."

"Yeah. Before that beaver moon."

She began to carry away the coffee cups while Chip walked to the front window and looked out over his property.

The ranch meant everything to him. He had big plans for it after Reese delivered the herd.

The problem now was that he didn't have the money to pay Reese. His own herd had been depleted and his pockets were empty.

A wave of sadness overcame him as he thought about his predicament.

How do you pay for something you badly need so that you can pay for something you

already have but are about to lose?
For now, Chip had no answer.

CHAPTER 47

Reese knew that he had to find water for his herd. He had only ridden through this country two or three times before. He knew there were streams here and there but could not remember exactly where.

The cattle were complaining with their loud and grumbling noises, and the horses were not faring much better.

The chuck wagon was slow over the rough ground because Checkers still had that lead cow in tow. He had not yet butchered it because, for the time being, his meat larder was full.

Reese knew he had to find water. So he whistled for Tommy to ride up to him from the rear flank.

"Yes, sir," Tommy said. "You wanted to see me?"

"Yes. I've got an important job for you. And I don't want you to get lost. You still have that compass?"

"Yes, sir, I still got it."

"Good. I want you to ride way ahead of the herd and find us a creek or a river that's near our trail. Can you do that for me?"

"Sure can, sir. I'll try. Just ride ahead of the herd and find a creek or a river."

"Way ahead of the herd. Then ride back when you've found some water. Might be just a tank. A natural water collector. Ought to be something out there."

"I'll look real hard," Tommy said.

"Get to it, then," Reese said.

Tommy saluted and rode off alongside the herd until he disappeared in the distance.

Reese slipped his bandanna from around his throat and covered his mouth and nose. The cattle were kicking up scrims of dust, and he was breathing every grain, it seemed.

Two hours later, Tommy rode up. He looked worn out. His shirt was soaked with sweat and his face had a sheen to it from perspiration.

"I found a creek," Tommy blurted out in a rush of breathless expulsion of words from his mouth. "And that ain't all."

"Get your breath and then tell me, Tommy," Reese said. "How far ahead is this creek and what else did you find?"

"Well, sir," Tommy said, after catching his breath, "they's a little creek, just as purty as

348

you please, and some Injuns camped right by it, big old teepees and kids half-starved, women skinny as rails. Big chief there speaks English pretty good."

"You talked to him?" Reese asked.

"Yep, sure did. His name is Red Beaver and he's a Blackfoot. They're all Blackfoot, I reckon."

"What did you tell him?" Reese asked.

"I told him we was drivin' a herd down to Cheyenne and the cattle and horses was thirsty. He said we were welcome. Or that was the gist of it, I reckon."

"How far is this creek?" Reese asked.

"About four or five miles. Real easy to find and it's right on the trail, accordin' to my compass."

"That's good news, son," Reese said. "You done good."

"Yeah, I could hear these cows a-moain' and carryin' on for more'n a mile when I rode back here."

"Did those Blackfeet seem friendly?"

"Yep. Red Beaver was the head man, and he was right friendly. So were the kids. They only got three teepees and maybe two other braves, a couple of women, and three little kids. They look like they're starvin'. I could see the ribs on the men and the kids. Women had on dresses, but they was all real skinny, looked like."

"I wonder why there are Blackfoot Injuns this far away from Fort Laramie."

"I don't know," Tommy said. "I didn't ask."

"Well, I will," Reese said.

"What do you want me to do now, Mr. Balleen?"

"Tommy, call me Reese, damn it. I've told you before. We're not formal out here and I ain't wearin' a tuxedo."

"No, sir, uh, Reese."

"You stay here and ride flank," Reese said. "I'm going to catch up with Checkers and tell him you found us a creek."

"He's goin' real slow, Mr., uh, Reese. Just a-tuggin' that ornery cow behind him."

"I know," Reese said. He rode off, leaving Tommy to ride flank. He caught up with Checkers and rode alongside him.

"What brings you up here?" Checkers asked as Reese pulled up next to where he sat in the driver's seat, next to Louella, who waved and tightened the light scarf that framed her face.

"Water ahead. A creek. Four miles maybe. The kid found it for us."

"I was expectin' a crick about now," Checkers said.

"Some Blackfoot Injuns there too," Reese said.

"I hope they're not on the warpath."

"Seems like they're friendly, so the kid says."

"Good. I hate fightin' so early in the day."

"That cow back there is still fightin' to get away," Reese said. "When are you going to butcher her?"

"Not right yet," Checkers said. "My meat locker is plumb full. And now that we've lost some men along the way, it's not goin' down so fast."

"I understand."

"I hate draggin' that cow behind me," Checkers said. "Slows me down somethin' terrible. Like I got an anchor on my prairie schooner."

Reese laughed. "This wagon ain't no schooner, Checkers. More like a whale-boat."

Checkers and Louella both laughed.

"Well, it gets me there," Checkers said.

Reese touched a single finger to his hat in farewell. Then he blew a kiss at Louella, who smiled and blew one back.

Checkers watched Reese ride off until he was out of sight. Then he heard a prairie chicken drum with his powerful wings.

"What's that?" Louella asked.

"Prairie chicken. And that's a good sign."

"How come?" she asked.

"Means there're water and grass. Usually don't find them chickens this far west. More of 'em in Kansas and Nebraska."

"So the horses will be able to drink soon," she said. "And that cow back there."

"I hope she drowns," Checkers said in an attempt to be funny.

Louella did not laugh.

CHAPTER 48

Reese saw the teepees first. They stood stark against the sky like old bones.

He rode up on the Blackfoot camp at a slow pace, prepared for any eventuality. He did not think there would be trouble since Tommy had said the Indians were friendly. But with a redskin, you just never knew.

There were three teepees. Their lodge poles crisscrossed the blue sky. There was no smoke. As Reese approached, he saw movement.

The children were the first to see him. They all ran inside their lodges. Women came out and stared at him. Then, from behind one of the teepees, Reese saw one man, then another, until three Blackfoot came into view.

They looked curious, not warlike.

Reese raised his right hand, palm facing the men on the ground.

One of them raised his right hand in the

universal sign of peace. The flat of the hand showed all that he held no weapon.

Nor were the faces of any of the Blackfeet painted.

Another good sign, Reese thought.

"How cola," Reese said as he rode in close.

"You speak the words of the Lakota," one of the men said. "But I know the tongue."

"Only Injun words I know," Reese said.

"I speak your tongue. I am Red Beaver. I am Blackfoot. You are the man with the cattle."

"Yes. I'm driving a herd of cattle to Cheyenne."

"The boy tells me that is so," Red Beaver said.

"We do not mean you any harm," Reese said. "We will water our cows and horses, then move on to the south."

Reese noticed the bare chests of the three men. He could see their ribs beneath the skin. The women wore buckskin dresses that concealed much of their flesh. Their dresses were beaded just below the shoulders. So were their moccasins.

The men wore unadorned moccasins and buckskin britches that bore marks of grease and other liquids. There were fringes on their britches.

"Come, if you have tobacco we will smoke

the pipe," Red Beaver said. He made the sign of a man dismounting a horse. A sign that Reese knew. Red Beaver straddled his left index finger with two fingers on his right hand and then showed one of them crossing over and walking away.

Reese swung out of the saddle.

"I have no tobacco, but some of my men do. When they come, we can smoke."

"Good," Red Beaver said.

Reese extended his hand.

Red Beaver closed his hand over it.

"I know," the Blackfoot said, "this is the way the white man greets another."

The two shook hands. The other two braves looked on approval.

Red Beaver was lean and his skin was dark with a reddish tinge. His long black hair was braided and hung down his back. He wore a single eagle's feather in his hair. The other two did not have feathers, but they too had their hair braided and tied with thongs. They looked younger than Red Beaver.

Red Beaver saw Reese looking at the other two men. He stepped back and waved a hand at them.

"These are my sons," he told Reese. "That one is called Blue Mouse and that one is called Red Deer."

"Why are you not at the fort?" Reese asked.

"We were at the fort, the one you call Laramie. But the agent there stole our food and our white man's clothes."

"The Indian agent?" Reese asked.

Red Beaver nodded. "A very bad man. He sells the food the army gives to us and he spends it on firewater. We were hungry, so we left the fort to hunt the buffalo. But there are no buffalo. Only the antelope and they are hard to catch. We have only our bows and they do not shoot the arrows far."

Reese thought that was quite a long speech for an Indian. But Red Beaver spoke English very well. And he seemed to know a lot of words.

Reese was impressed.

"You speak English right good," he said to Red Beaver. "How come?"

"I was scout for army. I listen and I learn."

"I am wondering if we will find more creeks like this one as we journey to Cheyenne," Reese said.

"Many creeks," Red Beaver said. "Much water. Much grass."

"Are you hungry, Red Beaver?"

Red Beaver rubbed a hand across the flat of his stomach.

"Much hunger," he said.

"The buffalo are all gone," Reese said.

"Yes. The white man killed all the buffalo. They take the hide and leave the meat to spoil. Will you sell me one or two of your cows so that my sons and our wives and children can eat?"

"Do you have money?" Reese asked.

"No, we do not have money. We have two beaver skins and some beaded moccasins. We will trade, no?"

Reese shook his head.

"If you will guide us to water and to Cheyenne, I will give you two cows," Reese said.

Red Beaver thought about the proposition for a moment. Then he smiled.

"I will guide you for two cows," he said. "Cheyenne is not far and my people will eat. You will feed me on the trail?"

"Yes, I'll feed you. The cattle will be here soon. They will drink. I have a big cow behind a wagon that I will give you and you may pick out another for your family."

"That is good," Red Beaver said. He shook Reese's hand again.

Then he turned and spoke to his sons in the Blackfoot language. He also spoke in sign language.

A woman peeked out of a teepee.

Red Beaver spoke to her in a loud tone of

voice. The woman came out and two others emerged from two separate teepees. Then the little children came outside and stared at the white man as they hid behind their mothers.

Red Beaver spoke to all of them in his native tongue. The women smiled and curtsied. The children rubbed their tummies and licked their lips.

"They have much hunger," Red Beaver said.

"They will eat soon," Reese said. "In fact, I can hear our herd now."

He turned and saw Checkers ahead of the herd, driving his horses hard.

"There is your first cow, Red Beaver," Reese said. "Behind that wagon. I will give it to you, but I will keep my rope."

"I will take the cow."

Reese looked at the small creek. It had plenty of water in it and ran fast across the prairie. It was a good watering place for his cattle.

Checkers rumbled up and stopped near the three teepees. He looked at Reese as if surprised to see him standing there, surrounded by several Indians.

"Checkers," Reese said. "You don't have to pull that cow no more. I gave it to Red

Beaver here. He's going to guide us to Cheyenne."

"Well, I'll be dad-blamed," Checkers said. He smiled. "Reese, you are a kindhearted man."

"I know," Reese said.

Louella laughed.

"I want to see the children," she said.

"Climb down," Reese told her. "They're harmless and right friendly."

"I can see that," she said as she climbed out of the wagon.

The women and children laughed and grinned as the white woman walked over to them.

The Blackfeet women plucked at Louella's clothes and one of them pinched her cheek as if to see if she was human. They all laughed and so did Louella.

"Don't get too friendly, Lou," Reese said. "You can't stay here."

She laughed. "Oh, it's just so nice to see other women after riding with Checkers for so many miles."

The two hugged and the Blackfeet women clapped their hands and looked on in approval.

Checkers climbed down from the wagon and untied the lead cow and the braves swarmed up and ringnecked the cow.

"Get my rope, Checkers," Reese said. "Then let them have that cow."

"Gladly," Checkers said. He removed the rope, and the two young men pulled the cow behind the teepees and out of sight.

One of them had drawn a knife from a beaded scabbard hanging from his waist sash.

Two of the women vanished behind the teepees. A third went inside one of the lodges and emerged with a large knife.

"Well, that takes care of my problem," Checkers said. "They don't waste no time, do they?"

Reese nodded.

Then, over the horizon, came the cattle herd. The smell of water had them on the run.

"Look out," Reese said to Red Beaver, "here comes the herd."

Red Beaver looked at the oncoming cows and smiled.

"They are pretty cows," he said.

"And you can pick out another one for your family," Reese said.

"I will take a big one."

The herd separated and streamed past the teepees and the three Blackfoot ponies, which were staked in between the small circle of teepees. The cattle lined up at the banks of the creek and began to drink.

The hands watered their horses as Chuck drove the feed wagon in close, followed by the remuda on ropes behind him, tethered in a straight line on two long lariats.

Tommy rode in to where Reese was standing with Red Beaver.

"Boy, them cows are sure thirsty," he said.

"Better water your horse," Reese said.

He watched as all the cattle line up and slurped water from the creek.

It had turned out, he thought, to be a very good day on a long trail.

Louella hugged him and he hugged her.

"It's wonderful to see them all drink," she said.

"Best sight I've seen all day," Reese said. He squeezed her and she looked up and smiled at him.

"I think," she said, "this is the happiest day I've had on this drive."

"Yes, hon. For me too."

He looked past the creek and up to the sky. The blue canopy seemed to stretch on forever. And beyond it, he knew, there was Cheyenne and the Flying U.

CHAPTER 49

Alsworthy lit a cigar and handed the humidor across his desk to Hamilton.

"What's your next move?" he asked.

"I can't wait too long to grab the Flying U," Hamilton said.

"No, you can't. Otherwise the whole thing will slip through our fingers."

"I can't let that happen."

"No. But I've talked to Jeff Brunswick, and he's prepared to sign a contract with us on behalf of his company. But he insists on closing the deal before the end of November."

"Why?" Hamilton asked.

"He's looking at a lease up in Johnson County that looks promising."

"And is he prepared to pay up real quick?"

"Upon signing, he'll give us a certified check," Alsworthy said.

"Well, your foreclosure won't be in time, will it?" Hamilton fixed the banker with a cold, steady eye.

"Not quite. These things take time."

"What I'm worried about is that Chippendale will stumble onto that section of his ranch and discover what we found there."

"That is a possibility," Alsworthy said. He shuffled through some papers on his desk, in the in-box. He looked a sheet over.

"There's a possibility I can block Chippendale from doing anything with his property, once he's in arrears on his mortgage," Alsworthy said. "There's a clause in his contract agreement that prevents him from destroying or altering anything on his property or home as long as the contract is in existence."

"What does that mean exactly?" Hamilton asked.

"It means that he can't dig up anything that we deem in violation. No drilling, no shoveling, no untoward development."

"But will it stick?" Hamilton squirmed around his hard-backed chair. The seat was hardwood and uncomfortable, as was intended by the bankers who furnished Alsworthy's office. His own chair was covered in soft leather, a high-backed baronial model that complemented his cherrywood desk that was polished to a high sheen and nearly devoid of clutter.

"It's admittedly a long shot."

"I don't like long shots. I like 'em short and sweet."

"The only thing sweet about this deal is that we won't have to wait long to foreclose. A little less than a month and a half."

"Meanwhile, I sweat bullets waiting for the ax to fall," Hamilton said.

"I will be somewhat nervous too until we can get Chippendale off the Flying U."

"It's only a question of time until he stumbles on what's he's got there," Hamilton said.

"It'll be difficult for Chippendale to find what you did."

"Sooner or later, he'll stumble onto that slough and then it's all over. I just hope he doesn't find it."

"That's my wish and my hope too," Alsworthy said.

"Well, see what you can do. I'm going to round up my old gang and take the Flying U by force if necessary."

"That could be messy," Alsworthy said. "Complicated for me."

"Well, there's too much at risk as long as Chippendale's on that ranch. I don't know if I can wait for you to foreclose on his note."

"I don't have much choice at this point."

Hamilton arose from his uncomfortable chair. He looked down on Alsworthy and donned his hat. He squared it and turned to go.

"I'll be in touch, Alsworthy," he said.

"For my sake, don't do anything rash just yet."

"I just want to get things lined up. Just in case."

"All right. But let's do some more thinking on this before we get too far ahead of ourselves."

Hamilton laughed low in his throat.

He strode to Alsworthy's opaque glass door with his name on it as president of the Cheyenne Savings & Loan. He opened the door and looked back at Alsworthy.

"We're not playing with tiddlywinks here, Alsworthy. There's big money to be made and I intend to make sure that I get the oil on the Fying U. There's bound to be a fortune in that swamp."

He walked out the door and closed it behind him.

Alsworthy took a deep huff of breath and stared blankly at his closed door.

That was what it was all about, he thought. Oil.

Black gold.

CHAPTER 50

Red Beaver pointed an extended hand and finger into the distance.

"Two suns," he said. "Big creek. Much water."

Reese smiled. "That's good," he said. "We can go two days."

"Much grass," Red Beaver said. "Big grass."

Reese laughed.

He liked the way Red Beaver talked. He had watched him as he picked out another cow for his wife and sons. The Blackfoot had looked over the herd very carefully and had chosen a large Hereford bull.

Lonnie had cut the bull out of the herd for Red Beaver, roped it, and led it to the small circle of teepees. Checkers had given the Indian an old piece of rope so that he could tether the animal until it was time to butcher it. Red Beaver had grinned and thanked both Lonnie and Checkers for his gift, which was payment for his services as a trail guide from that point all the way to Cheyenne.

Reese and Red Beaver rode well ahead of the herd.

When Reese took out his compass to check the direction of their route, Red Beaver saw it and commented.

"I have seen the soldiers use such a watch," Red Beaver said.

"It's not a watch, Red Beaver," Reese said. "It's a compass."

"I know. It shows the direction of the wind."

"Is that what the soldiers told you?"

"They said it points them to the four directions, like the smoke from my pipe."

Reese chuckled.

"So it does," he said. "But it points to every direction on the land. If you follow the arrows, you will get where you want to go."

That was the best explanation Reese could offer from the top of his head.

"How does it know where you want to go?" Red Beaver asked.

"It doesn't know exactly where you want to go, but it points to the west, or southwest, north, or east and you know which direction you want to go and it takes you there."

367

"Is it magic?"

"Not really. There are rocks in the earth. They have a magnetic quality. That is, they pull on the needles."

"So the rocks know the way you would go?" Red Beaver said.

"Sort of. The rocks know the directions and the compass can feel the magnetism. A magnet always points to the north. So if you want to go someplace else, you just turn the compass until the needle points in the direction you want to go."

"It is as if you hold the Great Spirit in your hand," Red Beaver said.

"That's a good way of putting it. But it's not the Great Spirit, Red Beaver. It's the way he made the earth and all the stars."

Red Beaver puzzled over Reese's explanation for a long time. And every time Reese checked his compass, Red Beaver stared at the spinning needle in rapt fascination.

And so they rode, toward Cheyenne, every mile on a ten- or twelve-mile day taking them ever closer to the Flying U Ranch.

When they reached the creek two days later, Reese was glad to see that it ran at an angle from the northwest to the northeast.

So the herd would have water the rest of the way.

The only thing Red Beaver had been

wrong about was the grass.

While there was plenty of grass, the hot sun had baked it dry.

And the cattle were starting to complain as they grazed on sere grasses that had fallen victim to the drought.

"Cattle can't go far on this here grass," Ben said to Reese on a hot afternoon.

"They don't have much farther to go," Reese said.

"Grass gets worse the farther south we get."

"I know. But in a few days, the grass won't be our problem anymore."

"What do you mean, boss?" Ben asked.

"I mean the herd will be in the hands of Chip of the Flying U," Reese said.

Then they lost the creek as it meandered to the southeast.

And there would be no more water for the cattle until they reached the Flying U.

Chapter 51

Chip followed his foreman, Archibald, "Archie," Lassiter as they rode to a far corner of the Flying U.

"You ain't gonna believe this, Chip," Archie said.

"Why won't you tell me what I'm going to see?" Chip asked.

"It ain't somethin' you can describe too good," Archie said. "Not and do it justice."

"I hate mysteries," Chip said. " 'Specially on my land."

"This is one you might like, boss."

Archie was in his late forties, a rawboned lanky man with weathered hands and a face crisscrossed with faint scars and a nose that had been broken more than once. But he was an experienced cowhand and a longtime friend of Chip and Carlene. They had met in Missouri at a livestock auction when Archie had just lost his job on a cattle ranch that had gone under.

Chip had asked him to go to Cheyenne with him and manage his herd.

It was a wise decision on Chip's part. Now that he was in trouble, Archie was doing the best he could to save what was left of the Flying U herd.

"Everything passes," Archie would say. "The good and the bad."

"So, what do I do about this damn drought?" Chip asked him.

"Ride it out," Archie replied. "There are better days ahead."

"I can't see 'em," Chip said.

"They're out there. You just got to have faith."

Encouraging words to Chip. But he still had his doubts, what with the mortgage coming due and Ned Hamilton ragging him to sell his ranch. He felt besieged on all sides.

After a long ride, Chip perked up.

"Looks to me like you're takin' me to that old slough, Archie," Chip said.

"That's where it is," Archie replied.

"That's the only part of my property that's totally useless," Chip said. "Just a lot of swamp water, dead plants, and mud up your ass."

"Now, don't go gettin' ahead of yourself, Chip," Archie said. "Just wait until I show you what the boys found this mornin'."

"Who found what?" Chip asked.

"Eli Dawson and Rudy Cameron chased a cow out here early this morning. Cow had full dugs and was bawlin' for her calf. It run down here and . . . well, you'll see."

In the distance, finally, Chip saw Eli and Rudy. They had a cow roped and were wrestling with something he couldn't make out. Probably the cow's calf, he thought. Their horses were ground-tied a few feet away.

Beyond, he saw the slough and began to smell the rotted vegetation.

"There they be," Archie said.

"I see 'em."

"That's a calf they got half-bulldogged," Archie said. "That's the calf's mother on that there rope."

"I figured that."

When Chip and Archie got close, Rudy and Eli let the calf go. It ran to its mother and she backed away from it.

Chip's jaw dropped when he saw the calf. It was almost unrecognizable.

"What in hell . . . ?" he said. "What happened to that calf?"

"It must've wandered down here and fallen in that swamp," Archie said.

The calf was covered in black slime that

glistened in the morning sun.

"What's that all over the calf?" Chip asked.

"Oil," Archie said. "Crude oil. I checked and it's bubblin' right up out of the ground. That slough there is some water and a whole hell of a lot of oil."

"Oil?"

"I checked it. Tasted it. Felt it. It's oil all right, and lots of it. Won't take much to get it out of the ground. You're sittin' on a gold mine, Chip. A black gold mine."

Chip sniffed the air. He could smell it. The calf shook itself and wagged its tail. Very little of the black slime flew off its body. He wobbled on shaky legs up to its mother. They touched noses, and then the mother cow turned away from her calf. The calf ran to her udder and began to nurse. The cow kicked one leg and held its head high as if to escape the stench of the oil.

Eli walked over to Chip and looked up at him.

"That calf was drenched in oil," he said. "We got it all over us gettin' it out of that swampy mess."

"Calf liked to have drownded itself," Rudy said. "It was in some kind of sinkhole. A sinkhole just a-bubblin' up crude."

"I see," Chip said.

He swung down out of his saddle and

walked to the edge of the slough.

There, on a small island of earth, he saw black bubbles that rose, sparkled, then sank back down. There were lots of bubbles, and there was a small lake of oil around the little islet.

"My God," he breathed. "I can't believe it."

"You got oil here, Chip," Archie said as he dismounted and stood beside his boss. "A fortune, maybe."

"Yes. Could be. This changes everything, you know."

"I expected it might," Archie said.

"I'll have to ask around, find a geologist in town."

"They's one there," Archie said. "I seen him in the saloon last week. He was holdin' court, talkin' 'bout the riches that was in the ground all over Wyoming. I thought he was just full of hot air."

"Where would I find this feller?" Chip asked.

"He's got 'em a small office on Main Street. I think you'll find this fellow there."

"Know his name?"

"Jeff somethin'. Didn't hear his full handle. Men there just called him Jeff. I think his last name was Brunswick, or some-thin' like that."

"I thought you didn't hear his last name."

"I heard a last name once. Just barely. Might not be Brunswick, but I think it's pretty close."

Chip turned away from the slough. He looked at Rudy and Eli. "You boys clean up that calf and get it away from this corner of the ranch."

"How do we do that?" Eli asked.

Chip frowned. "I don't know. Rub it off, wash it off, brush it off. Calf will die if you don't get all that oil off its hide."

"Sure enough, boss," Rudy said. "We'll clean it up."

Chip's mind was racing. If he could sell the oil rights, he'd be sitting pretty. He might even save his ranch and pay Balleen for the herd he was driving down from North Dakota.

Maybe there was a God after all, he thought.

CHAPTER 52

Ned Hamilton fairly bristled with controlled fury. It was all he could do to keep from punching Jeff Brunswick square in the mouth.

"I'm sorry," Brunswick said from behind his desk in the small office on Elm Street in Cheyenne. "Unless you can produce a deed to the property, Mr. Hamilton, I can't proceed any further."

"I'll have the deed in just a few days," Hamilton said.

"Fine. Bring it in and we'll do a title search on the property, buy insurance. You must understand that we must be careful in granting oil leases."

"Isn't a man's word good anymore?"

Jeff shook his head. His small office contained maps, some of which were on his oak desk, along with a compass, a slide rule, a magnifying glass, and an inkwell with a quill pen stuck in it.

"I'm afraid not, Hamilton. My company is not going to pay out hard cash on an oil lease unless we are sure that the lessee actually owns the property."

"Crap. I just don't have a deed yet. But I own the property in question."

"Fine. When you produce the deed, we'll pay up once you sign the necessary papers and we're satisfied as to your ownership of the land."

Hamilton leaned over the desk and braced himself with two balled-up fists.

"I'll be back," he said.

"With the deed?"

"Yes. With the damn deed." He turned and strode to the door, his neck reddening and swelling.

Brunswick did not watch him leave his office but turned to the maps on his desk and picked up his compass.

Hamilton slammed the door and stepped out onto the dusty street. He walked to his horse, put a boot in the stirrup, and grabbed the saddle horn to pull himself up onto his horse.

He rode straight to the Silver Slipper Saloon on Main Street.

As Chip and his foreman turned onto Elm, they both saw Ned Hamilton ride away from the oil company office.

"Isn't that Ned Hamilton?" Archie Lassiter asked.

"That's the man," Chip said. "Looks like he just left the office."

"So he's tryin' to horn in on your oil."

"He's been after me to sell my land for quite a spell. Archie, I want you and the other hands to arm themselves. Pack iron on your hips and carry rifles."

"You expectin' trouble from that Hamilton feller?"

"I am. I think he's desperate since I told him and Alsworthy that I was going to try and save my ranch, and in any case, I would not sell my property to Hamilton."

"I never liked that man."

"He's a crook. Just like Alsworthy."

"The banker?"

"Yeah. I think Alsworthy is in cahoots with Hamilton. I'm almost sure of it."

"Man, the lengths people will go to line their pockets."

"Let's see what this feller has to say when I tell him what's goin' on," Chip said.

The two men halted in front of the geologist's office and lashed their reins to the hitch rail outside.

They walked in and Jeff Brunswick looked up at them.

"I'm Leo Chippendale," Chip said, "and I

own the Flying U. I discovered oil on it."

Chip reached into his inside jacket pocket and produced a sheaf of papers, including a plot map of the Flying U.

He laid them in from of Brunswick. Jeff's eyes widened when he saw the plot map.

"I'm Jeff Brunswick," he said. He stood up and extended his hand to Chip.

Chip shook it. "This is my foreman, Archibald Lassiter," he said. Archie shook Brunswick's hand.

"Gentlemen. Have a seat while I look over what you have brought. Make yourselves comfortable."

Archie and Chip sat down as Jeff looked over all the papers Chip had brought.

"So you own the Flying U Ranch, Mr. Chippendale," Jeff said.

"Call me Chip. And, yes, I am the legal owner of the Flying U."

"Well, a man named Ned Hamilton has laid claim to it."

"He's been trying to buy, or steal, my ranch from me." Chip's gaze was steely and not lost on Brunswick.

"I see. He was just here and I told him unless he produced a deed to the property, my company would not enter into an oil lease agreement with him."

"That's good to hear," Chip said. "I have

a note due at the bank next month. If we can make a deal, I can pay up the note and I own the ranch free and clear."

"I see. Well, that's possible. I think there's a great deal of oil on your property."

"Are you willing to pay something on the lease up front?"

"We don't generally do that. But in this case, I'm authorized to put a substantial down payment on future earnings. If we drill and find oil, you will receive monthly royalties based on the number of barrels we extract from the well."

"I like that idea," Chip said. "When can we expect such a down payment?"

"Well, I have to do a title search on the land. Shouldn't take long. Then I'll have a talk with your banker, Frank Alsworthy. Shouldn't take long."

"I have a cow herd coming down from North Dakota. Should be here soon. I have to pay upon receipt of the cattle."

"It looks like you're in something of a bind, Chip."

"I would say so. A lot of balls to juggle."

Jeff chuckled at the juggler reference. "In the meantime, your papers look okay to me. I'll get out to see you right soon."

"I'm surprised you haven't come out already," Chip said.

"I was going on what Hamilton told me. I saw the oil and that was enough for the time being."

Chip's face contorted in displeasure, and then his mouth bent in a frown. "Well, you just saw a small corner of my ranch. I own five thousand acres."

"I see that, Chip."

"I'll expect you to come out in a few days, then."

"Yes. I'll see you soon," Jeff said.

Chip and Archie stood up. The men shook hands once again.

"I think we might have trouble with Hamilton," Chip said.

"He's pretty mad, all right," Jeff said.

"We'll deal with it," Chip said. Archie nodded.

"Good luck," Jeff said.

Archie and Chip walked out of the office and stood in front of the hitch rail for a few moments.

"Well, it looks like you might save your ranch, Chip."

"I hope so. It all depends on timing, though. And I haven't got much time left."

"Still jugglin' them balls, eh?"

"Only more balls are bein' tossed in and I'm runnin' out of hands."

Chip felt as if he had a lariat around his chest.

And it was being drawn tighter and tighter.

CHAPTER 53

The Silver Slipper was a large saloon. It was frequented by drifters and owl-hooters, mostly, and when Hamilton entered, he adjusted his eyes to the change of light and headed for the long bar where several men were seated.

He knew who he would find there. And sure enough, the men he wanted to see and talk to were at a back table. They were playing cards as he knew they would be. One of them looked up, saw him, and waved him over.

"Afternoon, Ned," one of the bartenders said to him, a man he knew only as Sully.

"Sully," he said, and strode to the far table. Sunlight streamed through the painted windows and the slats in the batwing doors. Light splashed on the floor of the large room and shimmered on the nearby tables.

"Howdy, Ned," one of the men at the

poker table said as Hamilton walked up. "Pull yourself up a chair."

"Sit in, if you want, Ned," said another. "Chips are two bits a piece, same as the ante."

"No, thanks, Charlie. I'm here on business."

"Haw," said the first man, one Reed Lawson, "what is it this time, stealin' horses?"

"Cattle ranch," Ned said.

The third man, Stu Larch, jiggled an empty chair, pushed it away from the table.

"We're flat on our last few pesos," Larch said. "So I hope you got somethin' that jingles our cash registers."

"Could be big," Ned said. "Bigger'n anything so far."

The men all stopped playing, cards in hand, and gave Hamilton their full attention.

"What you got, Ned?" Charlie asked. "A gold mine?"

"Somethin' just as good as a gold mine. Oil. Black gold."

Larch whistled a long, flat flute of surprise.

"Oil?" Reed said. "What we got to do? Drill for it?"

Ned sat down, scooted his chair in close.

"Put away your cards," he said. "We don't

384

have to dig or drill. Oil's just there for the takin'."

"Funniest way to get oil I ever heard of," Reed said, a smirk on his face.

"Yeah, Ned, you'd better lay it all out for us."

"But we're shore interested," Charlie said. He put down his cards. Facedown. So did the other men.

"All we have to do is kill a bunch of sodbusters," Hamilton said.

"How many?" asked Larch.

"A couple. Man and his woman."

"I ain't killin' no woman," Larch said. "I draw the line."

"I'll kill the woman," Ned said. "I just want to make sure one of us kills the man."

"Anybody we know?" Charlie asked.

"Chippendale. Flying U Ranch."

"Oh, that one. He ain't no sodbuster. Raises cattle, don't he?"

"He's got some cattle. They're doin' poorly in this heat. I want his ranch, and that's the only way I'm goin' to get it. Rub him out."

"Haw," Larch exclaimed. "Dry-gulch him, I say."

"Back-shoot him," Charlie said.

Reed nodded in agreement.

"I don't care how it's done," Ned said.

"Just so it gets done."

"When?" Charlie asked.

"Tomorrow, next day. Sooner, the better," Hamilton said.

"Day or night?" Larch asked.

"Day, I reckon. Hell, you got to see the man before you can put him down."

"That makes sense," Reed said.

"I'll take care of the woman. I don't want no heirs when this is over."

"Survivors, you mean," Charlie said. He had a wicked smile on his face.

A waiter drifted by. There was a bottle of whiskey on the table, but only three glasses. And each one was half-full.

"Sir, may I serve you?" the waiter asked Ned.

"I'll drink what they got. Just hand me a glass."

The waiter took a glass from his tray and set it in front of Ned.

"Bottle's paid for," the waiter said. "Is that all?"

"Yeah, that'll do," Ned said. "Thanks."

"You're welcome," the waiter said, and drifted away across the floor.

Charlie picked up the whiskey bottle and poured three fingers' worth of liquid into Ned's glass. Ned raised the glass in a toast.

"Here's to our success," he said.

The others lifted their glasses and drank.

"Hear, hear!" Reed said. The others grunted in approval.

"We'll go out to that ranch early in the morning," Ned said. "Just before dawn. Day after tomorrow. This gives you boys a day to rest up and practice."

The men laughed at the last reference.

"We don't need no practice," Reed said. "We all know how to dry-gulch a sodbuster."

The others laughed, even Ned.

"You're a good bunch," he said.

He drank more of his whiskey and felt its warmth in his belly. Now, it seemed, he was on the verge of getting rid of Chippendale and tapping in to the oil on his property.

A property that would soon be his.

And his alone.

Chapter 54

Jeff Brunswick went out to the Flying U prepared and excited. He hid his excitement as he dismounted in front of the Chippendale house fairly early the next morning.

Chip was not there when he knocked on the door and it was opened to him. He carried a small leather briefcase tucked under his left arm. It bulged with its paper contents.

Instead, Carlene greeted him.

"Hello, ma'am. I'm Jeff Brunswick. Is Mr. Chippendale in?"

"No," she said. "We didn't expect you to come out so soon. He's tending to our cattle. But I can bring him pretty quick. Won't you come in and have a seat in our front room?"

"Why, thank you, ma'am."

She ushered Brunswick in and sat him on the divan.

"Excuse me," she said. "I'll ring for Chip."

She walked outside and picked up a small iron rod. There was a triangle hanging from a post with an iron extension on it. She clanged the triangle with the rod. It set off a jangling sound that carried to the nearby pastures. She rang a prearranged signal and knew that Chip, or one of the hands, would hear it.

Then she went back inside.

"Mr. Brunswick, Chip will be here shortly. May I get you something? Coffee? A glass of water?"

"No, I'm fine, Mrs. Chippendale."

His hat was off and he looked as if he had taken a bath that very morning. He was clean-shaven and wore a light summer seersucker suit.

"Carlene," she said. "Call me Carlene."

"Yes'm. You have a nice house. I really like your fireplace."

"Why, thank you, Mr. Brunswick."

"Jeff."

She was about to engage Brunswick in small talk and pleasantries when they both heard hoofbeats outside.

"That'll be Chip," she said. She sat on a chair, her chair, in front of the small desk. A Currier & Ives print of a New York street and carriages hung on the wall behind her.

The door opened a few minutes later and Chip walked in. His face and clothes bore a patina of dust and his face was reddened from the sun.

"Mr. Brunswick," Chip said as he strode to the divan, "I didn't expect you to come out so soon."

"Sit down, Mr. Chippendale," Brunswick said. "We have much to discuss."

Chip sat down in an easy chair opposite the divan.

"Call me Chip," he said.

"And you can call me Jeff."

They both smiled at each other.

Carlene smiled too and folded her hands in her lap.

Jeff pulled the briefcase from his side and set it between his legs and the small table between him and Chip. He opened his briefcase but did not remove any papers.

"Chip, I inspected the slough again yesterday where you have oil bubbling up out of the ground. I also went over your plot map and papers. I find that you do indeed own the property known as the Flying U, and, while you have a small mortgage against it, you are the owner of the property where there may be oil."

"I told you that," Chip said.

Jeff smiled again. "I know. But we have to

check these things. You understand. Especially since Ned Hamilton claimed to own the land where I found oil."

"He wanted to buy my ranch, but I wasn't selling," Chip said.

"I know. I also checked at the bank where they hold your mortgage. A Mr. Frank Alsworthy."

"And?"

"And he verified that you are the sole owner of the Flying U and that particular piece of property where there might be substantial oil. He does hold your mortgage, but it's not past due until late next month."

"I know. He's threatening to foreclose on me, but I'm hoping to come up with enough money to pay him off."

"I may be able to help you in that regard," Jeff said. "Do you have a figure in mind for a possible down payment?"

"Yes, I do," Chip said.

"I hope you know that this is highly unusual. But I'm very confident that my company can extract a great amount of oil from drilling on your property. My resources are limited in this regard, though."

"I don't know much about oil," Chip said. "I know you'll get about four bits a barrel in today's market. Or less. Seems like it would take a lot of oil for me to earn any royalties."

"That depends on how much you want as a down payment on the lease."

"I'll tell you what I need. What my minimum is for me to get my head above water."

"So, tell me," Jeff said. "I promise not to swoon."

"I need sixteen thousand," Chip said. "That's five thousand to pay off my note at the Savings & Loan, plus eleven thousand to pay for the cattle I'm expecting any day now."

"I didn't know about that," Jeff said. "The cattle, I mean. It seems to me that you're just taking on more responsibility."

"I'm buying a herd of about a thousand head. I hope to sell them in Kansas, most of them. I may be able to sell some right quick to the army at Fort Laramie."

"I see. Well, sixteen thousand is quite a lot of money."

"You asked, Jeff. And I told you."

"That you did. All right. Before I came out here, I withdrew cash from my account. Once you sign the papers, I'm prepared to pay what you ask."

"The entire sixteen thousand?" Chip said.

"Yes. And part of it is a signing bonus, so you will not have to pay back the entire amount out of your prospective royalties."

"How much?" Chip asked.

"Two thousand is a signing bonus."

"That's mighty generous," Chip said.

Jeff dug into his briefcase and brought out a file folder full of documents. He laid them out on the little table.

"Do you have a pen, Carlene?" Jeff asked. "Otherwise I have one in my briefcase, along with an inkwell."

"Yes, in my desk here," she said.

She turned and opened the rolltop desk. There was an ink bottle, corked, and a quill pen. She handed these to Jeff, who set them on the table.

"Now, you both must sign these papers," Jeff said. "The lease is for fifty years, with an option clause to renew for another fifty years."

"We should live so long," Chip said.

"Your heirs, if any, will be able to honor the terms of the lease," Jeff said.

He handed some documents to Chip and duplicates to Carlene.

"Look these over carefully," Jeff said. "And if you're satisfied, I will require both your signatures on the designated place at the very end of the contract. You will keep one copy and I'll take the other to send off to my company."

Carlene and Chip began to read the documents after Jeff penned in the amount of the down payment and signed his own name at the bottom of the three-page document.

Much of the document was in legalese, but both Carlene and Chip could decipher all the "to wits," "second parties," and the option clause.

"I'm satisfied," Carlene said, who finished reading her document first. A few seconds later, Chip looked up from his papers.

"I'm ready to sign," he said.

"How soon can we expect the down payment?" Carlene asked.

"As soon as you sign. I have the money right here in this satchel," Jeff said.

Carlene breathed out a sigh of relief.

Chip gulped in air.

He and Carlene signed the documents above their names on both documents.

"You keep one for your records," Jeff said. "And I'll keep the other."

He blew on the ink to dry it since he had no blotter. Then he put the signed document back in its folder, returned it to his briefcase, and reached in and pulled out a large, bulging envelope.

He counted out sixteen thousand dollars in one-hundred-dollar bills.

He handed the bills to Chip. "Count it,

Chip, and I'll dig out a receipt for you to sign."

Chip counted the bills, then handed them to Carlene. She counted the money too, her eyes widening as the amount grew larger.

Jeff produced a receipt and filled it out with the amount he was paying the Chippendales.

"Both of you must sign my receipt," he said.

Carlene came over to the table and signed, then stood aside so Chip could do the same.

"There," Jeff said. "We're set. I imagine we'll start drilling in that slough in a week or so."

"That'll be fine," Chip said.

Carlene held the money in her lap. She wore a satisfied smile on her face.

Jeff put on his hat and stood up. He picked up his briefcase and closed it, then tucked it under his left arm. He extended a hand to shake Chip's.

The two men shook hands.

"Thank you both," Jeff said. "I'll be seeing you."

"I'll ride into town with you," Chip said. "I want to pay off my mortgage, get that out of the way."

"Fine. I'd enjoy your company," Jeff said.

"Honey, count out five thousand of that,

will you?" Chip asked.

Carlene counted out five thousand dollars and handed the bills to Chip.

"Be careful," she said. "Don't get robbed."

"I see he's armed," Jeff said. "Like you were expecting trouble out here."

"A precaution," Chip said. "I don't trust Hamilton. I'm armed and all my hands are packin' iron and carrying rifles on their horses."

"I hope you won't have trouble with Hamilton," Jeff said. "From what I hear, he's hard as nails."

"And maybe just one step ahead of the law," Chip said.

He stuffed the money inside two front pockets and hugged Carlene.

"Hurry back," she whispered to him.

Both men walked outside and unhitched their horses.

Carlene waved to them from the doorway as the two men rode away.

Then she realized that she still had a handful of bills and retreated to put the money in a safe place.

She counted the bills again before placing them in a strongbox they kept in their bedroom. She locked the box and put the key under her mattress.

Her hands shook from nervousness.

She walked back into the front room and opened the gun cabinet. She took out a loaded double-barrel shotgun and a box of shells.

Then she sat down in a chair she pulled over to the window.

"Just you try anything, Mr. Hamilton," she said to no one. "Just you try."

And she waited for her husband's return, her face a mask of eternal patience.

CHAPTER 55

Reese and Red Beaver crossed a small creek. It was still dark, just before dawn, when they splashed through the gentle waters of the meandering creek. The stars were still out, and so was the sliver of moon that glistened in its waters. Reese looked back and saw Lonnie on point, the herd just behind him. He waited on the other side of the creek for Lonnie to catch up.

"What's holding you up, Reese?" Lonnie asked when he reined his horse to a halt on the opposite bank. "Something wrong?"

There was a joyous smile on Reese's face.

"Nothing wrong, Lonnie. I just wanted you to be the first to know."

"Know what?"

"Red Beaver and I just stepped onto the Flying U Ranch."

"What? We're there?" Lonnie's face contorted in incredulity.

"Yep. See them wagon tracks behind me?"

Reese said. He pointed to a dim trail through the withered grass.

"Yeah, I see tracks."

"I've been here before, and we're on Chip's ranch land as sure as I'm sittin' in this saddle."

"Well, I'll be damned," Lonnie said. "That's good news."

"So, bring the herd across and just follow them wagon tracks. I'll ride on ahead and tell Chip that we're here."

"I'm on my way," Lonnie said. He turned his horse and rode back toward the head of the advancing herd.

"Well, Red Beaver," Reese said. "You got us here. Ready to ride back to your people?"

"Yes. I am ready. I will go."

"You take care," Reese said.

Red Beaver turned his pony around and recrossed the creek. His pony's hooves splashed through the water until he was on the opposite bank. Then Red Beaver turned his pony and waved farewell to Reese. Something he had learned on the trail.

Reese watched him ride off and disappear beyond the cow herd.

He felt a sadness flood through his heart. Over the miles, he had come to like and respect the Blackfoot brave. He had learned much from him on the drive. Red Beaver did not need a compass. He followed the stars at night, the sun during the day.

"There goes a man," Reese said. "There goes the West."

"Huh?" Lonnie uttered, seemingly dumbfounded. "I thought you didn't hanker to redskins, Reese."

"They had it all, Lonnie. And we took it away from them. The Indians. We thought they were dumb, and they were not. We thought they were weak, but they were not. We just had better and bigger horses, and we had repeating rifles and pistols. We took all this away from them."

"You've changed some, Reese."

"I hope so," Reese said. "We can't really know what's in a man's mind until we see through his eyes."

"Well, the Injuns would be better off if they'd foller the white man's ways. Learn how to till the earth and farm and raise livestock. They're a footloose and rootless bunch."

"Oh, they have roots, Lonnie. Deeper than ours maybe. It's just that they don't believe in land ownership. They believe the land was given to them by their Great Spirit and no man can own it, sell it, or give it away."

"Humph. Dumb notion, you ask me."

"Yeah, well, Red Beaver spoke a lot to me

and I learned a lot from him. Never mind. He's gone now. But he won't be forgotten. Not by me anyway."

Lonnie was silent.

Reese followed the dim wagon tracks, and after a time, he saw the ranch house come into view. The sky was turning pale in the east and some of the stars had winked out. But there was moon glow glistening on the roof and the barn and bunkhouse. He also saw lean cattle grazing on sparse dried grass and some were nibbling hay stored in slatted bins at intervals.

As he neared Chip's house, he saw men riding and one of them broke off and rode toward him.

He recognized the man as soon as he got near.

"Howdy, Archie," Reese said.

It was Archie Lassiter, whom he knew to be Chip's ranch foreman.

"Howdy, Mr. Balleen. You here already? The herd with you?"

"Herd's right behind me, Archie. Where's Chip?"

"He's in the barn. I'll get some of the boys to ride out and help your men."

"Just follow the old wagon tracks and you'll find them."

"And I know just where to put them

cattle," Archie said.

He turned his horse and rode back to the corrals at a gallop. He yelled at his hands to follow him.

Reese noticed that Archie was wearing his pistol and there was a rifle jutting from its scabbard on Archie's horse.

Both of the other men were carrying rifles too, and as they rode past, he saw that they were wearing sidearms too.

He rode to the barn where Chip was tossing hay into a wagon with a pitchfork. With him was another man, Rudy Cameron, who was in the loft, pushing hay from the loft down to where Chip was forking the hay.

"Howdy, Chip," Reese said as he rode up. The horses hitched to the hay wagon nickered and his horse responded with a matching neigh.

"Reese," Chip said. "You're here already. I'm mighty glad to see you."

Chip was sweating. He leaned on his pitchfork as he stuck the tines into the ground and wiped his forehead.

The sky paled as the dawn spread its cream over the eastern horizon. More of the stars winked out as if snuffed by an unseen hand.

"Climb down, Reese," Chip said as he looked upward toward the opening to the loft. "I got business to take care of. And we got enough hay to take out to them puny cattle in the west pasture."

Rudy started to back away from the opening, then stopped. He stared off into the distance.

"Chip, it looks like we got company," Rudy said. "I can hardly make 'em out. But looks like three or four riders headin' our way."

Chip and Reese turned and looked in the direction of Rudy's gaze.

In the hazy morning light, both men could see riders coming toward them. They seemed to be riding slow and with deliberateness.

"This ain't good," Chip said.

"What do you mean? Do you know those men, Chip?" Reese strained to make out the faces of the riders. Too far away.

"I think I know one of 'em. I'm pretty sure that's his horse. God knows, I've seen it often enough."

"A friend of yours?" Reese asked.

"If I ain't mistaken, one of those men is Ned Hamilton. And he's no friend of mine. In fact, he's been tryin' to buy, or steal, the Flying U. And those men ridin' with him look like hard cases to me. Even from this distance."

"I see you and your men are all wearing pistols. And there're two rifles leaning against the barn."

"Yep," Chip said. "I've been half expectin' Hamilton to come here and put my lamp out."

Rudy joined them a moment later.

"Chip, this don't look good," Rudy said. "Look, they're fanning out, like they was ridin' into battle."

It was true.

Reese saw four riders separate and ride toward them. Each was fifty yards apart when they finally settled on a course toward the ranch house.

Chip walked over and picked up one of the rifles. Rudy did the same a few seconds later.

"Reese, you'd better go inside the barn. I'm pretty sure there's goin' to be some shootin' right soon."

"I'll get my rifle and give you a hand," Reese said.

He pulled his rifle from its scabbard.

Chip and Rudy took up positions behind the hay wagon and at either end.

Reese stood just behind Chip.

And still, the riders came on. Slow, deliberate.

As they drew closer, Chip was sure. One

of the men was Ned Hamilton.

"That bastard," Chip muttered.

He had the deed to his property in his strongbox. He was free and clear. He now owned the Flying U, lock, stock, and barrel.

Alsworthy had not liked it when he laid out five thousand dollars on his desk. But the banker had no choice. He had marked the note "Paid In Full," signed it, stamped it, and taken the money.

The four riders came closer.

As Rudy, Chip, and Reese watched, the riders all pulled their rifles from their sheaths.

Chip levered a rifle cartridge into the firing chamber. Rudy and Reese did the same.

"Do you think they see us?" Rudy asked. There was a slight tremor in his voice.

"Hard to tell," Chip said.

"They don't see us," Reese said. "But they're lookin' for us."

The riders craned their necks, looking in all directions.

"When they get close enough, Rudy, you pick out that man on the far right of you. Drop him if you can."

"What about me, Chip?" Reese asked. "Which one do you want me to take out?"

"I'm going to shoot Hamilton," Chip said. "He's the one just to the left of the man on the right. You can take either man on the left. Whichever is easier."

"Maybe I'll empty both men's saddles," Reese said.

"We'll all be wading through a storm of bullets before this is over," Chip said.

He sighted down his rifle. The barrel hugged one of the wagon posts.

Chip lowered himself so that Reese could take a stance above him.

Reese laid his rifle barrel against the post and sighted down the barrel. He estimated the four men to be less than a thousand yards from them.

And they were still coming. Slow and deliberate.

As Reese looked at them, as if on command, each of the riders cocked his rifle.

"Uh-oh," Chip said, in a low voice.

"What in hell do they expect to shoot?" Reese said out loud.

"Probably my house," Chip said. "And Carlene's in there."

"Want me to check on her, Chip?" Reese asked.

"No, Reese. You'll get shot down before you could get there."

"Here they come," Rudy said. "Less'n five hunnert yards."

"Hold steady. See what they're goin' to

do and let 'em get closer," Chip ordered.

True to Chip's prediction, when Hamilton and his men were within a hundred and fifty yards of the house, they each brought their rifles to their shoulders, aimed them, and fired at the house.

Four puffs of smoke spewed from the muzzles of their rifles. Sparks flew from the barrels.

Glass shattered the front windows of Chip's home.

Carlene screamed from somewhere inside.

"Oh God," Chip exclaimed.

His hand was shaking as he tried to line up his front and read sights on Hamilton.

The four riders kept firing their rifles into the house.

Then Hamilton pointed an arm toward the hay wagon.

Chip could hear him yell something to the other men. All four rifles swung toward the hay wagon and barn.

"Let 'em have it," Chip said when the riders were a hundred yards away.

Even as he spoke, the four men began to fire at what they saw next to the wagon.

Bullets flew into the hay and caromed off the wagon posts. They whistled past the ears of Reese, Rudy, and Chip.

Chip fired first, his sights steady on Hamilton.

Rudy shot at the man on the right.

Reese aimed at the man on the far left and squeezed the trigger.

Hamilton jerked in the saddle as Chip's bullet smacked into his chest.

Chip fired again. He aimed for Hamilton's head.

The four outlaws were less than a hundred yards and were guiding their horses in a zigzag pattern as they approached the barn.

Rudy's target grabbed at his chest as a red stain spread over his linsey-woolsey shirt. He held on for a few minutes, then slumped over onto his saddle horn.

Rudy fired at the man again and saw the top of his head fly off like a sailing pie plate. The man fell from the saddle as his horse jumped sideways.

Chip kept firing at Hamilton and saw him jerk spasmodically as each bullet struck him. Blood spurted from three or four wounds. He dropped his rifle as he held on to his saddle horn with both hands.

Reese shot the next-to-last man on his left. He saw the man's hand grasp at his throat and the bullet tore through the larynx and ripped out half of his neck.

The man toppled from his horse. His foot

caught in one stirrup, and the horse dragged him forward, kicking its rear hooves in protest.

There was the acrid smell of smoke in the air.

The man Rudy had shot finally fell out of his saddle and landed on the ground with a heavy thump.

Hamilton reeled in his saddle, still amazingly alive, but bleeding profusely.

Chip kept firing his rifle at Hamilton, consumed with a hatred for the man that nearly blinded him.

Then, from inside the house, there was a shotgun blast. Then another.

Two loads of buckshot peppered Hamilton's body and he was thrown backward, his body sliding over the cantle and his horse's rump. Blood spurted from dozens of holes and he hit the ground a dead man.

"That was Carlene," Chip said proudly.

"She let him have it," Reese said as the last man fell from his horse and skidded to a stop.

The man caught in the stirrup rolled over and his foot came free. He was dead as his body slid to a stop.

A quiet descended over the small battlefield.

Wisps of smoke curdled in the still air of

morning. The sun rose and the men on the ground became riddled with sunlight, bathed in their shadows on one side.

Chip stepped away from the wagon and headed for the body of Hamilton.

Reese followed him, his rifle at the ready just in case any of the outlaws moved.

They did not come back to life. Any of them.

Chip stood over Hamilton's corpse.

"Well, he wanted my land," Chip said. "Now he's got a piece of it."

Carlene emerged from the house. She carried the double-barreled shotgun.

Chip turned to catch her as she rushed into his arms.

He hugged her tight.

"Good shooting, Carlene," Chip told her.

"Ooh, that man," she said. "That awful man."

Then Chip turned to Reese.

"Thanks, Reese," he said.

"My pleasure," Reese said.

Chip gave Carlene a last squeeze and turned to Reese.

"Come on in the house, Reese. I'll give you coffee and the money I owe you for your cattle."

"We'll wait until we get a final tally," Reese said. "We lost a few head on the trail. We come through some winter and deep river water."

"I'll take a little bit of that winter," Chip said.

And the three of them walked toward the house as Rudy stripped the dead men of their gun belts like some battlefield vandal.

One of the horses whickered and flicked its tail.

Then it headed for the wagon full of hay as the sun rose above the eastern horizon like a flaming beacon declaring peace over all the earth.

The employees of Thorndike Press hope you have enjoyed this Large Print book. All our Thorndike, Wheeler, and Kennebec Large Print titles are designed for easy reading, and all our books are made to last. Other Thorndike Press Large Print books are available at your library, through selected bookstores, or directly from us.

For information about titles, please call:
  (800) 223-1244

or visit our Web site at:
  http://gale.cengage.com/thorndike

To share your comments, please write:
  Publisher
  Thorndike Press
  10 Water St., Suite 310
  Waterville, ME 04901